BLOOD OATH

A CRIME THRILLER

WHEN HONOR DIES
BOOK 2

ROBERT VAUGHAN

**ROUGH
EDGES
PRESS**

Blood Oath
Paperback Edition
Copyright © 2024 (As Revised) Robert Vaughan

Rough Edges Press
An Imprint of Wolfpack Publishing
1707 E. Diana Street
Tampa, FL 33610

roughedgespress.com

Paperback ISBN 978-1-68549-538-1
eBook ISBN 978-1-68549-537-4

BLOOD OATH

CHAPTER 1

NEW ORLEANS, JUNE 7, 1926

As the police car in which he was riding turned west onto Decatur Street, Mike Kelly caught a glimpse of the sunset and saw that the sky was the color of liquid fire. To his left, the Mississippi River, sometimes called Old Strong by the locals, made a large bow of molten silver on its circuitous journey to the Gulf of Mexico, one hundred miles to the south. In the heart of the city newly built steel and concrete buildings, some as high as ten stories, loomed dark purple against the crimson sky, their windows reflecting a grid of melon-colored light. The streets were filled with the noise of automobile engines, grinding gears and jarring Klaxon horns.

When the car turned into the Vieux Carre, going north on St. Peters, Mike could hear a different sound. Here it was muted trumpets and wailing saxophones, played by musicians with shining black skin and dark, soulful eyes, spilling out through the raised windows and open doors of the nightclubs. This was the haunting symphony of blues and jazz, the Crescent City's major contribution to a time that took its very name, "the jazz age," from this New Orleans' sound.

Through the open window of the car Mike could smell distinctive night fragrances: the rich aromas of exquisite cooking, green bananas and pineapples just off the boats and the delicate flower scents from the honey-suckle, jasmine and wisteria that climbed along brick walls and overhung the elaborate grillwork balconies of the Quarter's elegant old homes. A different perfume was given off by the French Quarter's painted ladies, who lounged in doorways or on street corners to ply their trade, marking the night with their own sweet, sensual musk.

The habitués of the narrow, winding streets of the French Quarter were, with the setting of the sun, just now beginning to awaken. By day, they had slumbered as trucks and delivery wagons plied the alleys and twisting thoroughfares, off-loading their cargoes of vegetables and meat. Other cargoes arrived during the day as well, including bootleg shipments of whiskey and beer. Commerce in alcohol was forbidden by the Volstead Act establishing Prohibition. Bootlegging was an illegal but thriving business which, in New Orleans, was controlled almost entirely by a man named Charlie Matranga.

Matranga was deeply entrenched in New Orleans, a vital part of the city's subculture from bootleg booze to the numbers racket, and from political corruption to pros-titution. No criminal activity took place without his direc-tion and approval, and the small-time hood who might try to go into business for himself would find Matranga's law-enforcement activity even more effective than that of the local police.

Matranga dealt in moonshine and bootleg whiskey, which meant he often ran afoul of the federal government. In addition, because of his connections with criminal organizations in other cities, crimes plotted in one state were sometimes committed in another. Like bootlegging, interstate conspiracy to commit a crime involved the federal government, specifically the Bureau of Investigation. It was a case of interstate conspiracy that had brought Mike Kelly and Tim Clark to New Orleans. As agents from the New York office of the Bureau of Investigation, they were here to take into custody one Carmine D'Angelo, a member of Charlie Matranga's mob. D'Angelo was being held by the New Orleans Police Department on a state charge, but agents Kelly and Clark had already made arrangements with the state of Louisiana to take him back to New York.

Interstate conspiracy to commit crime was a little more difficult to prove than violation of the Volstead Act; by its very nature, such conspiracy was conducted in secret. On the other hand, violation of the Volstead Act was done openly and without shame. In general, the public did not support Prohibition, therefore national attitudes were conducive to violating that law. And in an atmosphere where one law was so blatantly violated, it was relatively easy for the public to turn their backs on other transgressions as well. As a result, not only New Orleans but every major city in the United States was undergoing a time of lawlessness unlike any period in America's history.

All across the country, organized criminal elements took advantage of the situation, and in many cases they linked up, forming corporations to make the business of crime more efficient. One of the most effective of these criminal organizations was created by Italian Americans, especially Sicilians. This was the Mafia and Charlie Matranga's mob was actually a Mafia organization.

The word Mafia was never used by the actual

members of the Mafia, nor by those who were subject to its power. The members called it the Family, the Arm, the Clique, the Outfit, the Tradition, the Office, the Honored Society, the Combination or La Cosa Nostra, but never Mafia. In fact, there were very few non-Italians who had ever even heard the word Mafia or knew of the existence of such an organization. Extreme secrecy, even as to its existence, was one of the strongest weapons in the Mafia arsenal. Mike had learned this firsthand.

The Mafia had been founded in Sicily in the 1600s as an underground army to fight against the oppressive rule of the Bourbons. When it began, the Mafia's aims were honorable, and it thrived on strong kinship bonds, a code of ethics and masculine honor. The individual Families were headed by "dons," or men of respect

For such an organization to work there had to be a very strong code of honor. This code of honor was a part of the dependence upon family, kinship and the Italian—particularly Sicilian—connection. The code was made up of many precepts that could never be violated, such as the precept of secrecy, expressed as the code of *omerta*, or code of silence. The code of omerta specified that no Sicilian would tell the police anything and in America, that honor dictated that even non-Sicilian Italians and those who were subject to the Mafia's control would follow the code. Violation of the code would bring quick death from Mafia enforcers.

Officially the Bureau of Investigation had no policy with regard to the Mafia. That was because J. Edgar Hoover, who had been head of the bureau since 1924, did not believe such an organization actually existed. He thought it was a myth perpetuated by the criminals to give them a sense of power greater than they actually possessed. But Mike Kelly knew better. One of J. Edgar Hoover's best agents, he did believe in the existence of the Mafia, and when he got D'Angelo back to New York, Mike would finally be able to prove it.

Mike was the son of a New York City policeman. In addition, both grandfathers, two uncles and a cousin had also been New York City policemen. Mike would have been a city policeman too had he not been put off by the high level of corruption within the department. Then he learned about the federal government's Bureau of Investigation. This was an organization that was above corruption.

Mike joined the bureau shortly before his own father was killed by a crooked cop. With his hatred of the corruption that had killed his father, Mike was as motivated toward rooting out and destroying the Mafia's corruptive influence as he was in combating its more conventional lawless activity. He frowned as the memories began to taunt him.

"How long it gonna take you fellas get to New York?" the driver of the car asked, speaking in a heavy Cajun accent. The driver, Eddie Mouchette, was one of two New Orleans police officers who had been assigned to escort Mike, Tim and their prisoner to the train. The question interrupted Mike's reverie, and he pulled his attention back to the task at hand.

"We're taking the Panama Limited to Chicago," Mike explained. "It leaves New Orleans at eight tonight and that'll put us in Chicago by three o'clock tomorrow afternoon. We'll catch the New York Special out of Chicago at four-thirty tomorrow afternoon and arrive in New York by seven the next morning."

"It be more better if you fly," Eddie suggested. "You get there faster. That what I'm goin' do when I go to New York one of these days."

"Ha!" Don Stanfield said. "Now, just what the hell

would a Creole boy like you do in New York? Will you tell me that, Eddie Mouchette?"

"Hoo boy, ain't no tellin' what all I might do. Maybe I show those New York ladies somethin', I bet," Eddie bantered. " 'Darlin', I'll say, 'You ain' had no lovin' 'till you been loved by a Cay-john man from N'arleans.' "

"I'll bet those New York women are just waitin' on that," Don offered dryly. The others laughed, then Tim spoke up from the backseat.

"Looks like the train is already here, Mike."

"Yeah, that's good," Mike replied. "I'm going to feel a whole lot better once we get Mr. D'Angelo on board. Park right over there, Eddie."

"Yes sir, you the boss man," Eddie replied, pulling the closed-body Chandler touring car into the parking spot Mike had indicated.

The train was standing still but the boiler relief valve of the big 4-6-0 Baldwin locomotive was opening and closing in rhythmic hisses, releasing feathery tendrils of steam to purple in the setting sun as it drifted across the crowded depot platform.

"There's quite a few people already on board," Don noted.

Inside the day-coaches of the Panama Limited, men and women, already anxious for the train to get underway, stared through the windows at the activity on the platform.

Mike made a thorough survey of the depot area and the station platform.

"Do you see anything?" Tim asked.

"No," Mike replied. "But I feel something."

"You feel something?" Eddie hooted. "What you feel? You feel the bogeyman puttin' his hand on your shoulder?" He laughed at his own comment.

"Not exactly," Mike replied, unperturbed by Eddie's teasing.

"I don't know, Mike, maybe you're being too cautious," Tim suggested, peering intently across the platform. "I don't see anything at all out there. And anyway, how would Matranga's people know we're here? Not more than half a dozen people know our plans."

"Don't underestimate him," Mike cautioned. He sighed. "Well, we can't stay here all day. Come on, we may as well get him to the train."

"What do you mean? You goin' to just take me over there without checkin' things out? What's the matter with you guys? You crazy?" Carmine D'Angelo complained. Carmine was sitting in the backseat, handcuffed to Tim. "You think the Matrangas just goin' to stand out there in the open so you can see them? They're here waitin' for me. I know they are."

"I tell you what. If it make you fellas feel more better, Don and me, we take us a little look around," Eddie suggested. "What you say, Don?"

"Okay by me," Don agreed. He looked over at Tim. "We'll give you guys the high sign if ever'thing is all right."

"You guys better look around real good," Carmine warned.

"What's the matter, D'Angelo, don't your friends love you no more?" Eddie teased.

"You're responsible for me," D'Angelo reminded him.

"I know my rights. You got to look out for me."

"D'Angelo, you don't worry about it none," Don growled. "We can do our job just fine without any help from you."

"You just mind what I said," Carmine replied. "And remember, I can't do nobody no good if I'm dead."

"It'd do me some good," Don growled. "It'd do me a lot of good if all you wop bastards were dead."

"You got no right to talk to me like that," D'Angelo complained. "Tell him, Kelly. He ain't got no right to talk to me like that."

"Yeah, Don, you know you don't mean that," Mike teased. "Don't forget, Mr. D'Angelo here is very special to us."

"Special, my ass," Don growled as he and Eddie walked out toward the platform.

D'Angelo was special. He was a particularly valuable prisoner because he had offered to talk about the Matranga Family. That meant he would be breaking the code of omerta. It was very rare to find a Mafia soldier who would go back on that oath and give evidence against the Mafia. However, D'Angelo had been persuaded by the logic of the situation. The federal government wanted him for conspiracy to commit interstate crime, but the state of Louisiana wanted him for murder. The way D'Angelo saw it, it was ten years in a federal pen or the electric chair.

Mike knew what Carmine D'Angelo did not know: the state's case was actually very weak. Mike had been able to talk them into dropping their murder charges if Carmine would plead guilty to the federal charges and answer several questions, not only about the Matrangas but about other families around the country as well. Carmine had agreed and was now being transported back to New York to fulfill his end of the bargain.

When Eddie and Don reached the platform, they looked around very carefully while Mike, Tim and Carmine remained out of sight in the car.

"Goddamn stupid cops," Carmine growled. "Look at 'em out there, gawkin' around like they're watchin' a parade or somethin'. They don't know shit."

"They knew enough to capture you," Mike reminded him, turning in his seat to look back at the prisoner.

"Aw," Carmine said, dismissing it with an impatient wave of his hand. "They was just lucky, that's all."

Mike turned back to watch the two policemen through the windshield. When Eddie and Don were satisfied that all was clear, Eddie looked back toward the car and waved.

"Okay, Timmy, my boy, this is it," Mike said. He opened the front door of the car. "Let's take this bum to New York."

Mike got out of the car and stood by as first Tim, then Carmine worked their way out of the backseat. Their egress was made slower and more awkward than normal because they were handcuffed together.

"Walk straight toward the train," Mike said quietly. "I don't want you to run, but I do want you to move it along."

"Okay," Tim agreed.

The three men started across the platform. Just to the left of the platform, on a track siding, stood a single boxcar. Suddenly the door of the boxcar slid open and six men jumped down onto the bricks. All were carrying weapons, submachine guns for some, shotguns for the others.

"*Morte soldati!*" D'Angelo shouted in terror.

"Tim! Look out!" Mike warned.

The six armed men stood in a little semicircle and began firing. Their faces were expressionless as they began dealing out death, moving their guns back and forth as calmly as if they were watering a garden.

D'Angelo started to run, dragging Tim along with him. Tim was fighting off D'Angelo while at the same time trying to draw his gun.

There were several bystanders on the platform. Some

were passengers getting ready to entrain, while others were there to see people off. When the first shot was fired, the civilians added their own screams and shouts to the bedlam as they started running in a mad dash to get out of the way. Some dived for the ground, others ran for cover.

The tommy guns and shotguns chattered and roared. Bullets whistled all around Mike, one hitting him in the thigh, another catching him in the side. Mike wasn't aware of going down; he knew that he had only when he suddenly realized he was lying on his stomach on the bricks, his gun stretched out before him. From this prone position he pulled the trigger, and the gun bucked up in his hand then kicked out an empty shell-casing. He was gratified to see his target grab his chest and fall.

The firing continued at a mad pace for about thirty seconds, although to Mike it seemed an eternity. He was hit again, this time in the shoulder, but he continued shooting and knocked down another of the gunmen.

Suddenly a large sedan roared out onto the station platform and the four gunmen who were still on their feet rushed toward it and jumped in. The driver whipped the car around in a tight circle, the tires squealing in protest against the bricks. Once back on the road, the car began to roar away. Mike tried to stand up to get a better shot at the speeding Buick but discovered he was unable to rise. In anger and frustration, he emptied his pistol at the back of the car, although he knew he wouldn't be able to hit anyone from this angle.

After the car was gone, Mike pulled himself into a sitting position, but he couldn't get up any farther than that. He lay his pistol on the ground beside him. All the ammunition had been expended and its empty condition was obvious to even the most casual viewer because the slide remained open after the last cartridge was fired.

"Tim! Tim, are you all right?" Mike called.

There was no answer.

"Eddie? Don?"

Mike looked toward the two police officers who had come with them. They were both down and absolutely motionless on the platform. Eddie's leg was twisted grotesquely.

"Tim!" Mike called again, and straining against the pain, he turned around to look behind him. "Oh, damn," he said at the scene that greeted him.

Tim was lying across the hood of the Chandler, his head resting in a pool of blood, his right arm dangling down, the gun hanging by its trigger guard from his index finger. Carmine was on the ground with his head against the bumper. They were still handcuffed together.

Gradually now, cautiously, as if expecting another attack, the bystanders who had bolted to safety at the opening shots began to reappear. They were drawn by morbid curiosity to the little islands of death that were scattered about the station. Some stopped at the bodies of the two men Mike had killed. Others stood over the two policemen, while the remainder stared at the grisly scene on the hood of the car. A few even came over to Mike, approaching him cautiously, for he had been one of the participants.

"Mister," someone asked. "Who the hell are you and what was this all about?"

"I am Federal Agent Mike Kelly of the Bureau of Investigation," Mike explained carefully, his voice strained by pain. "My partner and I were taking a prisoner back to New York. That's my partner back there on the car." He nodded toward the two downed policemen. "Those men are local police officers. They were escorting us to the train."

"Are you bad hurt?"

"I'm okay, what about the others?"

"You don't look okay. I'd better go call an ambulance."

"Get an ambulance for the others," Mike said.

"An ambulance ain't goin' to do none of the others any good, mister," the man said. "They're all dead. Every one of them."

Mike had been trying to stem the flow of blood by holding his hands over his wounds, but he was, at best, only partially successful. As the blood continued to flow he watched the world around him begin to spin, then grow dim until it was completely black.

"Great! Son of a bitch, that was great!" Vinnie Letto shouted as the Buick sped away from the depot. Vinnie was riding in the front seat with the driver, a strange, very pale man with white hair and pink eyes. In fact, The Albino, as he was called, had not gone out with the shooting team precisely because he was so identifiable.

The other three gunmen, who were much more average in appearance, were in the back. As Vinnie twisted around to look at them, a big grin split his face. "Did you see that sonofabitchin' stoolie go down when I gave him a blast from this?" he asked, holding up the shotgun he had used. "I opened him up from asshole to elbow."

"Yeah," one of the men in the back seat answered. "But I think maybe we should'a brought Willie and Ben with us. I didn't feel right just leavin' 'em lyin' back there like that."

"You know the rules, Carlo," Vinnie said. "You take your money and you take your chances. Anyway, what the hell difference does it make? They're both dead, ain't they? We couldn't do 'em no good by bringin' 'em with us."

"They was my friends," Carlo said.

"Yeah, they was all our friends," one of the others agreed. Paulie smiled broadly. "But we got to look on the bright side of things and Willie and Ben gettin' killed just means a bigger share for us." He took out his billfold and held it up. "When we get back, this baby is goin' to be full of money."

"Paulie, you dumb shit!" Vinnie shouted angrily, reaching over the back of the seat to hit the man holding the billfold. "What the hell is wrong with you? You know better than to carry a billfold on a job!"

"I didn't have it with me, Vinnie," Paulie answered, holding his hands up to ward off Vinnie's blows. "I didn't, honest!"

"Then where the hell did it come from?"

"Before we come on the job I stuck it down between the cushions of this car. I just now got it back!"

"Hell, that was just as stupid," Vinnie said. "This is a stolen car, you dumb asshole. What if the cops had stopped The Albino before he picked us up?"

"I wasn't thinkin', Vinnie," Paulie said. "I'm sorry."

"'I wasn't thinkin', Vinnie,'" Vinnie said, mimicking him. "I hope to hell Willie and Ben weren't that stupid. The cops are goin' to be crawlin' around on those two stiffs like flies on shit. And if either one of 'em has got anything on 'em, the cops are goin' to find it."

"You don't need to worry about Willie and Ben, Vinnie. They're clean," Carlo said. "We was talkin' about it this afternoon when you and Paulie was gone."

"Me and Paulie was gone?" Vinnie asked. He looked at Paulie. "What the hell does he mean? Where the hell were you?"

"I was nervous," Paulie said. "I went to the movies."

"You went to the movies," Vinnie said disgustedly.

"Yeah," Paulie said. "Listen, Vinnie, I didn't do nothin'

wrong. They didn't nobody say we couldn't go to the movies."

"I didn't think I'd have to tell you, you dumb shit," Vinnie said. "You knew damn well we had a job to do tonight"

"Yeah, well, I didn't do no harm goin' to the movies," Paulie insisted. "I was just killin' a little time, that's all."

"Yeah, Vinnie, lay off 'im. Calm down, for chrissake," one of the others said. "This was a good, clean job. The stoolie is dead and we didn't leave no witnesses except the citizens."

"Did you see them scatter when we opened up?" Paulie asked. He laughed. "I seen some fat old fart divin' behind a bush. That was funnier than shit."

"We didn't get all of 'em. We left one of the feds," Vinnie said. "He was still shootin' at us as we drove away."

"He might'a been shootin' but he ain't goin' to live. He was gut-shot," Paulie insisted.

"I don't know," Vinnie said. "I'm thinkin' maybe we should'a made sure of him. He was the only sonofabitch there who got a good enough look at us to identify us."

"With all the bullets flyin' around and ever'thing, he was probably scared as shitless as the citizens," Paulie suggested. "Hell, I'll bet we could walk in front of him right now and he wouldn't recognize a one of us."

"He'd recognize The Albino if he ever seen him again," Carlo quipped. The others laughed.

"Yeah, well, he might recognize us too," Vinnie warned. "Don't forget, he wasn't a local cop, he was a fed, a member of the Bureau of Investigation. Besides which, some of the bullets that were flying around came from his gun, remember? Especially the ones that got Willie and Ben."

"Is he the one that killed them?" Carlo asked.

"Yes."

"Then if the sonofabitch doesn't die, I may just take care of him myself...for free."

"What do we do now, Vinnie?" Paulie asked.

"What do you mean what do we do now? We been over this already, maybe twenty or thirty times."

"I know," Paulie said. "But you're already pissed off at me and I don't want to make no more mistakes."

"Okay, I'll go through it again," Vinnie said. "The first thing we do is we wash this car, then we dump it."

"What do we got to wash it for if we're just goin' to dump it?" Paulie wanted to know.

"Fingerprints, you dumb shit, fingerprints," Vinnie said with an exasperated sigh.

"Oh yeah, I've always wondered how they do that."

"Then we go to the bus station," Vinnie said, ignoring Paulie's remark. "After we get there you and The Albino will take the first bus goin' north. Me an' Carlo an' George will take the first bus goin' east. We'll change buses the first chance we get and we'll all meet in Chicago in two days."

"I got to travel with The Albino?"

"You got a problem with that?"

"Yeah, I got a problem with that," Paulie said. "The Albino is a freak and people are always starin' at him. An' when I'm with 'im, they stare at me too."

"The Albino can't help it what he looks like," Vinnie said. "Besides, when he keeps his hat on and his collar pulled up, folks don't notice him all that much."

"How the hell can you not notice someone's got a face like chalk and eyes pink like a rabbit?" Paulie asked. "I don't want to travel with him."

"Yeah? Well, how do you know The Albino wants to travel with you? Hey, Albino, what do you say? You want to travel with Paulie?"

"He don't bother me." The Albino grunted.

"The way he talks about you? That don't bother you?"

"No," The Albino said.

"You're a damn freak," Paulie said, reaching across the seat to give The Albino a shove on the shoulder.

The Albino, who was driving, brought the car to a screeching halt and in a flash, had his arm extended back over the seat with a knife in his hand. He put the point of the knife blade at Paulie's throat, then pushed enough to break the skin. A tiny trickle of blood began to stream down Paulie's neck, as if he had cut himself shaving.

"Hey, what the hell?" Paulie shouted in fear. "What you doin'? I thought you said my talk didn't bother you none?"

"You put your hands on me," The Albino hissed. He didn't push the knife any farther, but he didn't pull it away. "Don't ever put your hands on me."

Paulie held both his hands up, then made a show of pulling them back.

"I'm sorry, I'm sorry," he said. "I won't do it again."

There was a moment of tension in the car, then The Albino pulled his knife away from Paulie's throat, turned around and began driving again as if nothing had happened.

"Jesus, you're too good with that knife," Paulie said, taking out a handkerchief and dabbing at the tiny nick on his throat. He held it out and looked at the blood. "Look at that," he said.

Vinnie chuckled. "Of course he's good with a knife," he said. "Why you think he's with us? Sometimes we got a job only a knife can handle. When we do, The Albino is our man."

"I thought I was with you because I was so pretty," The Albino said. It was a humorous remark from a strange, brooding man who was without humor. As a result, it drew a bigger laugh than it deserved, especially from Paulie, who was now seeking to make up with The Albino.

"Okay," Vinnie said a moment later. "Now, are there any more questions about what you are to do?"

"What about the money?" Paulie wanted to know. He was still holding the handkerchief to the tiny cut on his neck.

"You'll get your traveling money before you leave," Vinnie promised.

"No, I mean—"

"I know what you mean," Vinnie said, cutting him off. "What I don't know is why you're askin'. You ever not been paid for a job?"

"No."

"Then what makes you think you're goin' to get stiffed now? You think the boss would like to know you're accusing him of welching on what he owes you?"

"No, Vinnie!" Paulie said quickly. "I wasn't accusin' him of anything! Don't say nothin' 'bout this to him! Please!"

"Then don't give me no more trouble," Vinnie said. "And shut up about when you're goin' to get paid. You'll get paid when you get paid, that's all you need to know."

"Yeah, Vinnie, that'll be fine," Paulie agreed contritely.

"Shit," Carlo said.

"Now, what the hell is your problem?" Vinnie asked, his temper growing shorter.

"Nothin'," Carlo answered. "I just sure as shit ain't lookin' forward to ridin' two days on a goddamn bus is all."

"Which would you rather be—ridin' two days on a bus, or spendin' time in a New Orleans jail?"

"Bus."

"Then shut the hell up," Vinnie said gruffly.

NEW YORK CITY

There was a fire somewhere over on Ludlow Avenue. The howl of sirens and blare of horns from the arriving fire engines pushed aside the normal evening cacophony of Little Italy. The fire was too far away from Joe Provenzano's apartment for him to see the flames, though some of the orange glow did slip in to mingle with the ambient light coming up from Rivington Street, seven floors below. Maria Vaglichio, who had been waiting in his apartment for him when Joe came home, was now standing at the open window. Her nude body was well enough lighted by the glow to be clearly visible.

Joe Provenzano had already taken off his jacket and shirt and now he sat on the edge of the bed to remove his shoes and socks. When he saw Maria standing by the window he stopped what he was doing and looked at her for a long moment, enjoying the view. She was nearly perfect in every detail, from the ember-tipped, conical breasts to the flat stomach to the flaring thighs and tapered legs. The orange fluorescence of the fire reflected from the dark bush of hair at the junction of her legs, making it appear like a spade of softly gleaming coals.

Maria turned from the window and saw Joe just sitting there with one shoe on and holding the other in his hand. She smiled at him.

"Is that all you're going to do?" she asked. "Are you just going to sit there?"

"Oh, I'm sorry," Joe said. He laid the shoe down, then took off the other. Finally, he slipped out of his trousers but when he lay back on the bed he was still wearing his shorts. Maria climbed onto the bed beside him, then leaned on one elbow as she looked down at him.

"What were you doing, just sitting there like that?"

"Looking at you."

Maria smiled again. "I like that," she said.

"You like what?"

"I like it when you look at me."

"That's not hard to do," Joe said. "You're a very beautiful woman and very easy to look at."

"You didn't always think so."

"When?"

"When you were in high school and I was in the sixth grade, you thought I was an ugly little pest."

Joe chuckled. "Well, you were an ugly little pest, then," he said.

"Well, if that's what you think, Joe Provenzano," Maria replied, and abruptly she started to get out of bed.

"Oh, no you don't," Joe shouted, laughing, reaching up for her and pulling her back to him. "I said you *were* an ugly little pest. But that's not true anymore. You're definitely not ugly and you're not even a pest. In fact, I like having you around."

Maria smiled again. "I am so glad I meet your approval, Mr. Provenzano," she said sarcastically. Using the red-nailed tip of her index finger, she began weaving little circles in the heavy growth of black hair on Joe's chest.

"You're my princess," Joe said.

The expression on Maria's face clouded and she sat up on the edge of the bed, looking down at Joe.

"Don't say that Joe. Please don't call me that."

"I'm sorry," Joe apologized. "I didn't mean anything by it."

"I know you don't," Maria said. "It's just that, well, that's what my father calls me."

"I'm sorry," Joe said again.

Maria lifted Joe's hand and held it to her lips. She kissed it, then he moved it down to her breast and let it rest there. Her nipple hardened under his palm and she made no effort to move his hand away.

"We make a fine pair, don't we, Joe? You being a policeman and me the daughter of a Mafia don?"

"I'm not a policeman," Joe corrected. "I'm a Federal Agent for the Bureau of Investigation."

"That's the same thing, isn't it?"

"No, it isn't the same thing. At least, not to me. Though I suppose some people might think so."

"Policeman or not, you go after men like my father and his associates and you put them in jail, don't you?"

"Yes, when I can," Joe admitted.

"That's what I mean."

"But, Maria, the fact that I am after your father and his associates has nothing to do with us," he insisted.

"I wish I could believe you."

"Do believe me," Joe pleaded.

Maria sighed. "What's going to become of us, Joe?" she asked.

"You could marry me."

Maria closed her eyes and shook her head. Despite the tightness with which she held her eyes closed, tears began to trickle down her face.

"No," she said. "I can't, Joe. You know I can't. It would kill my father." She was silent for a moment "Or he would kill you," she added quietly, so quietly that Joe could barely hear her. "I couldn't stand either one."

"I could quit the Bureau," Joe suggested.

"And what would you do then, come to work for my father?"

"No," Joe answered. "No, I could never do that."

"Good, because I wouldn't want you to. That would betray everything you have fought for, your entire life."

"There are other things I could do. Many things," Joe suggested. "There are new building projects going on all over New York. Maybe I could get a job with a construction company."

"Why bother? It doesn't make any difference what else you might do," Maria said. "You can't escape my father's influence."

"We could leave the city…get away from the Mafia."

"You should know by now that the Mafia is everywhere," Maria said. "New York, Chicago, Cleveland, Detroit, Kansas City, it wouldn't make any difference. No matter where we went, we wouldn't be free."

"No, I suppose not," Joe said with a sigh. "So, where does that leave us?"

Maria smiled. "That leaves us right here, right now, in this room and in your bed," she said. She leaned down over him and her breasts swung forward. "You can't argue with that, can you?"

"No, I guess I can't," Joe answered. "The question is, what are we going to do about it?"

"What are we going to do about it? I don't know. Maybe I can come up with something," Maria said teasingly.

Later, as they lay together side by side, holding hands and not speaking, Joe suddenly sat up.

"What is it?" Maria asked, surprised by his abrupt move. Joe didn't answer; instead, he cocked his head as if listening for something.

"Joe? What is it?" Maria asked.

"Sssh," Joe hissed quietly, laying his finger across his lips. Getting out of bed quietly, he padded, naked, across the room, then reached for the shoulder holster that hung from the dresser mirror. He slipped the .38 caliber, Smith & Wesson from its holster, then eased the hammer back with his thumb. There was a metallic click as a new cartridge-filled chamber was moved into position under the firing pin.

Maria pulled the bed cover up to her chin and watched through large, fear-brightened eyes as Joe held the pistol in his right hand, his arm crooked at the elbow, the pistol pointing straight up. He put his back to the wall, then slid along it, feeling his way with his left hand as he moved toward the door. At first, Maria had been puzzled as to what caused him to leave her bed, but now she too could hear footfalls outside the door. She waited with bated breath.

There was a loud knock at the door.

"Joe? Joe, are you in there? It's me, Bill." Bill Carmack was one of Joe's fellow agents in the Bureau. More than that, Bill was a close friend.

With a relieved sigh, Joe lowered his pistol. "Just a minute," he said. He turned toward the bed and signaled for Maria to get out of sight. Still using the bedsheet to cover herself, Maria moved over to stand in the shadows in the corner of the room. In the meantime, Joe slipped on a pair of trousers, then opened the door.

"Bill, what the hell are you doing here?" he asked. "You sure came at a bad time," he added sheepishly. Then, noticing the expression on Bill's face, he reworded his question. "What is it? What's wrong?"

"It's Mike," Bill said. "He's been shot."

"How bad?"

"Real bad, I'm afraid," Bill answered. "He's in the hospital. Tim's dead."

"Dead?"

"They were ambushed at the depot. Two New Orleans cops and our witness were also killed."

"Oh shit," Joe said. He sighed and pinched the bridge of his nose. "Is Mike going to pull through?"

"I don't know," Bill admitted. "But I'm going down there."

"You want me to come too?"

"No, you and Jason stay here and keep things going in New York. I think that's what Mike would say if he were here."

"Yeah, okay," Joe said. "How about Jason? Does he know?"

"No, not yet He's over on Long Island, visiting his family. I tried to call him but one of the servants answered. I didn't want to leave the message."

"I don't blame you."

"You try and get through, will you?" Bill asked. He looked at his watch. "I've got a train to catch."

"Call us, Bill, as soon as you know anything."

"I will," Bill promised. He started to leave, then turned back toward Joe. "I'm sorry about the interruption," he said quietly.

LONG ISLAND

The white marble chips covering the Vandervort driveway crunched under the tires of the big Cadillac as the chauffeur steered it majestically toward the front of the huge, palatial home. Jason Vandervort rode in the back with his mother and father. They were just returning from a party at the Long Island Country Club. Like his father, Jason was wearing a cutaway tuxedo. Unlike his father, Jason was carrying a pistol, though all through the evening, he had managed to keep it discreetly tucked away under the cummerbund so that very few people were even aware it was there.

"Shall I put the car away, sir?" the chauffeur asked as they stopped.

"Yes, we won't be needing it again," the senior Vandervort replied.

"Very good, sir."

"Phil, don't block off my car," Jason said.

"Jason, you aren't going out again tonight, are you?" his mother asked.

"I told Leah I might drop by for a while," Jason said.

"It seems a little late for that, doesn't it?"

"Oh, for heaven's sake, Mother, let him alone. He is a grown man," Mr. Vandervort said. "If he wants to go visit a young lady he can certainly do it without our say-so."

"Yes, of course, dear," Mrs. Vandervort agreed. "I wasn't raising an objection, I was just curious, that's all."

When they reached the library a moment later, Jason kissed his mother on the cheek, then went over to draw himself a cup of coffee from the great, just-filled silver samovar that sat on the credenza. As he leaned over to draw the cup his cummerbund slipped slightly, exposing the butt of the pistol he was carrying.

"Did you have to take that thing with you tonight?" his father asked.

"I'm a federal agent, Pop," Jason answered. "I'm supposed to be armed at all times."

"Even at a country club dance?"

"Even at a country club dance."

"Why? Did you expect someone to come out of the kitchen with a—what is it called—tommy gun?"

Jason chuckled. "I don't know, Pop. Those Wall Street sharks you run with are a pretty rough crowd. You never can tell who might show up at one of these events."

"Jason, all your father's business associates are fine, upstanding gentlemen. I do not find your attempt at humor in the least entertaining," his mother scolded.

"I'm sorry, Mom. I was just playing around, that's all. I was just having a little fun."

"Yes, well, I wish you would get your fill of playing around and having fun," the senior Vandervort said. "I wish you would quit this...this agency you are with, and come take your rightful place."

"My rightful place?"

"Yes. Your rightful place."

"And what do you think that would be, Pop?"

"In my office, with me, in the investment business."

Jason took a drink of his coffee and studied his father over the rim of the cup for a long moment before he spoke.

"Pop, I'm sorry if you think I'm just playing around and having fun. I'm really not, you know. My job with the Bureau is very important, not only to me but to the country. This is my calling, Pop, this is my rightful place."

"And the business I've built?" Jason's father replied. "What of it? You know, part of the satisfaction a man gets in building a successful business is the idea that he can pass it on to his son. Does what I have done mean nothing to you?"

"Of course it means something to me. But we've had this conversation before, Pop." Out in the hall, the telephone rang and Jason heard the butler answer. "I told you," Jason continued, "I have nothing but the greatest respect for you and for what you do. But I also have the insight to know that I have neither the talent nor the disposition to follow in your footsteps. On the other hand, I do have the talent and the disposition to be a federal law enforcement officer."

"Yes, well, I think both your talent and your disposition are being wasted," Jason's father said.

"Excuse me, sir," the butler said to Jason. "There is a telephone call for you."

"It's probably Leah," Jason said, smiling. "The girl just can't stay away from me."

"And that's another thing," Mr. Vandervort said. "Leah Sherman comes from a substantial family. How do you think her father would feel about his daughter marrying a policeman?"

"I'm not a policeman," Jason reminded him. "And who said anything about marriage? I just want to dally a little, that's all."

"Jason!" His mother gasped.

Laughing at his mother's response, Jason stepped out into the hall and picked up the telephone.

"Well, Leah. So what's wrong?" he asked. "Are you suffering from the deprivation of my company? What is it, my sparkling personality or my dashingly handsome looks?"

"Jason, it's me, Joe."

"Oh," Jason said, feeling a bit sheepish. "I'm sorry, Joe, I thought you were someone else."

"I need you in the city," Joe said. "Mike's been shot."

"My God! Was he killed?"

"No, he's still alive," Joe said. "We don't know yet for how long. Bill's on his way down to New Orleans to be with him. He wants us to keep things going here."

"I'll be right there," Jason promised.

CHAPTER 2

STEUBENVILLE, OHIO

gnatzio "The Hammer" Coppola was elegantly attired in the most appropriate sportswear for the golf course. He had on the most expensive cleated golfing shoes, yellow-and-brown argyle socks, brown corduroy knickers, a yellow pullover shirt and a narrow-billed flat hat. He teed up his ball, then selected the one-wood from a bag made of unblemished leather.

"Careful now, don't slice the ball," Jock O'Connell teased. Jock O'Connell, who was one of the foursome, was a captain on the Steubenville police force.

"Yes," Eric Adams added. Eric, one of the other members of the foursome, was a banker. "A good slice could crash through the clubhouse window and disturb all those nice folks having lunch."

"Wouldn't it be the shits if I could drop one right into the punchbowl, though?" Coppola laughed. "Ah, but I couldn't hit it that far on my best day."

"Really? Then why do they call you 'The Hammer'?"

the fourth and youngest member of the foursome asked. This was Stewart Dempster, a lawyer.

Coppola glared at him and the other two looked shocked, for it was well known by everyone that Ignatzio Coppola did not appreciate being called The Hammer. Coppola eased the situation, however, by smiling, and the others, including Stewart, breathed a sigh of relief.

"They used to call me that in my younger days," Coppola said. "But I don't like to be called that now. The name don't fit no more."

"I'm sorry," Stewart said in apology. "Of course, I'll never use it again."

"I should hope not," Eric said indignantly.

"You've got a big mouth, kid," O'Connell added.

"Ah, leave the kid alone," Coppola said generously. "He didn't mean anything by it and he said he was sorry." Coppola smiled warmly at the young lawyer, then he addressed the ball and stroked it cleanly, 275 yards right down the center of the fairway.

"Wonderful!" Stewart enthused. "Wonderful shot off the tee."

"Tell you what, kid," Coppola said. "You team up with me and we'll take these two on at ten dollars a stroke."

"Oh, Mr. Coppola, I'm not that good," Stewart said. "And if I bring you down and we lose, I'm afraid I wouldn't be able to afford it."

"Don't worry about it. If we lose, I'll make up the difference. But who's to say we're goin' to lose? What do you say? Are you game?"

"Yes sir, I'm game," Stewart said. "I'll do the best I can." A few seconds later he backed up his statement when his own tee shot flew straight and true to fall within twenty-five yards of Coppola's earlier shot.

Had any of the other three taken the time to notice,

really notice, what was going on, they would have seen Ignatzio Coppola at his best. Golf had nothing to do with it. What Ignatzio Coppola was doing was making a loyal and trusted subordinate out of Stewart Dempster. Coppola was a master of the game of psychological intimidation. He had, within the space of a moment, frightened Stewart, then defended, then befriended him. The result was a hireling who would be devoted for life.

Ignatzio Coppola got the name "The Hammer" for his battering opposition against competitors in the early days of Prohibition. As a Mafia don, Coppola started down the same path of bootlegging as many of his underworld contemporaries. He learned quickly, however, that the racket of supplying whiskey, so profitable to other dons in the larger cities, was less than satisfactory for him. Though he successfully fought off the competition, Steubenville was such a small market area that even controlling the entire city left little room for profit.

Then, a friend in another city, to whom Coppola owed a favor, asked if Coppola would take care of a "problem" for him. A police officer who was on the take was getting too greedy. Coppola's friend couldn't take care of the job because he was in the same city and the murder of a police captain would bring too much heat down. Coppola agreed to take care of it for a very generous fee. From that moment on, a new business was born.

Coppola reorganized his entire operation. He gave up bootlegging whiskey and though he sold small franchises in prostitution and gambling, he kept himself aloof from all the underworld activity going on in his own city. He became a model citizen, donating money to such worthwhile things as the hospital, the park improvement commission and the children's milk fund. He joined not only the country club but several civic organizations as well and he was held up as a sterling example of one who had completely "reformed his ways."

Ignatzio Coppola had a legitimate business which he used to front his operations. He was the sole owner of the Coppola Olive Oil Import Company. Most people accepted the ruse and didn't even bother to question whether or not the Coppola Olive Oil Import Company was really profitable enough to allow the style of living he maintained. Coppola did live lavishly and he spent freely. In addition to his club membership and his generous contributions, Coppola owned a huge home, staffed with servants, as well as a fleet of expensive automobiles.

Not everyone was totally blind to what was going on. Once Gary Blanton, a reporter for the Steubenville Times, wrote an article titled "Buying Public Opinion." The article dealt with Coppola's free spending of money in order to create a new image for himself. Blanton had intended to follow the first article up with another but the newspaper was so inundated with letters to the editor protesting the tone of Blanton's article that the newspaper refused to publish Blanton's next piece. Instead, he was assigned to a story on the reorganization of the school board. Shortly after that Blanton was found dead, an apparent suicide. The police dismissed as irrelevant the fact that Blanton though left-handed, had apparently shot himself in the right temple.

At the end of the golf game, which Coppola and his young partner won, Coppola offered to buy Stewart lunch. Stewart accepted and they were served in one of the private dining rooms of the club.

"I can make you a wealthy man, kid," Coppola said as he cut the piece of veal on his plate. He looked across the table at Stewart "That is, if you're smart."

Stewart was smart. He had graduated first in his law

class. He wasn't just book-smart, either. He had handled only two little jobs for Coppola but already he knew that there was much more than met the eye. The difference between the expense and income on the olive oil business was staggering. It was quite evident that Coppola was using the business as a means of concealing money he was making in some other way. And, even for the two little jobs he had done, Stewart had been paid three or four times what they would normally be worth.

"I like to think I'm smart," Stewart said, taking a sip of tea.

Coppola laughed. "Good, good. Kid, you've already had a glimpse of things around here, you know that I'm makin' a lot of dough, right?" He laughed and held his hand out to take in the elegantly furnished private dining room. "I mean, look at this. My ole man pushed a banana cart down the street. Hell, the bastards that run this place probably wouldn't even have let him on the grounds to take a piss behind one of their goddamn trees. But here I am, one of their most important members."

"You do seem to be doing very well," Stewart agreed.

"You're goddamn right I'm doing well." Coppola began buttering a roll. "The problem is, some of the things I do…some of the services I provide…could cause a little difficulty if the law ever got a burr in their ass and tried to come after me. When that happens, I need a smart lawyer to figure out ways to keep me out of trouble."

"Mr. Coppola, you realize of course that a lawyer is an officer of the court," Stewart tried to explain. "He can defend a lawbreaker after the fact. He cannot be a party to it before the fact, for if he is, then he becomes as culpable as his client."

"Yeah," Coppola replied. "I know that. So what that means is, you gotta work twice as hard, 'cause you gotta keep us both out of trouble." He smiled. "I figure that's the real beauty of it. When you're workin' for me, you'll be workin' for yourself too, so you'll do that much better of a job."

"Perhaps, but you failed to address the issue of what the incentive is that would cause me to put myself in such jeopardy in the first place."

"Incentive? Is that lawyer talk for how much am I goin' to pay you?"

"Yes, sir, I suppose it is," Stewart said.

"I like you, kid. You got balls and you cut right to the core of things. How does twenty-five thousand a year sound?"

Stewart had just picked up his fork and now he let it clatter back to his plate, stunned by the amount Coppola mentioned. This was ten times more than he was making at Norton, Norton, Ritter and Stead.

"I...I beg your pardon, sir?" he said weakly. "Did you say twenty-five thousand?"

"Not enough? All right, thirty thousand but not a penny more till I see how you're workin' out."

"Thirty thousand is fine," Stewart said quietly. "It's very fine."

"Good," Coppola said, finally taking a bite from the buttered roll he had been waving around. "When we leave here, you come with me. We can send for your stuff if you've got anything down at that law office where you was workin' that's worth sendin' for."

"There's nothing there I need," Stewart said.

Coppola laughed, spraying flecks of bread as he did so. "That means you're goin' to buy all new stuff, right, kid? I like that. Yes, sir, I like that. You're already learnin' to take advantage of the situation."

A man Stewart recognized as one of Coppola's associates came into the private dining room then and leaned over to whisper something in Coppola's ear. Coppola smiled, nodded, then sent him away.

"Something I should be involved with?" Stewart asked, after the messenger left.

"We've just completed a successful business deal in New Orleans and now we're goin' to Chicago."

"We are?"

"No, not us, not you and me personally. This business is bein' handled by my, uh, traveling salesmen, you might call them."

ABOARD A BUS, APPROACHING CHICAGO

The bus ride was two days long. It was also hot and sticky. Vinnie was very glad Illinois had paved roads. Those were in short supply west of the Mississippi and in the South. All up through Mississippi and Arkansas, as well as across the Bootheel of southeast Missouri, the roads had been gravel. At least they were supposed to be gravel. In fact, they were nothing but dirt roads and as a result of the bus's constant forty-mile-per-hour velocity, huge, billowing clouds of sand and heavy dust came pouring in through the open windows.

For almost two full days Vinnie had fought the stifling heat, the suffocating dust and the interminable boredom as he stared through the window of the bus. He was as torpid now as the listless creatures who were his fellow passengers. For hour after hour, the scenery outside had been nothing but rolling cornfields. Then, just over the past few minutes, the countryside had been undergoing a gradual change. A few buildings began appearing here and there, then more, and more still, until finally, it was obvious they were in a city. The bus was, at long last, in Chicago.

"Well, that's a welcome sight for sore eyes," Carlo

said. Carlo and George had made the trip with Vinnie. Vinnie and Carlo were sitting together, while George was in one of the two seats just behind. "I was beginning to think maybe we weren't goin' to ever get here."

"I never had no doubts about us," Vinnie said. "I'm just wonderin' about Paulie, that's all. He's such a dumb shit there's no tellin' if he made it or not."

"They left before we did, remember? And we had to go east for some distance before we could start north. Anyway, Paulie is with The Albino," George said. "He'll be all right."

"Yeah, The Albino is a good man," Vinnie agreed.

Half an hour later the bus pulled into the Chicago bus terminal and The Albino was standing on the platform, waiting for them as they climbed down from the bus. Vinnie wondered where Paulie was and he tried to read the expression on The Albino's face. He knew that was impossible, though; The Albino never had an expression. Some might say he didn't even have a face.

"Hello, Albino," Vinnie said. "Where is Paulie?"

"I tried to talk him out of it, Vinnie," The Albino said. "I tried to talk him out of it, but you know what a stupid sonofabitch Paulie could be."

"What the hell are you talkin' about?" Vinnie asked. They walked over to stand alongside the bus they had just come in on, to wait for their suitcases to be unloaded from the luggage bay.

"When we got here this mornin', Paulie got this idea. He figured to go ahead and take care of the job hisself. He figured if it was already done by the time you got here, he'd be back on your good side."

"So, what are you tellin' me? That the two of you tried to pull off the job and it screwed it up?"

"Oh, no," The Albino replied. "The job went all right. The guy we were after is down."

Vinnie smiled. "You mean it's all done? It's all taken care of?"

"Yes."

"Well, I've been misjudging Paulie. Maybe he isn't such a dumb prick after all. Where is he?"

"He's dead," The Albino said. "He did the job all right, but he got hisself killed while he was doin' it."

"Where was you?"

"I was waitin' in the car like I was supposed to be," The Albino replied.

Vinnie closed his eyes and pinched the bridge of his nose. "Shit," he finally said, letting out a long sigh. Then, remembering the incident in New Orleans, he looked up at The Albino. "He wasn't carrying anything with him, was he? I mean nothing the Chicago police could use to trace him?"

"No, nothin' like that. He was clean; we both made certain of that." The Albino said. "They got 'im laid out in the city morgue right now as a John Doe."

Vinnie smiled. "So, Paulie is dead, is he? Well, what was it he said down in New Orleans when Willie and Ben got it? That it would mean just that much more money for the rest of us?" He chuckled. "Pretty nice of him to chip in his share too, don't you think, boys?"

"Yeah," the others said, laughing along with him.

"What do we do now?"

"We go back to Steubenville."

"Not in a goddamn bus, I hope," Carlo complained. Vinnie smiled and picked up his suitcase. "To hell with the bus. We're goin' by train, boys. By first-class train," he said.

SISTERS OF MERCY HOSPITAL, NEW ORLEANS

Bill Carmack had been at the hospital for four days. He had gone in to see Mike every day since he arrived but Mike had been unconscious for the entire time. For the first couple of days, Bill thought that Mike's condition might be normal, but now he was beginning to worry. That was why today, after the doctor finished his examination, Bill stopped him as soon as he stepped out of Mike's room.

"Okay, Doc," Bill said. "Let's have it."

"I beg your pardon?"

"What's the story in there?" Bill asked, gesturing toward Mike's room with a jerk of his thumb. "Why doesn't he come out of it? How long is he going to be unconscious like this?"

"I'm afraid I can't say with any degree of certainty," the doctor said.

"Then say with uncertainty. Make an educated guess," Bill demanded.

The doctor sighed, then crossed his arms across his chest. He raised his right hand and began stroking his chin.

"Your friend was shot up pretty badly. He lost a lot of blood, and he had quite a shock to his system. We were extremely lucky he didn't die on the way to the hospital."

"Yeah, but he didn't die," Bill said. "So why's he like this?"

"Physically, his body needed a prolonged period of inactivity for complete convalescence," the doctor said. "That is nature's way and, so far, things have gone quite nicely. The physical healing is well under way. But now..." The doctor paused for a moment before he continued. "Now, the body has done its part. We'll have to see if his mind is up to the task. Will his mind allow him to regain consciousness?"

"Wait a minute. What do you mean allow him to regain consciousness? Are you telling me there's a possibility Mike won't come out of this?" Bill asked, surprised by the doctor's comment.

"Unfortunately, that is a possibility," the doctor replied. "He could go into an irreversible coma."

"A what?"

"Coma," the doctor said. "It comes from the Greek word koma, meaning deep sleep or lethargy. We don't know too much about it yet. We do know that people often enter comas as a result of an injury. As I said, nature makes good use of these periods of complete physical inactivity to allow the healing process to take place. But sometimes, for no reason that we can pinpoint, the patient just doesn't come out."

"What happens then?"

"They can stay in a coma for an indefinite period of time," the doctor said.

"How long is an indefinite period?"

"Indefinite means indefinite," the doctor replied.

"You're playing with words."

"It could be years," the doctor admitted.

"Years?" Bill asked in a weak voice. He looked back toward Mike's room. "You mean Mike could be like that for years?"

"Look," the doctor said. "I didn't want to have to tell you this but you were pressing me. I have to confess to you that I am a little worried about Mr. Kelly. As I said, he came through the surgery quite nicely. All of the bullets are out, there is no infection and his vital signs are strong. But...he is still comatose and I have no explanation as to why."

"So what you're saying is, he's in trouble and there's

nothing you can do about it? Is that it?" Bill asked sharply.

"I'm afraid so, yes."

"Why the hell can't you do something about it?" Bill demanded. "You're a doctor, aren't you?"

"Look, Mr. Carmack," the doctor said in an exasperated voice. "We can only do so much. Mr. Kelly will have to do the rest himself. If he is a fighter he'll come out of it all right. If not, he won't. It's that simple."

"He's a fighter," Bill insisted.

"Then you have nothing to worry about." the doctor said. "Now, if you'll excuse me, I've got rounds to make."

"Yeah," Bill said, almost distractedly. "Look, Doc, I'm sorry I mouthed off. I know you're doing all you can. I'm just worried, that's all."

"I know you are," the doctor said gently. "I will say this. If he is going to come out of it we should know by the end of the day."

"Is there anything I can do?"

The doctor looked pointedly toward the end of the hall, where a little door, marked by a crucifix, led into the chapel. He nodded. "You might try prayer," he suggested.

"Thanks," Bill said. "I guess I will at that."

Bill walked down the hall, then stepped into the chapel. The chapel was quite small, with two rows of two pews each. At the front of the chapel, there was an altar table and a stand-mounted cross. On the wall behind the altar was the ambry, with its little red light indicating a reserve of consecrated elements to be used for communion. On the side, just as he entered, there was a place for candles. Bill dropped some money in the box, took a candle, lit it, then knelt at one of the pews. He tried to pray, but it had been too long. He couldn't remember any of the prayers from the Missal and he wasn't the type who could extemporize. Instead of praying, Bill just thought about Mike.

Mike Kelly was chief of the New York office of the Bureau of Investigation, and that made him Bill's boss. Bill had been the second man to join the New York office and was second in charge, but his relationship to Mike went back much farther than that. Mike and Bill were more than partners and friends, they were first cousins. As children, they had played together, gone to school together and served as altar boys together. They had even gone to war together, serving in the "Fighting Sixty-Ninth," the New York regiment made up almost entirely of Americans of Irish descent.

Like his father and grandfather before him, and like his uncle, Mike's father, Bill, had joined the New York Police Department. Bill had expected Mike to join as well and was disappointed when Mike didn't. Later though, when Mike became a federal agent for the Bureau of Investigation, Bill was able to wrangle an assignment to work with him. Later, Bill resigned from the force, surrendering the time he had toward his retirement, in order to join the Bureau. The third man to join the New York office had been Joe Provenzano, while Jason Vandervort was the fourth.

That was six years ago. There were several agents assigned to the New York office now, but Mike, Bill, Joe and Jason were its core element

Bill sat quietly as two nuns came into the chapel, genuflected, then knelt for their own prayers. As they left, a few moments later, one of them reached out to touch Bill.

"How is your friend doing?"

"No change yet," Bill replied.

"He will be all right, you'll see. We are all praying for him," the nun said.

"Thank you," Bill replied. "If God won't listen to me, maybe He'll listen to you."

"God hears all prayers if they are honestly given," the other sister said.

"My prayer is honestly given, Sister," Bill replied. "The only thing is, it's been so long since I've been in a church that I'm not sure God will even know who I am."

The sisters smiled. "He knows, Mr. Carmack. He knows," one of them said.

A few minutes later Bill crossed himself, then left the chapel and returned to the little waiting area in the hallway nearest Mike's room.

A bright bar of sunlight spilled in through the open window. Just outside the window, a mockingbird was singing, while farther away still, there was the clack-clacking sound of someone pushing a lawnmower. The door to the room opened and a white-clad young woman came in, carrying a freshly cut bouquet. She was humming a soft tune as she put the flowers in a vase. For a moment or two, Mike was confused and he tried to figure out where he was. Then he remembered the shootout at the depot. This was obviously a hospital, though when and how he got here, Mike had no idea.

"Nurse?" he called.

Surprised, the woman turned toward the bed.

"Oh, my," she said, her eyes brimming with tears. "Thank the Lord. You're awake."

"Yeah. What time is it? Better yet, what day is it?"

"It's Saturday, sir."

"Saturday?"

"June 12th."

"June 12th? Do you mean to say I've been here for…"

"Six days," the young woman replied. "You were brought in here Monday night. Oh, there's someone outside who'll be glad you're awake. He's been here every day since Wednesday. I'll go get him."

"Wait, I…" Mike called, but the young woman was gone before he could finish his sentence.

A moment later a man came into the room. "Well, now, look at you," the visitor said, smiling broadly.

"Bill! What are you doing here?"

"What do you mean what am I doing here? I came down to see how you are getting along. I'm glad to see that you've finally come back to the land of the living. To be honest I had nearly given up on you."

"Yeah, well, I'd about given up on myself," Mike admitted. He laughed, dryly. "No, I'm lying to you. The truth is, I would have had to improve a lot to give up on myself."

The doctor came in then, smiling broadly. "Well, now," he said. "The nurse tells me someone is awake in here. Hello, Mr. Carmack. Hello, Mr. Kelly, I'm Doctor Presnell."

"The doc saved your life," Bill said.

"Thanks," Mike said.

"Well, it's no big deal. That's what I'm paid to do," the doctor said modestly. He turned on a tiny flashlight and shone the pinpoint beam into Mike's eyes. "I want to check a few things out. Follow my finger, would you please?"

Mike moved his eyes back and forth as directed.

The doctor snapped off the light and put it back in his pocket, then smiled broadly. "Yes, sir," he said. "You seem to be coming along quite nicely now. I think we might be out of the woods."

"Thanks, Doc," Bill said.

"I may not be the only one who deserves thanks," the doctor said.

"Pardon?"

The doctor nodded toward the crucifix hanging on the wall of this room, as it did in every room in the hospital.

"Yeah," Bill said sheepishly. "Yeah, I know what you mean."

"When can I leave, Doctor Presnell?" Mike asked.

"Oh, anxious to get out of here, are you?" the doctor teased.

"Yes."

"Well, I would like to keep you for twenty-four more hours," the doctor said. "If everything is still looking good, I'll let you go then. In the meantime, you take it easy, Mr. Kelly. I'll see you later, right now I have rounds to make."

"He's a nice guy," Bill said after the doctor left.

"I wouldn't know," Mike said. "I don't remember a damn thing since I checked in here."

"You do remember what happened at the depot, don't you?"

"Yeah," Mike answered. "I remember that, all right. There was a shootout. Oh, damn," he suddenly said. "They killed Tim, didn't they?"

"Yes," Bill answered. "Nasty business. Tim had a chest full of cutoff nail heads."

"Nail heads?" Mike asked.

"Whoever was wielding the shotgun had emptied the shot from his shells and replaced it with heads cut from ten-penny nails. You're lucky you didn't catch any of it."

"Poor Tim," Mike said. "What about his family? How are they getting along?"

"They're okay. They're strong," Bill said. "Well, as you know, Tim's old man is a policeman. That means that something like this is always in the back of their minds. Tim's funeral was Thursday. The two local cops were also buried Thursday."

"Damn," Mike swore.

"Mike, did you recognize any of the gunmen?"

"No," Mike said. "But I'd damn sure recognize them if I ever saw them again. And I'll testify about the two that I shot. You can believe that I don't intend to let the Matrangas get away with this."

"Yeah, well that's just it, Mike. The Matrangas have gotten away with it," Bill said, disgustedly. "They have ironclad alibis for last Monday evening. They weren't anywhere near the depot when the shooting took place."

"What difference does that make? Can't we connect the two gunsels I shot to the Matranga Family?"

"The New Orleans Police Department couldn't identify them."

"They couldn't identify them? Are you sure?"

"They tried, but they had no mug sheets on either one of them. They were clean as a whistle."

"Bill, that's impossible," Mike said. "These guys were professionals. They went about their business just as if they were delivering the mail. They knew exactly what they were doing. Somebody like that doesn't just come in out of the blue. They have to have a record."

"Maybe so, but they sure don't have one in New Orleans or in Louisiana and we didn't have anything on them in Washington. What they buried was two John Does."

"You mean they didn't even have a driver's license or anything like that?"

"They had nothing. Their pockets were as bare as Old Mother Hubbard's cupboard."

"Damn," Mike said. "Don't we have anything at all to go on?"

"We did find the car," Bill said. "It was a 1925 Buick, brown, four-door sedan."

"Yeah," Mike said. "Yeah, that was it. That was the car they used. How did you find it so fast?"

"Three of the eyewitnesses had enough presence of mind to write down the license number," Bill said. He chuckled. "We got three different numbers, but all three were very close, and only one matched up with a car that fit the description."

"Matranga's car?" Mike asked hopefully.

"No," Bill replied disgustedly. "It belongs to a doctor and his wife, right here in New Orleans. They had reported it stolen four days earlier."

"Shit. I was hoping we could make the connection."

"Yeah, I know. It would've been nice."

"Where'd you find it?"

"Down at the bus station. That probably means they're gone, though they could have left it there just to throw us off."

"Any prints?"

"Yes. They washed the outside of the car, but they left some pretty good prints inside," Bill said. "We sent them to Washington, they're trying to make a match now."

"What about Matranga? What does he say about all this?"

"Just what you would expect him to say," Bill answered. "He sent his regrets and flowers for the policemen who were killed and swore that he had never seen either one of the gunmen before. As I said, Mike, he's coming out of this without a scratch. He's gotten away with it."

"No," Mike insisted. "He hasn't gotten away with it. He may have put it off a little, but he hasn't gotten away with it."

The door opened again, and the nurse came back into the room carrying more flowers. This bouquet was larger and more elaborate than any of the many bouquets that already decorated the room.

"Look at that," Bill said. "That's not your ordinary

wreath of flowers. That looks more like something you'd hang around a horse's neck after winning the Kentucky Derby."

"Yes, aren't they lovely?" the nurse said enthusiastically. She looked around the room. "My goodness, I'll have to move some of the others for this bunch."

"Who are they from?" Mike asked.

"There is a card," the nurse said, brightly. "Would you like to see it?"

"Yeah, read it to me, will you, Bill?" Mike asked.

Bill took the little envelope from the nurse, then removed the card.

"'Get well soon,'" he read. "'Best wishes from your friend'..." Bill looked up at Mike before he read the name.

"Well, who?" Mike asked.

" 'Johnny S.,' " Bill replied quietly.

"Damn," Mike said. He sighed. "Nurse, would you please get those out of here," he asked dryly.

"What?" the nurse gasped. "Mr. Kelly, surely you don't mean that."

"Throw them in the trash."

"But...but, they are so lovely! I can't just throw them away."

"Then give them to somebody else, I don't care what you do with them," Mike said. "Just get them the hell out of here," he added more harshly.

"Yes sir," the nurse said, crestfallen at the harshness of Mike's words.

When Bill saw tears well in the nurse's eyes, he followed her out into the hall.

"Sister," he said. "You'll have to excuse my friend."

"I don't understand," the nurse replied. She looked at the flowers. "They are so lovely and I was just trying to bring some cheer to the room."

"You do understand that my friend is a law enforcement officer, don't you?" Bill asked. "And that he is here because he was shot in the line of duty?"

"Yes."

"The man who sent these flowers is no friend. His name is Johnny Sangremano and he is an outlaw, a gangster, just like the men who shot Mike. He meant this as a cruel joke."

"Oh," the nurse said, somewhat mollified now. "I see."

"Please give them to someone else," Bill suggested. "Tell them it's from someone who wishes them well."

The nurse brightened. "I could give them to Mrs. Abernathy," she said. "She has no family, bless her heart and no one has come to see her since she has been in here. I think she would appreciate the flowers."

"Good, good. Give them to Mrs. Abernathy with Mike's best wishes."

"Yes," the nurse said, pulling herself together now that the issue had been resolved. "Yes, I shall enjoy doing that."

"And you won't hold any hard feelings for Mike?"

"No, of course not. The poor man has already gone through enough," the nurse said.

Bill flashed his best smile. "Thanks. I knew you would understand."

"Did you apologize to her for me?" Mike asked when Bill returned.

"Yes."

"Good. I didn't mean to hurt her feelings. I was just angry."

"By the way, have you stopped to consider the idea that Sangremano may have meant it?" Bill asked.

"What the hell—are you taking up for that sonofabitch now?" Mike asked.

"No, I'm not," Bill said. "But the two of you were friends once. Good friends. And he did save your life. And he had nothing to do with what happened down here."

"He is the head of the Sangremano Family," Mike said.

"He is Mafia, one of the bad guys. We're the good guys, that puts us on opposite sides of the fence."

"Don't get me wrong," Bill said. "I'm not taking up for him. I'm just saying that he might not have meant any harm by sending the flowers."

"Yeah," Mike said. "I bet he can't wait to send me a funeral wreath."

NEW ORLEANS AIRPORT, THE FOLLOWING AFTERNOON

A large single-engine cabin monoplane sat on the apron near the terminal building. A fuel truck was parked just in front of it and a worker was sitting on top of the wing, putting gasoline into the fuel tanks. The letters SAFE were painted on the tail of the plane, while the words Southern Air Fast Express were just below. Though the fledgling airline depended on mail for most of its revenue, it also flew passengers from New Orleans to Chicago by way of Jackson, Memphis, and St. Louis.

As there had been no further complications, Mike was released from the hospital as promised and now he and Bill were approaching the airport, riding in the backseat of a wine-colored, four-door Dodge. A high chain-link fence surrounded the apron where half a dozen aircraft were sitting, including the large monoplane with the SAFE markings. The Dodge pulled up to the closed gate that led through the fence and the driver honked his horn.

"You can't get through here," a uniformed guard said, coming over to the gate. "You're goin' to have to go around."

"Open up," the driver said, showing a badge that identified him as a member of the Bureau of Investigation.

"Oh, yes sir, right away, sir," the guard answered and he put a key into the padlock that held the gate chained shut.

"Listen, you sure you don't want to rest a couple more days?" Bill asked Mike as the gate was being opened. "We don't have to go back today, you know." He smiled. "We could even go down to Bourbon Street and have a look around."

"A look around for what?" Mike asked.

"Oh, maybe a close-up look at sin, crime and/or evil," Bill teased. "Mostly sin."

"No, thank you," Mike replied laughing. "I want to go back now. Anyway, I'm feeling fine."

"Well, all right, but I think we ought to at least go by train. That way you could lie down when you get tired. I mean, look at this damn thing," he said, pointing to the airplane. "There's no room to stretch out."

"We're just going to fly as far as Chicago," Mike said. "I won't need to stretch out. From Chicago, we'll take the train to New York and I can lie down then. In the meantime, we will have saved a whole day."

"One day isn't going to make any difference to the bad guys," Bill grumbled.

"It will make a difference to me," Mike said resolutely.

"Hey, do you really work for this guy?" the driver asked Bill.

"Yes."

"Is he always this hard to get along with?" the driver teased.

"Always," Bill answered with a laugh.

When the gate opened, the car drove through, then across the apron and right up to the airplane. Bill got out first, then turned around to help Mike.

"You guys keep trying to find out who those two goons were," Mike said. "Somebody like that has to have a record."

"We'll do all we can, Agent Kelly," the driver replied.

"Wire my office in New York the moment you get a lead," Mike said. "Better yet, telephone me."

"We will."

"Come on, let's get aboard," Mike said, getting out of the backseat with some effort

The two agents from the New Orleans office waited until Bill and Mike were aboard the plane, then with a slight wave, they drove away. A moment later the pilot came out of the terminal building, signed a form that the mail clerk handed him, then climbed up into his seat. He looked back over his shoulder and smiled at Mike and Bill.

"You gentlemen ready?" he asked.

"As ready as I'll ever be," Bill replied. "Although I have to admit I don't like these things all that much."

"Relax," the pilot said. "It'll be over before you know it." One of the men on the ground swung the propeller through, then, as soon as the engine caught he pulled the chocks from the wheels. The pilot taxied into position for takeoff, turned into the wind and opened the throttle. With the engine roaring, the airplane raced down the runway, then lifted up. A moment later Mike and Bill were looking down on the roofs of New Orleans and at the great bend in the Mississippi River. The plane banked toward the north, then began climbing.

"We need to get one of these for our office," Mike said.

"Get what for our office?"

"An airplane," Mike said.

"I thought you had gotten all the flying out of your system."

"No," Mike answered. "Once you get the bug, you never get it out of your system."

As the plane continued to climb to altitude, Mike looked out the window at the cloud formations and let his thoughts wander back to another flight six years earlier. On that flight, Mike had been at the controls.

Mike was eight hundred feet above Long Island's Curtis Field when he chopped the throttle on the DH-4's liberty engine. It popped and snapped and threw back a spray of hot oil to stain the fuselage and splash on the forward windscreen of the De Haviland biplane. Mike rolled it into a left turn, then came out of the turn perfectly lined up with the grass runway at the little airport. The plane slipped down out of the sky, losing altitude rapidly as its guy wires and bracing hummed at just the right pitch to indicate that Mike's final approach was at the proper angle and speed.

Mike had come back from the war too restless to settle down. He had saved enough of his army pay to finish college but after he graduated with a liberal arts degree, he still didn't know what he wanted to do. Then, at an air show, he ran into Johnny Sangremano, the same young man who once landed on a road in France to rescue Mike from what was going to be a German firing squad. The two of them became reacquainted and when Johnny offered to teach Mike to fly, Mike accepted the offer. Mike was a quick learner and became a good flyer, though he wasn't as good at it as Johnny and willingly admitted that he never would be. However, he discovered that flying was something he very much enjoyed doing.

Johnny was the one who found the surplus DH-4 airplane sitting disassembled out behind a hangar at Roosevelt Field. The two men were able to buy it with what little money they had left. The barnstorming trip across the country, however, was Mike's idea. He had talked Johnny into it and they were set to leave within a few days.

"How are you doing?"

Bill's question brought Mike back to the present and he looked back from the window at his friend.

"I'm doing fine," he said.

"No pain anywhere?"

Pain? Yes, Mike thought, there is pain. There is a deep and abiding pain over circumstances that conspired to turn Johnny Sangremano, once his best friend, into his mortal enemy. But that was not a pain that could be shared, or even understood, except perhaps by Johnny himself.

"No," Mike answered with a small smile. "There is no pain."

"How far have we come?" Bill asked the pilot.

The pilot looked out the window, then shouted back over his shoulder. "About a hundred and fifty miles," he said.

"Really?" Bill replied. He smiled broadly. "Damn, that's moving right along, isn't it? I think you're right, Mike. I think we should get one of these. We're going to be in Chicago in no time."

It took ten hours to reach Chicago and they scooted in just in front of a fast-building thunderstorm. By the time they were taxiing up to the terminal the rain was already coming down in sheets and Mike had resigned himself to getting wet during the walk across the apron. Then he saw a car drive right up to the plane. When he wiped the window and looked through it, he saw Joe Provenzano and Jason Vandervort, smiling up at him from the front seat of the car.

"Hey!" Bill said. "Look who's here to meet us."

"What are they doing here?" Mike grumbled. "Why aren't they in New York where they belong?"

"You really are a hard one to get along with, aren't you?" Bill teased. "Have you ever stopped to think that they might have been worried about you? Maybe they just wanted to come see how you are doing."

Joe and Jason met Mike and Bill on the apron, opening the cabin door of the monoplane the moment the propeller stopped. Bill hopped out of the plane; Mike stepped out a bit more gingerly.

"What are you doing here?" Mike asked.

"What are we doing here? We're working, that's what we're doing here," Joe replied.

"Working? In what way?"

"Well, to be honest, Jason and I thought we would come meet you and Bill and ride back on the train with you. But when we arrived this morning, one of the guys from our Chicago office had some information he thought we might be interested in."

"What was it?"

"Come along to the morgue and we'll show you," Joe said mysteriously.

"The morgue?"

"If you're up to it, that is," Joe added. "I mean, how do you feel?"

"I feel fine," Mike said. "Who's at the morgue?"

"We've got a John Doe," Joe said. "But I have a feeling you are going to find him interesting."

"In what way?"

"That's what we want you to tell us," Joe said.

It was cold in the morgue. Mike shivered and turned the collar of his jacket up as he followed the coroner between two rows of tables. Most of the tables were empty, but two had bodies, covered by gray sheets, with bare feet sticking out from beneath. One of the bare feet had a white nametag tied to its big toe. This tag read "Leo Miller, DOA." On the big toe of the other body, there was a yellow tag. The yellow tag read, "John Doe, DOA."

"They were both brought in this morning," the coroner said. "Leo Miller is a known associate of Dutch Heinie's gang. A police patrol car found them both in an alley, just off Pierpont Street."

"What's the theory?" Mike asked.

"Leo was a collector for Dutch Heinie," Joe explained. "The cops think he may have leaned too hard on John Doe. John Doe resisted and they shot each other."

"Plausible," Mike agreed.

"They found a gun only for Miller, nothing for John Doe," Joe said.

"Really? How do the cops explain that?"

"They say someone must have stolen John Doe's gun."

"Stole John Doe's but left Miller's?"

"Yeah, I pointed that out to them, but they said sometimes it happens," Joe said.

"But you don't believe it."

"No, and neither will you when you see him. Take a look at him, Mike," Joe invited.

"Yeah, well, that's why you brought me down here," Mike said. "But I don't know what I'm looking for. I mean, this is pretty much a job for the Chicago police, isn't it?"

"It probably is," Joe admitted. "But I want you to take a look anyway."

Mike pulled the sheet down to expose the naked body

of a male Caucasian in his late twenties or early thirties. His skin had a slightly blue tint to it "Well, I'll be damned," Mike said.

Joe and Jason laughed. "I knew it," Joe said.

"Knew what? What's all this about?" Bill asked. He was the only one who was still in the dark.

"This was one of the shooters at the depot in New Orleans," Mike said, pointing to him. "One of the ones who killed Tim." He looked over at Joe and Jason. "The question is, how did you two know who he was?"

"Well, like your mobsters down in New Orleans, this fellow was stripped clean, so the Chicago PD hasn't been able to run a make on him yet," Joe explained. "But our friend in the Chicago office thought seeing how you were in New Orleans, we might be interested in this. It was in the band of his hat." Joe held up a red ticket stub.

"What is that?" Bill asked.

"It's a ticket from a movie house in New Orleans," Jason explained. "It's to a matinee that just happened to be playing the same day Mike was shot."

"He must've come up here to get away from the cops down there," Joe suggested.

"Did either our people or the Chicago police find anything else on him?" Mike asked. "I mean anything, other than the ticket stub, that would tie him to New Orleans?"

"No."

"What about his clothes? Where are they?"

"Over there," the coroner said, pointing to a cardboard box.

"Mind if I take a look?"

"Go ahead, be my guest."

Mike dumped the dead man's clothes onto the countertop, then began looking at them closely. The box contained a dark pin-striped suit, a felt hat, a pair of oxblood shoes, a silk shirt, a black tie and cotton underwear.

"Something about these clothes bothers me."

"They're sort of typical clothes, if you ask me. Just about every hood you ever see wears clothes just like this," Joe suggested.

"Yeah," Mike agreed. "Every hood in New York, or Cleveland or Chicago. But you don't see anyone wearing stuff like this down in New Orleans...not even any of Matranga's people. New Orleans is hot and humid and everyone dresses to be comfortable."

"But you did say that you saw this man in New Orleans?" Jason asked.

"Oh yes, I saw him all right. And he was wearing clothes just like this too. In fact, I realize now that I actually noticed the clothes the moment he and the others jumped from the train car. I knew then that something was wrong, I just wasn't able to put my finger on it. But dressed like this, all these guys stood out like sore thumbs, even without their guns. The reason no one in New Orleans had ever heard of them is that they weren't from there. They came to town just to kill D'Angelo." He looked into the face of John Doe. "The question is, where did they come from and where are the others?"

STEUBENVILLE, OHIO

"If you ask me, it was a pretty sloppy job," Coppola said.

"No it wasn't, boss," Vinnie said in defense. "I was told to take out D'Angelo and Miller. Well, we done that, just like we was supposed to."

"And got three good men killed."

"Two good men," Vinnie corrected. "Paulie wasn't worth a cup of warm piss. We're just as well off without him."

"Willie and Ben were good men."

"Yeah, they were," Vinnie said. "So are The Albino and the others who came back. So am I. We was all standin' up there, takin' our chances. That goes with the territory. The important thing is, we done a good, clean job, and there ain't no way the New Orleans or the Chicago police can trace anything back to us."

"Yeah," Coppola agreed. "Yeah, that's the important thing."

"What's next?"

"I'm goin' to let you take a few days to rest," Coppola said. "Then I've got some more business for you."

"Yeah? Where, this time?"

Coppola smiled. "You don't need to know yet. I'll let you know in good time."

LONG ISLAND, AT THE HOME OF DON LUCA VAGLICHIO

That evening the Vaglichios were holding a very important meeting. Present were Don Luca Vaglichio, the head of the Vaglichio Family, his brother, Mario, his chief enforcer Guido Santini, and his consigliore, Ben Costaconti.

Luca Vaglichio sat in his big leather chair and puffed contentedly on a Havana cigar, listening to his brother, Mario. Luca was in his middle fifties, about five feet seven, with a broad face, heavy brows and high cheekbones. He tended to squint whenever he was discussing anything intently, which, because of the cheekbones and brows, turned his eyes into narrow slits. Mario, Luca's younger brother and Maria's father, was a much more handsome man. Mario was talking about the problems they were having with the blacks who were moving their numbers rackets into Vaglichio territory.

"Ah, numbers are small potatoes anyway," Luca said, dismissing it with a wave of his cigar. "Let the niggers have it. I'm more interested in how things are going with our new venture."

"You mean dope?"

'Yeah," Luca said. "See, the way I figure it is, the niggers will make a few bucks on the numbers, then they'll give it all to us because we'll have what they want. Right?" He laughed.

"If we can get everything going all right," Mario agreed. "But we've got a few problems right now."

"What kind of problems?"

"What we need are some dealers down in Lower Manhattan and over in Queens," Mario said.

'You mean Sangremano territory," Luca said.

"Yes," Mario agreed. "That territory is wide open, thousands of potential customers over there and nowhere for them to go to get taken care of."

Luca took his cigar out and studied it for a moment, then he looked up at Ben Costaconti. "What about it, Ben? Do you think we can work something out with the Sangremanos?"

"I doubt it," Ben replied. "Johnny Sangremano has made it pretty clear he doesn't want anything to do with the dope business."

"Maybe we can make a deal with him," Mario suggested. "If he doesn't want to handle it, we can handle it for him."

"What do you think, Ben?" Luca asked.

"It's certainly worth a try," Ben agreed.

"Why don't we set up a meet?" Luca asked.

"All right," Mario said. "Maybe we can get Don Pietro Nicolo to mediate for us."

Don Pietro Nicolo was the head of one of the other families of New York. There had been several intermarriages between the lower echelons of the Nicolo and the Sangremano families, and between the Nicolo and the Vaglichio families. As a result, the Nicolos had, on occasion, acted as peacekeepers between the Vaglichios and the Sangremanos. In the past, this often proved to be very difficult, for the Sangremanos and the Vaglichios had been at each other's throats for years. Also, peacekeeping was nonproductive and often frustrating, so it wasn't a role the Nicolo Family relished. It was, however, one that had been thrust upon them and they had no choice but to accept it.

"If you will allow me, Don Mario, I have a suggestion," Ben said. In the strictest sense, Mario wasn't a don, since Luca was actually the head of the family. However, Luca and Mario shared responsibility so evenly that it was sometimes difficult to tell who was in charge. As a result, Ben treated them nearly equally.

"Yes, what is it?" Mario asked.

"As you may know, Johnny Sangremano is about to get married. Perhaps we could call on him then?"

"Yes," Mario agreed, smiling broadly. "Yes, that's a splendid idea. What do you think, Luca?"

"Sure," Luca agreed. "I don't know why not." He smiled. "Besides, that's the traditional time to make a request."

"He ought to be in a good mood," Mario suggested.

"And if he's not I know just the gift that will put him in a better mood," Luca said.

"What kind of gift? What can you give someone like Johnny Sangremano that he doesn't already have?" Mario asked.

Luca smiled. "Something very special," he said. "Actually, I got it for Mama, but this is a better use for it."

"What about Mama?"

"This is business," Luca said easily. "Mama will understand."

GREENWICH VILLAGE, NEW YORK

There were four men sitting together at a table in the back of the Sons of Italy Restaurant The restaurant, being in Greenwich Village, was in the territory controlled by the Nicolo Family, and sitting at the head of the table was Don Pietro Nicolo's oldest son, Enrico. Enrico, who was in his early thirties, had not yet "made his bones," an expression the Sicilians used meaning, "to prove himself."

There seemed little likelihood that Enrico would ever get the opportunity to make his bones. The Nicolos were a small family, with a small territory. Don Pietro Nicolo, Enrico's father, had established himself as a peacemaker over the years, the mediator who worked out compromises between the other families, either to prevent a war, or to stop a war once one had begun. It was Don Nicolo who finally negotiated an end to the war between the Vaglichios and the Sangremanos.

As a result of Nicolo's mediation, the Village had become to the Five Families of New York what Switzerland was to Europe. The Nicolos were never involved in a war. The advantage of their peaceful disposition was that no one else coveted their territory, nor made any claims against the various enterprises—booze, numbers, prostitution and so forth—by which the Nicolo Family supported itself. The disadvantage was that the Nicolo Family paid for this security by being forever relegated to the position of one of the smaller families.

Sitting at the table with Enrico were three of the Nicolo underbosses. Like many other members of the Nicolo Family, the underbosses were related by blood or marriage, to people within the Sangremano and Vaglichio families. These interconnected relationships made the job of peacekeeping somewhat easier.

Enrico Nicolo rolled the spaghetti up with his spoon and fork, then shoved it into his mouth.

"Well, I'll tell you this," he said, speaking with his mouth full and using his fork as a pointer. "If there was one man who could take the best ideas of the Sangremanos and the Vaglichios and put them together, he'd have one hell of an organization."

"What do you mean, Enrico?" Jerry Martelli asked. Martelli was married to the sister of one of the underbosses in the Vaglichio operation.

"Well, now you take Johnny Sangremano, for example," Enrico said. He picked up a piece of bread and began buttering it "He has all the theater owners working for him, not just in the Lower East Side but all over the city."

"No, he don't. We got the numbers and prostitutes workin' the theaters here in Greenwich Village," Martelli insisted.

"Small potatoes," Enrico said. "I'm talkin' about the movies themselves. Did you know that every theater in town, even the fanciest ones, has to get their movies from Sangremano? He controls every bit of the distribution. You want to show a movie, you show the one Sangremano tells you to show and you pay him his price. And what's the good of owning a theater if you got no movies to show?"

"Yeah, I see what you mean," Martelli said.

"But, and here's the thing I was talkin' about," Enrico went on. "Johnny Sangremano don't want nothin' to do with dope, so he's leavin' that business up to the Vaglichios. He could make a million, maybe two million real easy. Dope's goin' to be as big a thing as booze, but Sangremano don't want nothin' to do with it."

"Would you get into the dope if you was him?" Gino Conti asked.

"Sure I would," Enrico answered. "And if you ask me, Sangremano's crazy for not gettin' in on it."

"Why don't we do it then?" Conti asked.

"Yeah, boss. Why don't we get into a little of that action?"

Enrico waved their suggestions off.

"Don't think I wouldn't like to, but the way things are now, it wouldn't work for us," he said. "We don't control enough territory to make the dope profitable and since the Sangremanos control all the movies, we can't do anything there either. That leaves us pretty much stuck with what we got."

"Yeah, I guess so," Martelli said. "But you got to admit that what we got ain't bad," he added, smiling broadly. "I mean, look at us all here. Sittin' around the table, all of us wearing silk suits, all of us got a little money in our pockets. We weren't doin' this we'd be doin' what—workin' down at the docks?"

"Or in the fish market," Georgio Sarducci suggested.

"Yeah," Conti agreed. He looked across the table at Enrico. "Thanks to you and your father, the don, we're all doin' pretty well for ourselves. We got no complaints."

"I have always known I could count on your loyalty," Enrico said and he put his left hand out to have it joined by the others so that their arms formed a star across the table.

CHAPTER 3

NEW YORK, LATE SPRING, 1926

Johnny Sangremano's home on Long Island was large by any standard. He had built it to resemble a French villa that had caught his fancy during the war and like the villa, Johnny's house had nineteen rooms, turrets, dormer windows and a red tile roof. The five well-tended acres on which it sat ran from the portico in front, across the clipped grass lawn, around half a dozen marble statues, through a formal garden, across flagstone walks, past a large swimming pool and finally ended at a boathouse and dock down at the shore.

There were only two ways to reach the house: by private road or from the bay. The private road was guarded twenty-four hours a day, every day, and there were enough underwater impediments in the bay to force any approaching boat to use a specific channel. Johnny Sangremano did not like drop-in visitors and the precautions he took with the private road and water access ensured that no one would be able to pay him an unexpected visit. His aversion to visitors was not idiosyncratic; it was, in fact, very practical for these times and for someone in Johnny's position. Johnny Sangremano was the head of the Sangremano Family, a Mafia empire built by his father. When Johnny's father, Giuseppe, died, the position went to the oldest son, Tony. But first Tony and then the second son, Vinnie, were killed in a gang war. That left Johnny as the new don.

On this particular Saturday in July there were many visitors to the Sangremano estate, all of them expected. In fact, a very large canopy had been pitched on the lawn to accommodate them. There were also two long tables, which would soon be loaded with food, and enough smaller tables scattered around to seat 150 people. Balloons and twisted strips of red, white and green crepe paper festooned the tables and hung from the trees, all in preparation for a wedding.

The actual marriage ceremony would not take place until four o'clock in the afternoon. The service would be a relatively private affair attended only by family and a few of Johnny's closest associates. The reception, however, was open to hundreds of Johnny's people, and it would start before the wedding, continue through the marriage rites and last far into the night.

Johnny Sangremano was taking a bride and though the young lady he had chosen, Clara Ricco, would have preferred getting married in a church, she was perfectly satisfied that the marriage would be properly sanctified.

"Why go to the church when we can bring the church here?" Johnny asked her, and indeed, a bishop, two priests—one of them the bride's brother—and a dozen altar boys were more than enough to convert the large parlor into a chapel. In addition to this holy entourage, an altar and reredos had also been brought in to complete the transformation.

Johnny had many reasons for getting married at

home. The one he expressed most frequently was that, since the celebration would last from early morning until far into the night, it wasn't fair to the other parishioners to tie up the church for such a long time. Also, a great deal of spirits would be consumed by the guests. Since drinking was illegal, it wouldn't do to compromise the church in such a way. The bishop and the priests were happy with the arrangement, not only because they didn't want the church tainted by illegal behavior, but also because Johnny Sangremano had made a large enough donation to the parish school to build four new classrooms and put on a new roof.

There was another reason. As evidenced by the demise of Johnny's two older brothers, being the head of the Sangremano Family was a dangerous job. It was much easier to protect him at home than in a church. Jimmy Pallota, better known as Weasel, was responsible for Johnny Sangremano's safety, and he breathed a sigh of relief when he learned that the wedding and the party would be at Johnny's Long Island home.

As the guests began arriving for the wedding they brought gifts for the bride and groom. Some of the gifts were as elaborate as a yellow Duesenberg convertible with red leather seats; others were as modest as a home-baked cake.

In this case, it truly was the thought behind the gifts that counted, for Johnny Sangremano's many business enterprises had already made him a wealthy man and there was very little likelihood that any one gift could improve his situation. A homemade quilt that was dear to the giver in terms of time and money for material was as appreciated as the finest silver service set from one for whom the silver service was easily managed. It was in this way that Johnny could measure the respect being paid him by his many friends.

Because his appreciation for the smallest of the gifts was as genuine as his gratitude for the most ostentatious, even the poorest of the people came away uplifted. "He is truly worthy of the position of don," they said to each other. "He is someone we can trust, someone we can turn to in our time of need."

Most of the wedding guests and friends of "Don" Johnny Sangremano were first- or second-generation American citizens. They had not yet learned to think in terms of federal, state or local government for functions and sendees. In their minds, the police, city hall, the state-house, and the federal government were all entities that were, at best, composed of confusing regulations and unfathomable mysteries. At worst they were corrupt organs of governmental bureaucracies whose only purpose was to oppress the people.

Therefore, when a businessman within the Sangre-mano territory wished to establish a grocery store, a laun-dry, a bakery or a restaurant, he didn't go to the chamber of commerce. And when a woman wished to make arrangements to bring someone over from the old coun-try, she didn't go to Immigration. When seeking redress for a grievance, the injured party didn't go to the Justice Department. Where one went on all these occasions was to Johnny Sangremano. Everyone knew that he had the connections and the resources to cut through the red tape and get things done.

Johnny was not only the one they came to when they needed help against some transgression, he was also the one they feared when they were the transgressors. He was the final authority, the benevolent dictator, the godfather of them all, and when he was spoken to it was always with a respectful "Don" before his name. And, just as Don Sangremano never turned down an earnest request, neither would anyone ever turn him down if he should happen to call upon them for a small favor.

This relationship was based not only upon fear and dominance, but also upon respect and honor. Honor was a very important thing to the Italians, more important than any other virtue.

A long white chauffeur-driven Lincoln arrived on the scene. Though the parking lot was already filled with expensive automobiles, this car, with the exposed front seat for the uniformed driver and the elaborate scrollwork around the enclosed or "saloon" part of the limousine, stood out. Those who were closest to the road turned and stared unabashedly, while others moved to get a better look. When the car stopped under the portico, a valet stepped down from the porch and opened the door to help the occupants out. "It's Katie Starr!" someone said.

Katie Starr, whose real name was Katherine Sangremano, was Johnny's younger sister. She was also one of the biggest stars in Hollywood. It was no secret that her career had been helped by her family. The Sangremanos had invested money in the movie that gave her her start. The producer had used Katie as a means of getting the funding he needed. To his and everyone else's surprise, however, Katie Starr was a smashing success. A movie critic had put it best when he reviewed her first role:

Who is Katie Starr, you ask?

Katie Starr had only one scene in Glory Dust but that scene was the salvation of the entire picture. How can one describe the innocent sensuousness of Katie Starr? It is, perhaps, a little like discovering a beautiful young wood nymph at her bath. You feel guilty at invading her privacy... but you enjoy the view.

Every producer in Hollywood would like the opportunity to feature Miss Starr in one of their own films, but the word is that the wily Mr. Solinger has her sewed up tighter than a drum with an exclusive contract to her services.

After three more pictures, Katie was the biggest box office attraction in Sammy Solinger's stable. She was particularly profitable to him because he was still paying her the same thing he had paid her for her first picture. Al Provenzano, the Sangremano consigliore, who was also a lawyer, had written a very polite, businesslike letter to Sammy Solinger asking that Katie's contract be renegotiated. Solinger refused, so Johnny had gone to Hollywood to talk to Sammy in person to see if he could make him "listen to reason".

Those who knew the Sangremanos knew that term had an ominous quality behind it. It was the last opportunity one had to avoid incurring the full wrath of the Sangremanos. Sometimes, when one didn't "listen to reason," the Sangremanos would "make an adjustment." Such adjustments often proved fatal.

When Johnny had spoken with Sammy Solinger on behalf of his sister, he asked, in all sincerity, for Solinger to listen to reason. Solinger had laughed it off.

"Mr. Sangremano," Solinger said, "perhaps it is time we got something straight. In New York, your brothers thought they were King Shit. But they are both dead now and the Sangremanos got no power anymore, not in New York, and sure as hell not out here. Out here, I am the king of the jungle. People cringe when I roar. Do you understand what I'm telling you, guinea? I've got ways you've never even heard of to protect my interest. You mess with me and I'll ruin your sister and disgrace your entire wop family, what there is left of it. Now, get out of my house, you wop bastard. And get out of my town."

Johnny had smiled politely, apologized for the intrusion and excused himself. Shortly thereafter, Solinger's head turned up on a tray of luncheon meats. The mystery of Solinger's murder was still unsolved but his death had automatically released Katie Starr from her contract. She was with a new production company now and her affairs were being handled with exacting honesty.

Katie returned to New York, and her brother's wedding, as a star. But she had not come to the wedding alone. She brought Vic Mason with her. Vic was a tall, straw-haired man who had held his looks well enough to enable the studio to pass him off as thirty-five when he was actually forty-four. A few years earlier he had been a legitimate contender with Rudolph Valentino for the unofficial title of most romantic male actor in the movies.

Unfortunately for Vic, the public has fickle taste. The blond hair, perfectly chiseled features and clear blue eyes that had gotten him into the movies in the first place now became his downfall. The women who went to the movies now developed their sexual fantasies around dark, smoldering Latin men. As a result, all the producers started looking for Valentino types. Vic Mason went out of style and he quit getting parts.

Vic Mason hadn't worked for three years. He managed to maintain a degree of visibility because he paid publicists to get his name in the gossip columns. He was still invited to parties, but people were beginning to talk of him in the past tense. "Whatever happened to Vic Mason?" someone would ask, or worse, they couldn't even think of his name and would say such things as, "Do you remember that blond fellow who used to be a romantic lead?"

Then someone said that a handsome blond leading man would make a good counterpoint in Katie Starr's newest picture, Sun and Rain. The leading man's blondness and Katie's dark, sultry looks would be the perfect combination. Katie, who did remember Vic Mason, suggested that he would be good for the role, and because she was the star, she was able to get her wish. It was a good picture, Vic Mason had a good part and already people were beginning to talk about his "comeback."

After the picture was finished, Katie invited Vic to come back east with her to attend her brother's wedding. Vic was not only grateful to her for getting him back into pictures, he also saw her as the key to his future. Therefore, he gladly accepted her invitation.

Vic had no idea of what to expect at the wedding and the grandness of the house and grounds, as well as the number of people who were in attendance, surprised him. It was even larger than an event at the home of the biggest producer in Hollywood.

"Miss Starr, could I have your autograph?" someone asked.

"Certainly," Katie replied. "And I'm sure you'll want Vic's as well," she added generously.

"Oh, yes, I'd like your autograph too, please," the autograph seeker said. Actually, the young woman was just being polite. She was too young to remember Vic Mason from his own pictures and the one he had just completed with Katie had not yet been released.

Vic was embarrassed that Katie had to explain who he was, but he signed every piece of paper that was thrust before him, affixing his signature with a flourish.

The first autograph seeker was followed by dozens of others, who rushed to the car and thrust odd bits of paper, old envelopes, and even table napkins toward the two movie stars. Katie and Vic were soon surrounded by fans, some of whom wanted their autograph and others who just wanted to be close.

Johnny was upstairs in his bedroom, in his underwear, having just taken his bath. The tuxedo he would be married in was laid out on the bed. Weasel was in the same room with him, standing over by the window, looking down on the scene below.

"What's all the noise down there?" Johnny asked as he pulled on his socks. "There" came out "dere," because Johnny was sucking on an ever-present lemon drop. A sack of the confections was on the dresser, another was on the bedside table and still another was downstairs in the den.

"Your sister," Weasel answered. "Everyone's crowdin' around her, askin' for her autograph."

Johnny smiled. "Well, it's what she wanted."

"That old guy is with her," Weasel said.

"What old guy?"

"You know," Weasel answered. "The old guy she got as her costar on this picture."

Johnny laughed. "That would be Vic Mason," he said. "He's not really that old. He just hasn't worked in a while. Anyway, Katie likes him and she asked me if he could come to the wedding."

"I wonder how much she likes him?" Weasel mused.

"What do you mean?" Johnny asked quickly.

"Nothin'," Weasel answered. "I don't mean nothin'. It's just, well, him comin' all the way out here to go to your weddin'. That's pretty important when a man does somethin' like that, ain't it?"

"Yeah," Johnny replied. "Yeah, you may be right. Maybe I should look into it." Johnny put on the bright red cummerbund, then stepped in front of the mirror to take a look. "How do I look?" he asked.

Weasel smiled. "I should look like you," he said. "I'd have to beat the women away with a stick."

"Why beat them away?" Johnny teased.

The cummerbund set off Johnny's slender waist and broad shoulders. For a Sicilian, he was a little taller than average. All the other features were there though, the dark hair and eyes, the olive complexion and the full lips. Johnny was a very handsome man and had been, for some time, a ladies' man. The fact that he was now about to settle down and get married surprised not only Weasel but several others. At his bachelor party, someone had mentioned it to him.

"Whoa," Johnny had replied. "I may be getting married but who said anything about settling down?"

Most laughed, but Weasel and a few others knew there was a degree of truth in Johnny's statement. Johnny's mother had long wanted him to get married.

"You are the last of my sons," she had told him. "Your papa, your two brothers, may their souls rest in peace, are gone now. Without you get married and have the children, who will there be to carry on the Sangremano name?"

"Besides," AL Provenzano had told him, when he spoke for Johnny's mother, "it is expected that the godfathers be married. Surely there is someone?"

There was.

Clara Ricco was a beautiful young girl whose large brown eyes and blue-black hair had captured Johnny the first time he ever saw her. She was from a good family; her father was a legitimate businessman who owned a small tailor shop and her brother was a priest. That was important. If her family was in "the business" there would be too many opportunities for jealousies and differences of opinion to arise.

Another thing that was important to Johnny was the fact that Clara was a virgin. Johnny was surprised that he considered this important. After all, he had spent his entire life since puberty trying to change that status in as many girls as he could. But it was important and the fact that he had not been able to get Clara into bed raised her worth in his eyes. Therefore, if to satisfy his mother and to live up to the image of a godfather he had to marry, Clara Ricco was as likely a choice as anyone he had ever run across. Maybe getting married wasn't going to be so bad after all. He began whistling a happy little tune.

Someone knocked on the door to the bedroom and Weasel answered it. The visitor was a heavyset gray-haired man in his sixties. Weasel recognized him as Ben Costaconti, consigliore to the Vaglichio Family. During the late war between the Vaglichios and the Sangremanos, Tony and Vinnie Sangremano had died at the hands of the Vaglichios. Johnny had personally killed Sam Vaglichio, the patriarch of the Vaglichio Family. However, all that was in the past. There was now and had been for the last few years, an uneasy peace between them.

"Hello, Mr. Pallota," Costaconti said, smiling warmly. "I'd like to speak to your boss."

"Yeah," Weasel said, stepping back from the door and holding his hand out toward Johnny. "He's right here."

"Johnny, Johnny, it is your wedding day. What a happy day this is," Costaconti said, striding across the room with his hand out Johnny took it.

"Ben, it's good to see you," Johnny said. He stuck a lemon drop in his mouth.

"The Vaglichio Family sends its best regards," Costaconti said.

Johnny laughed. "Really? Best regards from the Vaglichios? Why don't I believe that?"

"But you should believe it, Johnny," Costaconti said. "Those bad days are all behind us now. We've had four years of peace. That should prove we can all work together."

"Yeah," Johnny said. "As long as we stay out of each other's way," he added pointedly. Johnny turned back to the mirror and began tying his bow tie, a bright red match to the cummerbund.

"Believe me, Johnny," Costaconti went on, "Luca and Mario want only the best for you. And as a token of their esteem, they have sent a very special wedding gift to you."

"Yeah? What did they send, a cobra?" Johnny teased.

"Please, I wish you would take this seriously," Costaconti said as if personally hurt by Johnny's remarks.

"Okay, counselor," Johnny replied. "No more wise-guy remarks," he promised. "What is this special gift from the Vaglichios?"

"The Madonna from the church in Misilmeri," Costaconti said, smiling broadly. "That is the church in Sicily where your father was baptized."

Johnny looked at Costaconti in surprise. "Yes, I know of the church in Misilmeri," he said. "But how did the Vaglichios come by its Madonna?"

"As you may or may not know, the church in Misilmeri is also the church where the senior Vaglichios were married. In honor of what would have been their parents' sixtieth anniversary, Don Luca Vaglichio made a very generous donation to the church," Costaconti explained. "And of course, they bought a new Madonna. The point is, they went to great expense and trouble to present you with a wedding gift that would be to your liking. You do like it?"

"I am genuinely touched by it," Johnny admitted. "My mother especially will be most pleased."

Costaconti smiled broadly, then wiped his face with a handkerchief.

"Good, good," he said. "I will tell the Vaglichios. They will be very happy that they have pleased you."

"The Vaglichios," Johnny said, as he slipped on his jacket. "They are coming to my wedding?"

"They are coming to the reception, Don Sangremano. They were not invited to the marriage mass."

"Please apologize to them for that oversight," Johnny said. He smiled at Costaconti. "Tell them I would be most honored if they would attend."

"Yes," Costaconti said. "I'll tell them."

Costaconti left. As Weasel closed the door behind him, he turned toward Johnny.

"I don't know, boss," he said. "The Vaglichios want something."

"Of course they want something," Johnny agreed easily. "The question is, what do they want?"

"They've never forgiven you for rubbin' out their old man. Maybe they're plannin' some way to get even with you."

"No, the score is more than even," Johnny replied. "Don't forget, the Vaglichios killed both my brothers."

"Yeah, well, that's why I don't trust them now. I mean, bringin' gifts like that."

Johnny laughed. "The old adage reads, 'Beware of Greeks bearing gifts'. It doesn't say anything at all about Sicilians bearing gifts."

"Nevertheless, I think you ought to be careful."

"Why, I am being careful, Weasel. That's why I have you around all the time," Johnny replied. "Now, come on, let's go downstairs. I hear there's going to be a wedding down there."

There were tears in the eyes of the father of the bride as he gave Clara away. There were tears in Clara's mother's eyes too. Johnny's mother and sister also cried and as Katie explained later, the beauty of a wedding could always be measured by the amount of tears shed. In the case of this wedding, enough tears were shed to float a battleship; therefore, it qualified as one of the most beautiful.

After the wedding, the bride went outside to the lawn reception, where she greeted the hundreds of guests who were there. Johnny promised to join her later but for now, he had to attend to a ritual that was almost as old as the wedding service itself. Whenever there was a wedding in a don's family, the don would hold court to receive well-wishers and visitors. It was customary also for such visitors to make requests of the don and, if it was within his power to grant the requests, he was bound by tradition to grant them. The fact that it was the don himself who was getting married did nothing to decrease Johnny's responsibility and obligation to the tradition.

For the most part, the requests were simple things to grant, such things as adjusting a utility bill that was wrong, or speaking on someone's behalf to a landlord or an employer. These were problems that seemed insurmountable to the poor soul who was suffering them, though they could often be taken care of by a simple word from the don. That didn't lessen the degree of anguish the people were going through, nor did it diminish their gratitude for having the problems solved.

For more than two hours a steady stream of favor-seekers came into the parlor to make their petitions to the don and Johnny sent them away relieved of their anguish. Then, during a lull in the visiting, Johnny leaned his head back on the great leather chair, the same chair his father had used to receive visitors when Johnny was a boy. He could hear the music and the laughter outside and, from somewhere, the high, excited squeal of one of the children at play. Johnny plucked at the bridge of his nose with his thumb and forefinger.

"How about it, Weasel?" he asked. "Is there anyone else out there?"

"The Vaglichios," Weasel replied.

Johnny raised his head and looked at Weasel in surprise. "The Vaglichios are waiting to see me?"

"Yes, Padrone."

This was most unusual. These request times, granted not only at weddings but at birthdays and holidays, were reserved strictly for the ordinary people, the "subjects," so to speak, who were under the don's administration. People who were "connected" never infringed upon this time, especially if they were connected to another family.

"Did they say what they wanted?"

"No, Padrone."

Johnny sighed. "All right, send them in," he instructed.

At Weasel's invitation, the two Vaglichios came into the parlor.

"Okay, gentlemen, I've agreed to see you," Johnny said. "Now, what do you want?"

"First, we want to offer you our heartiest congratulations," Luca said.

"Thanks," Johnny replied. He was standing, and he made no move to sit down, nor did he offer the Vaglichios a seat.

"You, uh, got the present okay?" Luca asked. "The Madonna?"

"Yes," Johnny replied. "Well, I mean, I haven't seen it yet, but Mr. Costaconti told me about it. It is very generous of you."

"Listen, we're glad to do it," Luca said. "I mean, we've had a few differences of opinion in the past, I admit. But at the bottom we're all Sicilian, right? And we got to all stick together. I mean, if a Sicilian can't trust another Sicilian, then who the hell can he trust?"

"Yes indeed," Johnny replied. "Who can we trust?" He walked over to the sideboard and opened a fresh sack of lemon drops, then popped one in his mouth. He held the open sack toward the Vaglichios, but they declined. "Now, what can I do for you?"

"We have a proposition we'd like to offer," Luca said.

"One that could make us all a lot of money," Mario added.

"I already have a lot of money," Johnny replied.

"This will make much, much more," Luca insisted.

"Why are you sharing this with me?" Johnny asked. "If it is such a good proposition, why don't you do it yourselves?"

"We can't do it ourselves," Mario admitted.

"That is, we can," Luca put in, quickly. "But it will be a lot more productive, for both of us, if we have your cooperation."

"What is this proposition?"

"Dope," Luca said.

Johnny shook his head. "I have heard it before," he said. "I didn't like it then and I don't like it now. I'm not going to get involved with dope."

"We aren't asking you to," Luca said.

"Then what are you asking?"

"Look. We've got a steady supply of dope…more than we'll ever be able to use in our own territory…"

"So we want to expand into your territory," Mario finished. "We'll handle everything and cut you in for a percentage."

"Dope is bad stuff," Johnny said.

"Yeah, bad for the dumb bastards who use it. But for us. it's better than bootleg whiskey," Lucca insisted. "The thing is, once the users get the craving, it creates a guaranteed market. They'll buy as much as we can come up with."

"And they'll do anything they have to do to come up with the money," Johnny said. "That means a lot of uncontrolled criminal activity in the neighborhood. I don't want to be responsible for anything like that."

"Don't worry. You won't have anything to do with it. Like I said, we'll take care of everything," Luca promised. "All we want from you is the right to sell it in your neighborhood. We'll make all the buys and collect all the money. You'll be given a full and equal share, even though you won't have to do a thing."

"I still don't like it."

"You just don't understand. You might remember, when we started selling bootleg whiskey, we had this same conversation," Mario said. "Your brother, Tony, didn't want to sell whiskey."

"So you had him killed," Johnny said.

"Pop had him killed," Luca corrected. "And you killed Pop. But I didn't bring this up to stir up old wounds. I brought it up just to remind you that there was a time when you didn't understand whiskey, either. But look at it now. Would you willingly give up the bootleg whiskey business?"

"No," Johnny admitted.

"Believe me, if you get into the dope business, you won't give it up either. There's a lot of money to be made."

"I'll think about it," Johnny promised. He smiled. "Anyway, today is my wedding day. You can't expect me to give you an answer to such a question on my wedding day, can you?"

"No, of course not, Don Sangremano," Luca said easily. "And I ask your forgiveness for choosing such a day to make the proposal."

"That's all right," Johnny said, starting toward the door and, by that action, moving the Vaglichios out as well.

'You are not angry with us?" Luca asked.

"How can I be angry with anyone who would bring such a thoughtful gift?" Johnny asked.

Luca smiled. "Good, good," he said. "Enjoy it in good health."

Out in the garden, Vic Mason sat alone and watched the hundreds who were enjoying the wedding party. The band was playing a lively tune, led by an accordionist, and the flower-bedecked wooden platform was crowded with dancers. Though Vic's table was empty, all the others were crowded with guests who were enjoying the food and the wine. Children played tag, running in and out of the tables, unrestrained by their indulgent parents. Clara Ricco, who was now Clara Sangremano, sat in white-gowned, bejeweled splendor at a special raised table. The groom's chair right beside her was empty now but everyone realized it was because Johnny was attending to important business. The others at the raised table were Mama Sangremano, Clara's parents, the maid of honor, the bridesmaids, and the ushers.

Katie was supposed to be at the table with Vic but she was off dancing and had been almost from the moment of the wedding. She was with one of the ushers now and behind that usher a whole line of young men waited for their own opportunity.

"You're going to wear yourself out dancing all day," Vic said once when Katie came over to wipe her face and take a drink of punch. "Tell them to take a walk."

"I can't do that," Katie said. "These are my people."

"We can't let our fans run our lives for us just because we are movie stars," Vic insisted. "Anyway, have you gotten a whiff of any of them? Every damn one of them smells of garlic."

"You don't understand," Katie said. "These people

aren't dancing with me because I'm a movie star. They are dancing with me because I am Johnny's sister. In their eyes, that is much more significant."

Despite Vic's protestations, Katie returned to the party, and she continued to dance, mix and mingle with the guests. Even when she wasn't dancing, she was sitting at the bride's table, exchanging giggling "girl talk" with her new sister-in-law.

Finally, with a sigh of disgust, Vic got up from the table. He told himself he was bored with the whole thing, but in fact, he was piqued because he was being ignored, not only by Katie but by all the others as well. Who the hell were these people? Didn't any of them ever go to a movie? Didn't they know there was a world beyond their own guinea neighborhood?

As Vic moved through the guests he could overhear bits and pieces of conversation. Some of the guests were speaking in Italian, so he had no idea what they were talking about. And even the conversations he could understand seemed strange to him. He was sure that Katie's brother's name was Johnny, yet people kept referring to him as Don, only not just Don, but "the" Don. Vic walked around half a dozen marble statues, wandered through a formal garden, moved across flagstone walks and passed a large swimming pool, until he finally ended up at a boathouse and dock down at the shore.

As Vic stood looking out over the water, he heard someone behind him. When he turned, he saw a young man trudging along the road, carrying a shotgun slung over his shoulder. What was he doing here? Surely he wasn't hunting.

"Hello," Vic called.

Though the armed man nodded in reply, his face remained expressionless. He continued to trudge on down the road and Vic turned his attention to the boathouse. He walked out on the dock, then pushed open the door and stepped inside. There, nestled in the water slip inside the boathouse, was a very large cabin cruiser. Vic let out a low whistle and stepped on board, feeling the boat rock gently under his weight.

Vic stepped into the cabin of the boat and looked around. He smiled. When he got back on top he was going to buy a boat just like this. It would be a perfect place to take women. Not Katie, who was too powerful in her own right, and also too smart, but young women with beautiful bodies and empty heads. And he would have a strict rule. As soon as a woman came onto his boat, her panties would come off.

"Hello."

When Vic heard the woman's voice, he turned to look toward the open hatch. Almost as if she had been materialized by his musings, a beautiful young woman was standing there, smiling down at him. From the dress she was wearing, he realized she was one of the bridesmaids.

"Hello yourself," he said. He took in the boat with a wave of his hand. "It's quite a boat, isn't it?"

"Yes," the young woman replied. She stepped through the hatch and came down to stand close to him. She was young and supple, with coal-black hair and piercing brown eyes. Her skin was olive-complexioned and, warmed by the sun, gave off a subtle fragrance of its own. "Do you have a boat like this out in Hollywood?"

"Well, not at the moment," Vic hedged. "But I'm going to get one," he added.

"This boat belongs to the don. One time he gave a party on it and I was a guest."

"I'll bet you had a fine time."

"Yes," she said. "I was the only guest." She smiled, then her eyes grew distant. "I thought after that party that he and I would be, uh, that is..." She blinked a couple of times, as if forcing whatever thought she had to go away before she said something she didn't wish to say. "But of course," she went on in a lower voice, "I'm just thrilled to death that he married Clara. She is one of my dearest friends. Clara and Gina, everyone used to say. If you want to find Clara, look for Gina. If you want to find Gina, look for Clara."

"You're Gina?"

"Yes. I went to school with Clara."

"I see."

"Oh, but I'm out of school now," Gina added quickly. "I mean, I wouldn't want you to think I'm...too young... or anything."

"Too young? Too young for what?" Vic asked.

"Oh, for anything," Gina said. She put her fingers on his face, then traced them down his jawline. "Tell me, Vic. Do you think I'm pretty?"

"Yes, of course."

"Am I as pretty as the girls you know in Hollywood?"

Vic smiled at her, then he reached up and caught her wrist in his hand.

"If you want me to make love to you, why don't you just come out and ask?" he said.

Gina gasped and tried to pull away, but Vic held her wrist too lightly for her to escape.

"I...I don't know what you're talking about," Gina said.

"Sure you do," Vic said. "You want to get even with the don for marrying someone else, don't you? Wouldn't you like to make love on his boat?"

"No, I, uh, it's nothing like that," Gina insisted.

Vic picked her up and lay her down on the long, wide couch that ran along the side of the boat's cabin. It didn't take long, and it didn't matter at all to him that he had left her hanging and unfulfilled.

As Vic started to pull away from Gina, she wrapped her arms around his neck and pulled him to her, pleading with a soft little cry, deep in her throat, for him to stay.

"Shhh, shh," Vic said. "This isn't right...someone might come in on us. How would that be?"

"I don't care," Gina pleaded. "Don't leave me, not yet, not like this."

"You'd better get yourself put together," Vic said. "I'll wait for you outside the boathouse."

Vic left the boat and the frustrated young woman behind him. When he stepped out of the boathouse a moment later, he was surprised to see someone standing on the dock, right next to the door.

"Mr. Mason?" the man said.

"Yes," Vic answered nervously. Who was this? Was he here for revenge? Vic knew that Italians were big on such things as avenging the honor of their women.

"My name is Jimmy Pallota," the man said. "The Don would like to see you."

"The Don?"

"Mr. Sangremano," Jimmy explained.

"Oh, you mean Katie's brother. Sure, sure, I'd be happy to talk to him."

"This way," Jimmy said, starting back through the guest-filled garden to the house.

"I must confess you startled me, standing on the dock like that," Vic said.

"Why?" Jimmy asked. "The girl you screwed in there ain't nothin' to me."

"Oh...uh, I just didn't know what to expect," Vic said. He had thought to protest, to tell the young man with the cold eyes that he and the girl hadn't done anything. Then he thought better of it. It was obvious the man knew better and telling an outright lie would just make matters worse.

"I guess you got a right to be nervous, though," Jimmy said. "I mean, if the girl had meant anything to me, I would have handed you your balls."

When Weasel showed Vic into the parlor a few moments later, Johnny Sangremano was standing over in front of the big window, looking out onto the party going on in his garden. Vic heard the door close behind him and he knew that the man who brought him had discreetly withdrawn. Vic stood there for a moment; then, when he wasn't sure Johnny knew he was here, he cleared his throat.

"I know you're here, Mr. Mason," Johnny said without turning around. He stood at the window for another full minute before he did turn. Though Vic had been in the makeshift chapel for the wedding, this was the first opportunity he had to really study Johnny up close. Johnny wasn't very old, but there was something in his eyes...some ancient qualify that made him look years older.

"Mr. Pallota said you wanted to see me," Vic said. For some strange reason, he had the feeling of a recalcitrant schoolboy, reporting to the principal.

"Are you having sex with my sister?" Johnny asked calmly.

"What?" Vic gasped.

"I want to know if you are having sex with my sister," Johnny asked again.

"I...no! Why would you even ask?"

"I know about you, Mr. Vic Mason. I know that two studios have dropped you because you can't keep your pecker in your pants. One of them had to pay off the parents of a young girl to keep you out of prison on a statutory rape charge."

"The girl was seventeen," Vic said. "She told me she was twenty-four and she looked it."

Johnny brushed his protest aside with an impatient wave of his hand. "I'm not interested in all that," he said. "What I want to know is, are you having sex my sister?"

"No, I swear to you!" Vic said.

"You expect me to believe that?"

"You must believe me," Vic said. "Look, I admit, I would sleep with her if I could, but your sister won't have anything to do with me. She's still a virgin, for God's sake! Can you imagine anyone like her in this day and age, living in Hollywood, still being a virgin?"

"Yeah," Johnny said, smiling broadly. "Yeah, I can imagine it." He got a serious expression on his face and he pointed to Vic. 'You want to marry my sister, you come around and talk to me," he said. "Otherwise, you stay the hell away from her."

CHAPTER 4

NEW YORK, ONE NIGHT LATER

Martin Milsaps was a projectionist for the Orpheum Theater on Delancey Street in Manhattan's Lower East Side. He had no intention of making this his life's work but he had been, thus far, unsuccessful in getting a job in the field for which he was educated. Martin had studied at CCNY and he had a degree in theater arts, an irony that wasn't lost on him. Roy Loomis, the manager of the Orpheum, who had no concept of theater beyond movie houses, thought a theater arts degree was the perfect background for a projectionist.

It was Thursday night and the Orpheum had been showing Little Lord Fauntleroy, starring Mary Pickford, for a week. This was to be its last night and already the marquee out front had been changed for the next day's showing. Tomorrow would be the first day for Katie Starr's newest picture, *Poor Little Princess*. Martin was looking forward to the changing of the film. It wasn't that he didn't enjoy Little Lord Fauntleroy, but as the projectionist, he had already watched it more than twenty-one times and he was more than ready for a change.

After the last showing of the evening, Martin put Little Lord Fauntleroy in the film can, then went downstairs to the lobby to wait for the delivery of *Poor Little Princess*. It was a little past midnight and all the customers and other employees of the theater were gone. By now, even Mr. Loomis's office was locked. It was always like this on the night the film was to be exchanged, but Martin didn't mind. By the end of the week, he was sick of the old film and he was paid two dollars extra for locking up.

As Martin walked down the stairs from the projection room he noticed that it seemed unusually dark in the lobby. The lobby was normally brightly lighted but tonight the only illumination Martin could see came from the ambient light of the colored, frosted-glass wall fixtures of the theater itself. Even that light had to spill between the cracks of the heavy red curtains that hung over the doors between the lobby and the theater. Martin figured the concession stand operator must have turned off the lobby lights when he left and he cursed him for his thoughtlessness.

"One might wonder just how he proposes that I get around?" he grumbled to himself. "Am I to feel my way about with a white cane?"

The lobby smelled of popcorn. The tangy, buttery aroma was enticing to the theater audiences but the smell had grown old to Martin, who had to abide it night after night. Martin set the film can down by the front door, then walked over to turn on the light. To his surprise, he discovered that the light switch was already on. "Oh my," he said. "The light bulb is burned out."

Martin considered changing the bulb but decided to wait and do it the next day. The light fixture was too high for him to reach without a ladder and in the dark, with no one here to hold the ladder for him, it would be too dangerous a job.

Suddenly, and for no discernible reason, Martin felt the hair rise on the back of his neck. There was someone in the lobby! Or at least he felt as if someone was here.

"Hello? Hello, is someone here?" he called.

There was no answer.

"Mr. Loomis? Mr. Loomis, is that you? Are you still here?"

No answer.

"Mr. Loomis, if you are here, please don't play games with me. I find this most vexing."

When there was still no answer, Martin's irritation changed first to apprehension, then to genuine fright.

"Listen, if there is someone here, I think you should know that I am just the projectionist. Do you understand? I show the movies. I have absolutely nothing to do with the money. Mr. Loomis takes the money to the bank every night. There is no money here. There is nothing here except a few candy bars. I hope you clearly comprehend that."

Though Martin neither saw nor heard anything specific, he couldn't shake the uneasy feeling that someone else was here with him. Finally, he decided it might be the unexpected darkness that was giving him the willies. Whatever it was, he didn't want to stay around in the lobby any longer, so he picked up the film can and walked out onto the street. It was dark outside as well, but there at least the darkness was somewhat ameliorated by the corner streetlamp. He would just wait in front of the theater for file film exchange.

It didn't take that much to make Martin nervous. He always felt uneasy about this part of his job anyway. The film exchange was frightening enough by itself. That was because Nino LaRosa and Joey Bendetti, the two men who always brought the new film and picked up the old, were two of the most sinister-looking characters he had ever seen. When he once jokingly told Mr. Loomis that LaRosa and Bendetti looked like people whose pictures should be on wanted posters, Mr. Loomis told him that it was no joke. It was then that Martin learned that this theater, as well as every other theater in New York, was controlled by the mob.

"The same people who own the speakeasies and the gambling joints also control the movie business," Mr. Loomis explained.

The only reason Mr. Loomis told Martin at all was so that Martin would understand he should never do anything to upset Nino or Joey. He was to make certain that the sealed envelope the manager gave him every week was inside the can of film when he turned it in. Martin had never looked inside one of the envelopes but he was reasonably certain the envelopes contained money.

Nino LaRosa and Joey Bendetti were frightening but at least they were a known fright. Martin had been dealing with them ever since he had gotten this job and he could handle that. Whatever or whoever was inside the theater was an unknown fear, so, given his choice, Martin would rather face LaRosa and Bendetti. But he did wish they would get here and get this over with.

A few minutes later a black four-door Chevrolet pulled to the curb in front of the theater and Nino and Joey got out. Joey was carrying the film can for tomorrow's movie. Martin never thought he would be happy to see them, but he was.

"Good evening, Mr. Bendetti. I must confess to being relieved to see you," he said.

"What are you doing out here?" Joey asked gruffly. "The exchange is supposed to be inside."

"The lobby light bulb is burned out," Martin explained. "I didn't want to wait for you in the dark."

Nino laughed. "Scared of the dark, are you? What's the problem?"

"I...I thought I saw someone in there, that's all. It made me feel uneasy."

"So, who do you think is in there—the Big Bad Wolf?" Nino asked. Nino pushed the door open and stepped into the lobby. Within seconds he came backing out.

"What is it, Nino?" Joey asked, laughing. "You see him too?"

Nino turned around. His eyes were open wide, and he was making a rattling, choking sound.

"Nino?" Joey asked.

Nino fell against Martin. "Marty sold out," he gasped. He staggered, then fell to the sidewalk. It wasn't until then that Martin saw a knife sticking out of his chest.

"Oh, my God!" Martin said. He looked at Joey. "I didn't sell anyone out, I swear!"

"Nino!" Joey shouted. He took only one step toward Nino, then thought better of it, dropped the film canister, and turned to run back toward the car.

Martin, who was too terrified even to move, stood there with both hands over his mouth, looking on in fear and confusion. Suddenly the night was shattered by a loud blast as a brilliant flash came from within the lobby of the theater. The glass of the door exploded out onto the sidewalk, while at the same time Joey's blood-splattered body was slammed against the side of the Chevrolet. A man came out of the theater then and Martin saw that he was carrying a gun, the same gun he had used to shoot through the glass door. The assailant pointed the gun at Joey and pulled the trigger. Again the night was interrupted by a bright flash and a loud blast.

With a little wisp of smoke curling up from the end of his gun, the gunman looked over at Martin. "I'm not goin' to have any trouble from you, am I?" the gunman asked in a low, husky voice.

"No!" Martin said. "Oh, please!" he begged. He got down on his knees and held his hands out in prayerful supplication. "Please! Please, don't shoot me!"

"Tell your boss he's dealing with the wrong people," the gunman said. "You got that? He's dealing with the wrong people."

"The...the wrong people," Martin said. "Yes, sir. I understand."

A blue Jewett pulled up to the curb, and the gunman got in, then pointed the gun toward Martin, who was still on his knees. "Put your head down onto the sidewalk!" he ordered.

"Y...yes, sir!" Martin answered, complying with the order as the car roared off.

Almost as a reflex action, Martin raised his head to watch the car drive away. Then he realized that the gunman might think he was trying to get the license number and that would be disastrous. Quickly he put his head back down, though before he did so, he managed to notice that the license plate was from New Jersey.

"How did it go?" The Albino asked as the car drove away.

"You saw it," Vinnie answered. "They're both down."

"Yeah, it looked like a good job."

"How far to where the car is stashed?"

"Not too far," The Albino said. "Only about ten more blocks or so."

"Once we change cars, how long will it take us to get back home?"

"We'll be there by sunup," The Albino promised.

"Good, you drive, I'll sleep." Vinnie twisted around in the car and looked through the back window.

"What you lookin' for?"

"Nothing. Anything," Vinnie said. "Just keepin' an eye open, that's all."

"Why are you acting so nervous?" The Albino asked. "It was a good job, wasn't it?"

Vinnie turned back to the front "Yeah, of course it was a good job. What do you think, I can't pull off a simple job like this?"

"Somethin's makin' you nervous."

"I didn't like leavin' the eyewitness," Vinnie said. "I mean, if the client wants it, I'll rub someone out, but I don't like leavin' an eyewitness to the job just so he can deliver a message. That's not very professional."

"Yeah," The Albino said. "I know what you mean. But what can you do about it?"

"I can tell the boss when we get back. If he's got any more jobs for me I want to do them clean. Nothin' else like this."

"I feel the same way. I'll back you up."

Vinnie chuckled. "You're goin' to stand up to the boss, are you?"

"Well, not exactly stand up," The Albino replied. "But I'll agree with you if you talk to him."

"That sure takes a load off my mind, Albino," Vinnie said sarcastically. "How much farther to the car?"

"See that garage up there?" The Albino replied. "Our car is in the alley just behind it, all gassed up and ready to go."

"Good. I'd just as soon put this place behind us. I never cared much for New York."

"No, me either," The Albino agreed.

Vinnie leaned back in his seat and dropped his hand

to his belt. He moved his hand around to let it rest famil-
iarly on the handle of his knife, but there was nothing
there. That was when Vinnie realized his knife was missing. He gasped and twisted around in his seat to look,
once again, out the back window. It was at that moment
that he realized where his knife had to be. He had used it
but he hadn't recovered it. His knife was still sticking out
of Nino LaRosa's chest!

"Damn!" he said aloud.

"What is it?" The Albino asked. "Somethin' wrong?"

"My knife," Vinnie said. "I left my damn knife back
there."

"I told you, you got a job needs a knife, that's the job
you give to me," The Albino said.

"Now that would'a been real smart, wouldn't it?"
Vinnie growled. "All that projectionist would'a needed
was one look at you. It'd be the same as leavin' a picture
behind."

"At least I wouldn't have left my knife behind," The
Albino said.

THE NEXT MORNING

It was just before seven A. M. and the Manhattan South
Precinct station was a hustling, bustling beehive of
activity as policemen and civilians passed in and out of
the front doors. Feet tapped noisily on the tile floor and
telephones jangled incessantly. Dozens of people sat on
the benches awaiting the disposition of cases that were
still pending from the night before. Some had already
been there all night and a few were even stretched out
asleep.

The day watch had not yet begun but the oncoming
uniform officers were already present for duty. As they
waited for watch mount they stood around in clusters,

drinking coffee and eating doughnuts, engaged in their own topics of conversation. Periodically a few policemen would drift from one cluster to another, thus changing slightly the dynamics of the groups.

As Mike Kelly stepped into the station he was greeted effusively by some of the police officers and looked at with askance by others. Some of the officers respected the work Mike and the Bureau of Investigation were doing, while others felt that the bureau's activities interfered with city police work. There were even some, notably those who were "on the take," who regarded Mike and the bureau as potentially dangerous to them.

The man behind the desk was Sergeant Marshal Moore. Moore had come onto the force with Mike's father and Mike had known him for a long time. Mike trusted Moore implicitly and knew that the sergeant was one of the policemen in his camp.

"Hello, Mike," Moore said, greeting him warmly. "What brings you down to Manhattan South?"

"Up at Midtown, they told me there were two men killed over on Delancey Street last night," Mike said.

"Yeah, happened around midnight, I think," Sergeant Moore said. "It was a robbery attempt, but they sure didn't do a very good job. The manager had already taken the day's receipts to the night deposit and the killers left behind an envelope that had a thousand dollars in it."

"An envelope with a thousand dollars?" Mike asked.

"Yes. It was in one of the film cans."

"Who were the two men who were killed?"

Sergeant Moore reached across his desk and picked up a piece of paper. "Let's see, here is it. The two men were Nino LaRosa and Joey Bendetti."

"LaRosa and Bendetti. I see," Mike said. "It's beginning to make sense now."

"Is it? Well, if you're making sense out of it I sure wish you'd tell me," Sergeant Moore said. "Why would somebody kill two men, then just walk off and leave a thousand dollars behind?"

"May I help you, Agent Kelly?" a stern, disapproving voice suddenly asked.

"Good morning, Captain Dillon," Mike said, turning toward the sound of the voice. A large, uniformed officer, wearing the rank of captain, was standing in the door that led into his own office. He was leaning smugly, almost contemptuously against the door jamb. The police captain was definitely not in Mike's circle of friends.

"What are you doing here?" Captain Dillon asked.

"I was just trying to get a little information on the shooting over on Delancey last night," Mike explained.

"Come into my office," Dillon said. It was more of an order than an invitation.

"Be glad to," Mike said, complying with the order.

"Now then," Dillon went on, closing the door behind them. "Would you be for tellin' me what interest a simple murder and robbery holds for the federal boys?"

"It wasn't a simple murder and robbery," Mike said.

"And what would you be meanin' by that?"

"For one thing, there are two dead, not one," Mike explained. "And where's the robbery? They left a thousand dollars behind them."

"How did you know about the one thousand...never mind. Sergeant Moore was shooting off his mouth, wasn't he? I'll have to have a talk with Sergeant Moore."

"Sergeant Moore wasn't telling me anything that won't be in the newspaper today," Mike said, defending his friend. "So what is your big interest in it?" Dillon asked again.

"I believe this was a gangland killing."

"Oh, a gangland killin' is it? And would you be so kind as to tell me why you think so?"

"Because the killer left behind an envelope containing a thousand dollars."

"Maybe they didn't know about it."

"They?" Mike asked. "Are you telling me there was more than one killer?" He smiled. "Well, thank you. That's more than I got from Sergeant Moore."

"One man did the killing," Dillon said. "The other drove the getaway car."

"But neither man took the money," Mike said.

"You keep coming back to that. Why? It was just a botched job all around, that's all," Captain Dillon insisted. "The killer came to rob the place, but he got there too late. The manager had already left with the deposit. When LaRosa and Bendetti came to deliver the new movie, the killer panicked and killed them while he was trying to escape. He didn't know about the money in the envelope."

"Oh, he knew the money was there, all right," Mike said. "He knew all about it. You see, this was a mob rubout. LaRosa and Bendetti worked for Johnny Sangremano."

"They worked for the Manhattan Film Exchange Company," Captain Dillon said.

"Which is owned by Johnny Sangremano," Mike explained patiently. "What do you think the thousand dollars was for? It was part of the cost of doing business with the mobs. No one in this town, not one theater, can show a movie unless they are willing to pay Sangremano for the privilege. Only, somebody doesn't like that arrangement, and he decided to send Sangremano a message."

Captain Dillon looked at Mike for a long moment, then he pulled out a cigarette and lit it, taking a puff before he answered.

"If he wanted to send a message to Sangremano, why the hell didn't he just write a letter?" Captain Dillon finally asked. His words dripped with sarcasm.

Mike ignored the comment. "Captain Dillon, are you aware that, in addition to the two men who were killed in front of a theater, there were four movie theaters that burned last night?"

"New York is a big town. In a city this size, there are bound to be fires, just like there are bound to be murders. There've been fires and murders goin' on here for two hundred years, and I suspect there will be for another two hundred. And when they happen they are, always have been, and always will be, the responsibility of the New York City Fire Department, and the New York City Police Department. We neither need nor want any interference from the federal government."

At that moment there was a knock on Dillon's door. Dillon called out and Sergeant Moore opened it, then stuck his head in.

"We just sent Mr. Milsaps back to his apartment," Sergeant Moore said. "I hope you don't mind. We kept him all night for questioning."

"No, that's all right," Dillon said brusquely. "You got a complete statement?"

"Yes sir," Moore said. "It isn't going to be much help, though. About the only thing he could tell us was that the car had Jersey plates."

Mike smiled broadly. "Did it now?" he asked. "Goddamnit, Moore, that's classified information!" Dillon shouted angrily. "You know better than to come in here, blabbering in front of civilians!"

"Beg your pardon, Captain," Sergeant Moore said. "I didn't know Agent Kelly was a civilian. I thought he was one of the good guys." Moore smiled at Mike, and Mike realized then that Moore had purposely tipped him off about the Jersey plates.

"Back to your desk with you," Dillon ordered. "And how about getting some of these people processed and out of here? They've been here all night, and this place is a goddamned madhouse."

"Yes sir," Moore said easily.

"And you. Don't be for tryin' to make somethin' out of the Jersey plate," Dillon said, returning his attention to Mike. "It doesn't mean a thing."

"Oh, but it does," Mike said. "It means there is a possibility that whoever killed poor old Nino and Joey came from New Jersey, crossing a state line to commit a crime. And that means that the bureau now has a stake in this murder. We have the right, by law, to start our own investigation."

"All right," Dillon said. "All right, you can investigate. But I'll not be havin' you botherin' any of my men in their investigation, do you hear me? I won't have it."

"I'm sure we'll be able to work together splendidly," Mike said. "I wonder if you would be so kind as to provide me with a copy of the police and coroner's reports? Also, I would like to talk to Mr. Milsaps."

Now it was Dillon's turn to smile. "I'll send a copy of the reports over to your office," he said. "But as for Milsaps, you heard the desk sergeant. We've already let him go. You'll have to find him and make the arrangements on your own."

Mike assigned Bill and Jason the task of interviewing Martin Milsaps. One hour later, they stood just inside the door of Martin's apartment, holding up their badges and identification cards.

"Are you gentlemen with the police?" Martin asked. "Because I have already spoken at some length with the police."

"No, we're with the Bureau of Investigation," Bill explained. "Sometimes it's called the Federal Bureau of Investigation because we are federal agents."

"My, my. Federal officers," Martin said. "So, you are like the Treasury men who go after the bootleggers?"

"Yes, something like that," Bill agreed.

"Well, I wouldn't be surprised if Mr. LaRosa and Mr. Bendetti weren't involved in bootlegging too. They just had that look about them, you know what I mean?"

"Yes sir, I know what you mean," Bill said.

"By the way, you don't mind if I water my plants while we speak, do you?" Martin asked, picking up a watering can and walking from potted plant to potted plant "It's so difficult to raise plants in an apartment. One must balance the light and the water, the heat and the cold just so."

"No, go ahead," Jason said.

"How long had you been paying LaRosa and Bendetti off?" Bill asked.

Martin looked up in surprise. "Paying them off?" he asked. "What makes you think I was paying them off?"

"There was a thousand dollars in that envelope last night. That was for LaRosa and Bendetti, wasn't it?"

"I, uh, didn't know what was in the envelope," Martin said nervously.

"Look, Mr. Milsaps, we aren't investigating you," Bill said. "We're investigating a murder. We'd like to keep you as an innocent witness, but if we need to, we can expand this investigation until you are drawn right into the middle of it. Is that what you want?"

"No, no," Martin said. "I wouldn't like that."

"You did know there was money in the envelope, didn't you?"

"Well, I must confess that I suspected there was money in the envelope," Martin admitted. "But I never actually looked. I never wanted to look, I didn't want to know."

"So you decided to just stick your head into the sand, is that it?" Jason asked.

"I suppose you could put it that way if you wanted to. I prefer to say, 'See no evil, hear no evil,'" Martin replied.

"How long have you been paying?"

"I really can't answer that question. Mr. Loomis—that is, Roy Loomis, my employer—would bring me an envelope every Thursday evening to be put into the film can for the exchange that night. We change movies after the last showing on Thursday evening. That's so there will be a fresh movie for the weekend," he explained. "I've been working here for over a year and we've been doing it all that time."

"Has there ever been any trouble with it?"

"No," Martin said.

"Has anyone other than LaRosa and Bendetti ever tried to put pressure on you to pay them?" Jason asked.

"No."

"What about the manager? Has anyone ever tried to put the pressure on him?"

"Oh, I wouldn't know about that," Martin said. "Like I told the police last night, I'm just the projectionist. If such a thing had happened, I'm quite sure Mr. Loomis would not have taken me into his confidence."

"Did the police ask you anything about the payoff?" Bill asked.

"No," Martin replied. "The police seemed to think it was a robbery attempt."

"Do you think it was?"

"Well, I don't know. I mean, it would have to be, wouldn't it?" Martin answered. "Although I must say he certainly didn't do a very good job with it. The whole thing was so…so queer. I mean, if you had been there…if you had seen it."

"Suppose you tell us," Bill suggested. "Tell us everything you can remember…don't leave anything out."

"Well, of course, I told the police everything already," Martin said. He smiled. "But to tell the truth, it was such an adventure that I don't mind repeating the story."

Martin began his story, explaining how he would exchange the film once a week with the two men who were killed. He told about coming downstairs from the projection room and finding the light burned out in the lobby.

"The police said that the bulb had been unscrewed," Martin said. "Whoever it was had done it so that I wouldn't see him."

"I'll check with the police lab," Jason said. "But I'm sure there were no prints on the bulb."

"I wouldn't think so, either. The killer would have had to use gloves or a rag or something to get the bulb out," Bill said. "It would have been too hot to handle, otherwise. Go ahead, Mr. Milsaps."

Martin continued the story, how he waited outside, then how Nino, laughing at his fears, had gone into the lobby only to come staggering out a moment later with a knife in his chest.

"And then…the most frightening thing," Martin said. "He spoke to me. He called me by name. I didn't even know he knew my first name. But he used it and he accused me of selling him out."

"What did he mean by that?"

"I have no idea," Martin said. "I assure you, I didn't sell him out, whatever that is."

"What, exactly, did he say?" Bill wanted to know.

"Well, to begin with, he called me Marty," Martin said. "When you think of it, that is strange in itself. I mean, I don't go by that name...I never have. Even as a child my parents called me Martin. He said, 'Marty sold out.'"

"Did he say 'Marty, you sold me out'?"

"No, he said, 'Marty sold out.' "

"Okay. Go on."

"Well, shortly after that, or actually, almost at the same time, there was a loud bang and a very bright flash from inside the lobby. The police told me later that the killer was using a shotgun and he shot right through the door. That is a very big gun, isn't it?"

"You saw it, didn't you?" Bill asked. "How big was it?"

"It seemed big," Martin said. "It was long and black. I wasn't sure what kind of gun it was, but I knew what it wasn't. It wasn't a six-shooter." He smiled. "I've certainly shown enough Westerns in my day to be able to recognize a six-shooter when I see one. Anyway, the killer shot once from inside the lobby, right through the glass door. That shot knocked poor Mr. Bendetti down, then the killer walked right over to him and shot him again. Then"—Martin paused and shivered—"then he pointed it at me."

"What happened?"

"I...I don't mind telling you, I begged him not to kill me. Then, after I assured him he wouldn't have any trouble with me, he told me to tell my boss he was 'Dealing with the wrong people.' "

Bill and Jason looked at each other.

"It's just like Mike said, Bill. Somebody's making a move on Sangremano."

"Anything else, Mr. Milsaps?" Bill asked.

"No," Martin said. "I've told you all I can remember."

"What did the killer look like?"

"I can only give the most general description," Martin

said. "He wasn't very tall. I have the impression that his eyes may have been brown, though as it was dark I couldn't see them that clearly. He was wearing a hat, so I couldn't see his hair. He had a narrow face, rather dark complexioned."

"You've just described half the male population of America," Jason suggested.

"I'm sorry, that's the best I can do."

"What about the shotgun the killer used? Was it single-barrel or double-barrel?" Bill asked.

"Oh. Well, that I can tell you. It was a single-barrel," Martin replied. "Yes, yes, I'm quite sure that it had only one barrel. I remember, distinctly, looking at it when he pointed it at me. It had only one barrel, but it was a very big barrel, if that is of any help."

Bill chuckled. "They're all big when they're pointed at you," he said.

"What about the driver of the car?" Jason asked. "Can you tell us anything about him?"

"Not even if it was a him," Martin said.

"What do you mean? Are you saying the driver could have been a woman?" Bill asked.

"Could have been," Martin said. "I'm just saying I didn't even get a glimpse."

"Was there anything that made you think it might have been a woman?"

"No."

"What about the car?" Bill wanted to know.

"It was a blue Jewett," Martin replied. "A '25 model." He smiled. "My sister's husband has one just like it. A different color, but otherwise just the same."

"And you said it had a New Jersey license plate?"

"Oh, yes, I'm quite sure of that."

"Okay, we're just about finished, Mr. Milsaps, but I want you to think for a moment," Bill said. "Is there anything you may have told the police that you haven't told us, or that you may have told us that you didn't tell the police?"

"Let's see," Martin mused. "No, I think I gave both of you pretty much the same story. Maybe the gun is all. I don't recall the police asking me how many barrels it had."

"I see," Bill said. He smiled and reached out to shake Martin's hand. "Thank you, Mr. Milsaps. You've been a great help."

"I wonder if we'll be able to show the picture tonight," Martin said.

"I beg your pardon?"

"Poor Little Princess. It's a Katie Starr picture that I haven't seen yet, and I'm really looking forward to it. Will we be able to show it?"

"That's up to the New York City Police," Jason said, "but I'm sure you will."

By the time Bill and Jason returned to their office, Mike and Joe had already reviewed the police and coroner's reports. Bill briefed them on the interview.

"'Marty sold out,'" Joe repeated after Bill finished his briefing. "That's what he said?"

"Well, that's what Milsaps said he said."

"That's odd," Joe said.

"Yeah, that's what I thought."

"No, I mean that's very odd. I knew Nino. I knew him for many years but he never called me anything but Provenzano."

"What are you getting at?"

"It was a quirk of his. He just didn't call people by their first names," Joe said. "Not unless they were blood relatives or something. It seems strange that he would say something like that to Milsaps as he was dying."

"Maybe so, but that's what Milsaps said he said. 'Marty soldout.' "

Mike's eyes opened wide, as if he suddenly got an idea "Say that again," he ordered.

"What? You mean, 'Marty sold out'?"

"Yes, only say it the way you just did, running the last two words together."

"Marty soldout," Bill said.

"Damn, that rings a bell," Mike said. "I've heard that before, somewhere." Suddenly he snapped his fingers. *"Morte soldati!* I remember now! D'Angelo yelled that, just before he was shot."

"Morte soldati?" Jason asked. "What the hell does that mean?"

"Death soldiers," Joe explained.

"Death soldiers? Well, what the hell does that mean?" Bill asked.

"I don't know," Joe said. "I mean, I know the words but I have no idea what it means. I've never heard the term before."

"Whatever it means, I believe that's what LaRosa actually said," Mike said. "Not 'Marty sold out.'"

"And you say D'Angelo shouted that too?"

"Yes. The moment he saw the men jump down from the boxcar. Joe, I know you say you've never heard the term before, but have you ever heard of anything that might be connected to it?"

"You mean like a special death squad within the Mafia?"

"Yes, something like that."

"Well, yes. I mean, each family has their enforcers," Joe said. "But I've never heard them referred to in that way before."

"But you've never really been inside, have you? I mean, actually inside."

"No," Joe admitted.

"So, 'Death soldiers' could be a way of referring to the enforcers?"

"Yes, I suppose it could," Joe said.

Mike smiled. "Gentlemen, I think we have just learned one more little piece of information we can use. And, since that term popped up in New Orleans as well as here, it must be a fairly universal term."

"What about the police and coroner's report?" Jason asked.

"Not much to go on, I'm afraid. It's pretty thin," Mike replied. He pointed to the inventory of evidence. The list included such things as the clothes the two victims were wearing, the knife that killed Nino, and the contents of their pockets.

"The knife?"

"Yes. With prints. I've got pictures, we're sending wirephotos to our lab in Washington."

"Sure would be nice if they could come up with something," Joe said.

"They might. They have the biggest collection of fingerprints in the world."

"Maybe so, but they couldn't do anything with the prints we lifted off that car in New Orleans."

"I wonder where the empty shell casings are?" Jason asked.

"Beg your pardon?"

"The empty shell casings," Jason said. "Bendetti was shot twice and Milsaps says it was a single-barrel gun. But there are no empty shell casings listed as part of the evidence. I recall my days on the skeet range, using pump-action shotguns. You could scarcely walk for the empty shell casings."

Mike smiled broadly, then looked at Bill and Joe. "Damn, he's right, you know," he said. "If it was a single-barrel shotgun then there would have to be an empty shell. The first cartridge would have to be ejected. What I want to know is, why didn't you professional policemen think of that? Why did it have to come from a rich playboy like Jason?"

"I guess neither one of us ever spent that much time playing skeet or shooting polo ponies," Joe quipped, and he and Bill both laughed.

"Anyway, maybe it was a single-shot and he opened the breech and took it out himself," Bill suggested.

"You know anyone who would plan something like this with a single-shot shotgun?" Mike asked.

"Can't say as I do," Joe admitted. "But that brings us back to your question. Why isn't the empty shell, or shells, part of the evidence?"

"Maybe the police don't have it," Jason suggested.

"But they must. That's a critical piece of evidence, they wouldn't just overlook it like that."

"They might overlook it if they don't know anything about it," Jason said. "Remember, Bill, Milsaps said he didn't mention to the police that it was a single-barrel gun. The police may have thought the gun was a double-barrel."

"Yes," Bill said. "And if it had been a double-barrel and if the empty shells weren't in plain sight, the police would naturally assume that the shells remained in the breech and were taken away from the scene by the shooter."

"The theater hasn't been open since the shooting. Why don't the four of us go down there and take a look around? Maybe we can find them." Mike suggested, starting for the door with the others trailing behind him. It took them half an hour to find it. In the excitement of the moment, the shooter had operated the pump action with such force that the ejection sent the empty shell casing flying all the way across the lobby, behind the concession counter. Joe was the one who found it. It had rolled under the popcorn popper, and Mike picked it up with a pencil, then dropped it into an empty popcorn sack.

"Are we going to tell the police we have it?" Joe asked.

Mike smiled. "Well, it's this way, Joe," he explained. "The police have their investigation going and we have ours. If this leads anywhere, we'll let them know."

Greenwich Village, New York

"I don't like it," Don Pietro Nicolo said, putting the newspaper down on the dining room table and slapping at it with the back of his hand. "Those crazy bastards, what do they think they are doing?"

"What crazy bastards are those, Pop?" Enrico asked as he poured himself a cup of coffee.

"The Vaglichios," Don Pietro said. "They've killed a couple of Sangremano's men. If Sangremano returns the favor, we could wind up with a full-scale war on our hands."

Enrico took a drink of his coffee, slurping it through extended lips to cool the hot liquid.

"So what if they do kill each other off?" Enrico asked. "The way I look at it, it's no sweat off our balls."

"Oh? That's the way you look at it, is it?" Don Pietro asked disgustedly. "Well, let me tell you something, just so you understand. The secret to success for any business like ours is to make as little noise as possible. When such things as this happen, there are many stories in the newspapers. When the newspapers run many stories, the people get concerned and they go to their politicians and ask that something be done. The politicians go to the police and the police bring heat down on everyone."

"So, the cops make a little noise and a few people get

arrested. So what? I still say that it isn't any of our concern and I don't know why you continue to try and keep peace between them all the time."

"Maybe I should explain a few things to you, Enrico," Don Pietro said as clearly as he could. "Not even the biggest police crackdown is strong enough to do any harm to the big families. The Sangremanos and the Vaglichios have nothing to fear from the police. The smaller families, such as ours, have much to fear."

"Why? We didn't start anything," Enrico said.

"No, we didn't. But that won't protect us, once the war gets started. In addition to the possibility that our family might get caught up in the war itself, there is also the police department to consider. If they can't deal with one of the larger families, they'll take it out on us."

"So, what are you going to do?"

"I'm going to do what I can to keep peace between the two families," he said. "Otherwise, the whole thing is liable to break up."

"Pop, have you ever considered that when something breaks up, there are always pieces left lying around?"

"What do you mean?" Don Pietro said. "Don't talk in riddles."

"What I mean is, let them fight it out," Enrico said. "The longer they fight, the more damage they are going to do to each other. What if we just stood by and did nothing?"

"We can't stand by and do nothing," Don Pietro insisted. "It is our role to be the mediator."

"Wouldn't our position of mediator be strengthened if we were more powerful?" Enrico asked. "Think of the 'peace' you could impose if you controlled not only Greenwich Village but the Bronx and the Lower East Side as well."

"Why should I waste my time with such foolish thoughts? Nothing like that would ever happen."

"It could," Enrico said. "If we were smart and played our cards just right."

"No, I won't have it," Don Pietro said. "And I don't want to hear you ever saying such things again."

"All right by me, Pop," Enrico said easily as he took another slurping drink of his coffee. "We'll be just what you say we should be. We'll be the peacemakers. I was just wondering what would happen if we let them fight it out, that's all."

CHAPTER 5

SATURDAY MORNING, SOMEWHERE IN PENNSYLVANIA

Katie Starr and Vic Mason had taken adjacent compartments on the Continental Express leaving from New York at eleven o'clock Friday night. It was nine the next morning, and they were somewhere in Pennsylvania, breakfasting in Katie's compartment.

"Are you going to eat any more of that?" Vic asked, pointing to the bacon on her plate.

"What? No," Katie answered, distractedly. She was reading a newspaper the porter had brought with the breakfast. "Oh, dear. Oh, dear."

"What is it? What's wrong?" he asked as he helped himself to a couple of the crisp strips.

"According to this article, the public is soon going to be demanding sound in all the pictures made."

"That's what I hear," Vic said. "Do you have a problem with that?"

"I find it a little frightening," Katie admitted.

"Why? You're a big star. What can happen to you?"

"What can happen to me? They can get a load of this accent, that's what can happen to me," Katie said. "How can I play a desert princess, or a gypsy dancer, and talk like a girl from the Lower East Side?"

"They have voice coaches," Vic said easily. "You'll learn."

"And if I don't learn, what happens then? I could lose an important part."

"No problem. Just have your brother pay a visit to the producer."

"What do you mean by that?"

"Nothing. I was just thinking about what happened to Sammy Solinger a couple of years ago, that's all."

"Are you suggesting that my brother had something to do with Sammy's death?"

"Come on, Katie, you aren't deaf," Vic said. "You know what people have been saying."

"What do I care about what people think? They've got it all wrong."

"What difference does it make whether they have it wrong or not?"

"Well it makes a difference to me," Katie insisted.

"Maybe so, but it doesn't change anything. You must remember that what people perceive is almost as real as the truth itself. And people perceive that your brother was responsible for Solinger's death."

"All right, I'm not deaf. I have heard my brother's name in conjunction with that," Katie admitted. "But the only reason his name came up in the first place was because he had come to California to talk to Sammy, to try and make him listen to reason."

Vic chuckled. "Evidently, he wouldn't listen to reason."

"It's no laughing matter," Katie said.

"No, I suppose it isn't. Especially to poor old Sammy."

"Poor old Sammy? Are you taking up for him, now? He was a no-count bum and everyone in the business knew it."

"You're right, everyone knew what a no-count bum he was and everyone hated him. But not everyone killed him."

"Someone did," Katie said. "And it wasn't Johnny. Even Sammy's butler said that he saw Sammy alive after my brother left. The police didn't even call Johnny in for questioning. But maybe you would like to."

"Oh, no! I wouldn't want to do anything like that," Vic said, holding out his hands as if waving her away. "Anyway, I've already had one talk with your brother, and that one talk was uncomfortable enough for me."

"You had a talk with Johnny?" Katie asked. "What was your talk about? What did he say?"

"Your brother wanted to know if you were putting out for me."

"How did you answer it?"

"Well, what do you think I said? I did want to come out of there alive, after all," Vic replied. "So, naturally, I lied. I told him that I had the utmost respect for you and for your virginity".

Katie smiled. "Now, that is the first intelligent thing you have said in this entire conversation."

Vic walked around the little table, then leaned down to kiss Katie. The kiss was long and demanding and when it was finished, he held her under the chin as he smiled down at her.

"Ah, Katie, Katie. From all that I have heard, you were the most innocent, naive young woman ever to come to Hollywood. But look at you now."

"How I live my life is my own business," Katie said.

"Now is that any attitude for a nice young lady to have? Is that how you were raised?"

"I was raised to go to church, say my rosary, keep my mouth shut and my legs crossed," Katie said. "But you will find I am not like that anymore."

"I'm sure this would all come as a big surprise to your brother."

"Surely you aren't entertaining any ideas of telling him?"

"Now, why would I want to do a thing like that to the young lady who is going to help me become a star again?" Vic asked.

"Is that all I am to you, Vic?" Katie asked. "Am I just someone who is going to help you make a comeback?"

"Oh, no, you're more than that, baby. You're much more than that," Vic said. His hand slipped in under Katie's blouse and cupped the warm flesh of her breast. "You're good to me and I'm good to you. That's why your secret is safe with me."

"I'm glad my secret is safe with you," Katie said. "But just in case you ever do decide to tell him, I think you should know that my brother is the old-fashioned kind... the real old-fashioned kind, if you know what I mean."

Vic pulled his hand out from under her blouse. "No, I'm not sure that I do know what you mean," he admitted.

"Well, in his own way, Johnny is like a king in his kingdom. And, like the kings of old, he would not treat too kindly any messenger who brought him bad news. You do understand what I'm saying, don't you?"

In an almost involuntary gesture, Vic put his finger to his collar and pulled it away from his neck. "Yes," he answered. "Yes, I think I do."

Now it was Katie's turn to smile. "Good," she said. "But, what do you say we put all that behind us?" She reached up and pulled his face back to her and kissed him again. This time her mouth opened and her tongue met his. Then, as suddenly as she started, she broke off the kiss. Vic looked at her in confusion.

"If we're going to go on with this, don't you think we would be more comfortable in bed?" she asked.

"What about the porter? Won't he be coming back for the tray?"

"Set it out in the aisle," Katie ordered. "Then lock the door."

Vic set the tray out into the aisle, then locked the compartment door as requested. After that, he converted the seat into the bed it was designed for. In the meantime, Katie began stripping out of her dress. Then nude, she stretched out on the bed and watched as Vic removed his own clothes. Behind him, she could see the Ohio countryside rolling by. She held her arms up toward him.

When Katie first came to Hollywood she had denied her own passionate nature for as long as she could, but she lost her virginity one sin-filled night a couple of years ago. For about a week after that incident, she experienced a tremendous guilt and she confided her transgressions to a friend.

"What was the harm?" her friend had asked. "I do it. All the girls I know do it. There's nothing wrong with it as long as no one gets hurt."

From that moment on the guilt was gradually stripped away, until now Katie felt no guilt whatsoever and she took her pleasure whenever and wherever she could find it. After all, didn't the same blood that ran through her brother's veins run through her own? And hadn't she heard stories about him for as long as she could remember? Why should Johnny be allowed to live any way he wanted while she should be denied, just because she was a woman? She should have as much freedom as he. As a matter of fact, now that Johnny was married, she should have more freedom, for his sexual exploits would have to be curtailed whereas she, being single, had no such restrictions.

Vic didn't come to her right away but held himself poised just above her for a long moment, supporting himself on his outstretched arms, one hand to either side of her shoulders. Katie smiled, for she knew he was showing off the flat and muscular body he was so proud of.

"Are you just going to hold yourself up there posing for me, or are we going to have some action here?" Katie teased.

"Oh yeah, baby, we're goin' to do it," Vic said.

During the final moments of their lovemaking Katie had been aware, though only dimly, of the slowing of the train. Now, as they lay together with the sensations all played out and nothing left but limp relaxation, Katie realized for the first time that the train had actually come to a complete stop. She turned her head toward the window, and as she did so, she saw that they were standing in the station. Not only that, someone was standing on the platform, looking in. He moved closer to the train, then bent down to get a better look through the window. That was when he saw what was going on inside. His eyes grew wide for a split second, then he turned away in quick embarrassment.

"Oh my God!" Katie gasped. Without even attempting to cover herself, she hopped out of the bed, then reached up and jerked down the shade.

"What is it?" Vic asked, lying on the side of the bed after having been unceremoniously pushed aside by Katie's abrupt action.

"On the station platform," Katie said, reaching for her dress. "He was looking in. He saw us."

Vic laughed. "What's the matter? Was someone getting a cheap thrill?"

"It was Weasel," Katie said in a small, terrified voice.

"The don is worried about you," Weasel said when Katie let him into her compartment a few moments later.

"What is he worried about?" Katie asked defensively. "I'm a big girl, Weasel. He doesn't have to wipe my nose every time I get the sniffles."

"No, I ain't talkin' about what I just seen," Weasel said. "Fact is, they didn't any of us know anything about any of this. I'm talkin' about somethin' else, somethin' worse."

"Something worse?" Katie barked a short, humorless laugh. "What could be worse than what you saw?"

"Dyin' could be worse," Weasel said. "Maybe you ain't seen no newspapers yet, but LaRosa and Bendetti got themselves killed."

Katie inhaled a quick, short breath. "No," she said quietly. "I didn't know. I'm sorry to hear about that. I knew Joey Bendetti. He took me to my first dance. You said they were killed—what happened?"

"That's what we don't know," Weasel answered. "I mean, they weren't doin' nothin' dangerous. They were just changing the film at the movie houses, that's all. That's why the boss is nervous. He figures someone must be tryin' to move in on him."

"Johnny knows the risks of his business," Katie said dryly.

"Yeah, sure the don knows it," Weasel said. "The thing is, do you know it?"

"What do you mean?"

"Figure it out," Weasel said. "If somebody is after the boss, there's no tellin' where they'll stop. They might even try to get to him through you. That's why he put me on the plane this mornin' and sent me out to catch up with you.

He wants me to watch over you till you get out to Hollywood." Weasel smiled. "I'm goin' to be your bodyguard."

"You mean you are going to California with me?"

"All the way," Weasel said.

"How long are you going to stay?"

"Till the boss thinks it's safe for me to come back," Weasel said.

"And I suppose, in the meantime, you'll be spying on me?" Katie challenged. She gasped, as if suddenly remembering what Weasel had seen. "Weasel, you...you aren't going to tell my brother about Vic and me, are you?"

"I got to."

"What do you mean? Why do you have to?"

"I got no choice. I owe him my loyalty and my life," Weasel said.

"Do you think he is going to want to hear this news?"

"No," Weasel said. "It's goin' to break his heart when he hears it."

"Then why tell him?"

"I got to."

"No, you don't. Please, Weasel."

Weasel sighed. "All right. The boss could have my head for this," he said. He pointed at Katie. "But your friend, Mason, ain't goin' to get off that easy. Where is he now?"

"I don't know where he went. When we saw you out on the depot platform, he got scared and left."

"Yeah, he should have been scared. Where did he go?"

"I don't know."

"You may as well tell me, Katherine," Weasel said. It was the first time Weasel had ever called her anything but Miss Sangremano. "Because if you don't, I'll turn this train inside out until I find him. And when I do, I won't go easy on him."

"No! Wait!" Katie called. Weasel stopped. "What... what are you going to do to him when you find him?" she asked in a frightened voice.

"That depends on whether I have to work hard to find him. I work hard I get frustrated, you know what I mean? And if I get frustrated, I might just take it out on your boy."

"What if I find him for you? What would you do to him?"

"I don't know," Weasel said. "I got to figure out what the don would want."

"Would you...would you kill him?"

Weasel sighed. "I guess not. That is, not if he listens to reason," he said. "Now, where is he?"

"Please, let me go to him. Let me talk to him first," Katie pleaded.

Weasel ran his hand through his hair and looked at Katie and at the fear in her face. Finally he relented. "All right," he said with a sigh. He ran his hand through his hair. "I shouldn't do this, but I'll let you talk to him first. But after you talk to him, you send him to me. I got a few words I need to say to him."

"All right," Katie said. "You stay here, in my compartment. I'll bring him to you."

"No, don't bring him, send him to me," Weasel said. "I don't want you around when I talk to him."

"Please don't hurt him," Katie said. "Promise me?"

"I can't make no promise like that," Weasel said. Then, when he saw the expression on Katie's face, he relented somewhat. "All right, I ain't goin' to hurt him. Leastwise, not if he listens to reason." Weasel saw an empty plate. "Hey, you got any food left? The don had me on an airplane before daylight this mornin' just so I could catch up with this train. I ain't had no breakfast."

"I'll see the porter and have some breakfast brought to you," Katie promised. "Then I'll bring Vic to you."

"Send Vic to me, you mean," Weasel reminded her.

"Yes, send him," Katie agreed.

"Good. And don't worry, everything is goin' to be fine." Shortly after Katie left Weasel in the compartment, she passed one of the porters moving quickly and importantly down the long, narrow corridor. She stopped him and ordered breakfast for Weasel. After that, she moved on to the rear of the train to the club car, where she knew she would find Vic. Vic was there, just as she thought he would be, sitting at a small table at the back of the car, nursing a cup of coffee and smoking a cigarette. The train had already resumed its journey and as Katie walked toward Vic, she could see the track playing out behind and the little town they had just come through, falling off in the distance.

"So tell me," Vic said, motioning for Katie to join him. "Did Weasel get all excited from watching us?"

"I don't think that was what he had in mind," Katie said. The club car attendant brought her a cup of coffee, then took the money from a little pile that Vic had lying on the table. After that, he withdrew.

Vic snorted. "That may not have been what he had in mind, but you can't tell me the sonofabitch didn't enjoy it. Well, where is he now? Did he get off the train?"

"No," Katie said. "He's still in my compartment having breakfast. Vic, Weasel wants to talk to you."

"Does he now? Well, I don't want to talk to him."

"You must."

"I must? Why must I?"

"Please, Vic. If you don't talk to him, there's no telling what he might do. You...you would be in great danger."

Vic laughed. "Are you serious? Me, in danger from that punk? What is he, twenty, maybe twenty-one years old? And have you taken a good look at him? He's all skin and bones. Why, I could break him in two like a matchstick."

"Don't underestimate him, Vic."

"Shit," Vic scoffed. "What's he doing here, anyway? Surely he didn't come just to peek into our window."

"Johnny sent him to protect me," Katie said.

"Protect you? Protect you from what? Or, maybe I should say, from who? Is he supposed to protect you from me?"

"No," Katie said. "It's…" She sighed. "It's my brother's business. Some of his…associates…were killed last night. Johnny feels that his, uh, competitors, may have been behind it. If so, I may be in danger."

"So he sent that dried-up little punk to protect you?"

"I am very honored," Katie said. "Weasel is Johnny's personal bodyguard."

"Just what, exactly, could this…Weasel…do to protect your brother or you?"

"He's very inventive," Katie said. "I'm sure if Sammy Solinger were still around, he would vouch for that."

Vic's eyes narrowed. "Look here, are you telling me?" He stopped in midquestion, not sure how to go on.

"I'm not telling you anything," Katie said. "I'm just asking you to go talk to Weasel and avoid doing anything that would make him mad."

Vic ground out his cigarette and stood up. "All right," he grumbled. "If you think it's all that important, let's go see him."

"No," Katie said in a quiet voice.

"No? What do you mean, no? I thought that was what you wanted."

"He doesn't want to see us; he wants to see you, alone," Katie said.

"Alone?" The bravado and scorn suddenly left Vic, to be replaced by an uneasy feeling. The hair stood up on the back of his neck and a tiny line of perspiration beads broke out on his upper lip. "Listen, Katie. What the hell is this all about? What's goin' on here? Why does he want to see me alone?"

"I don't know."

"I mean, he's not...he's not going to do anything stupid, is he?"

"He promised me he wouldn't hurt you, but...Vic?"

"Yes?"

"Do whatever he tells you to do, no matter what it is."

Weasel was halfway through his scrambled eggs when he heard a quiet knock on the door. "Come in," he called, without interrupting his breakfast

The door opened and Vic Mason stepped in. He closed it behind him.

"Katie said you wanted to see me," Vic said. There was no bravado or challenge to his voice.

"Yeah," Weasel replied. "I asked Katherine to send you down to me. Katherine, that's what everyone called her before she left New York, before she became a Hollywood movie star."

"Yes. Well, lots of people change their names when they get into the movies," Vic said.

"Yeah? Did you change your name?"

Vic cleared his throat "What uh, what does this have to do with anything, Weasel?"

Weasel's eyes flashed angrily and he held up his hand with the fork still in it. He shook it slowly, dropping pieces of egg.

"Only my friends call me Weasel," he said. "You call me Mr. Pallota."

"I'm sorry. I meant no insult."

Weasel smiled, though the smile didn't reach his eyes. "That's okay," he said. "Anyway, I was just tryin' to make pleasant conversation. The truth is, I don't have to ask you did you change your name, 'cause I already know that you did. Your name used to be Arnold Fenton. You come from Cleveland, Ohio, and you got parents that still live there. You got a sister in Chicago. Her name is Louise Mitchell. Her husband is an insurance agent. His name is Bob."

"How...how do you know all this?" Vic asked. "How do you know so much about my family? Not even my agent knows that much."

"The don," Weasel said, wiping up the last of the yellow with the single remaining piece of toast, "has friends everywhere. He has them in Hollywood, in Chicago and in Cleveland. He's done all of those friends favors and when he needs a favor, they are willing to do one for him. He's been keepin' tabs on you pretty good."

"I'm not sure I like that," Vic said.

Weasel's features hardened.

"Well, let me tell you something, Mr. Fenton. It don't matter much whether you like it or not. I only told you all this so you would understand, if the don was after you, no matter where you might go, he would find you. And you wouldn't want that, would you?"

"No," Vic agreed. "I don't think I would want that."

"All right, since we are agreed on that, I'm goin' to try and reason with you."

There was that terrible phrase, Vic thought, *What did it mean? Why was there such trepidation in that one innocent remark?*

"I want you to get off the train," Weasel continued. "I want you to get out of Katherine's life."

"If I get off the train, how am I supposed to get back to Hollywood?"

"No, you don't understand, Mr. Fenton. When I said I want you out of Katherine's life, I meant all the way out. You don't have to worry about getting to Hollywood 'cause you ain't goin'. You're givin' up show business."

"What?" Vic gasped. "You can't be serious! I'm not giving up Hollywood! My whole life is in Hollywood!"

"No, Mr. Fenton, that is where you are wrong," Weasel said. He held up his hand, palm forward, fingers extended and spread. "I got your whole life right here, in the palm of my hand." He made a fist. "Don't ever forget that. You see, from this moment on, your life is worth exactly what I say it is."

"But what will I do? Where will I go?"

"I don't give a shit," Weasel answered. "Go to Cleveland...work in a laundry. Just get the hell off this train and out of Katherine's life."

Though Weasel had shown him no weapon, nor even made a move to suggest he had one, there was something about him that stilled any protest Vic may have made. At first Vic couldn't understand what it was he was feeling, what he saw in Weasel that made him believe Weasel was someone who could carry out his threats. Then, with a gasp, he realized what it was. When Vic looked directly into Weasel's eyes, he realized that he was looking at a man who could kill another human being with as little regret as if he were stepping on a bug.

"All right," Vic said. "All right, if you insist, I'll get off at the next stop."

"No."

"No?"

"Get off now."

"What do you mean get off now? How'm I goin' to do that? The train is moving."

"Jump," Weasel said easily.

OFFICE OF THE BUREAU OF INVESTIGATION, NEW YORK

"The car was stolen," Captain Dillon said. He smiled. "It belongs to a real estate agent over in Hoboken."

"I figured it would be stolen," Mike replied. "Did you come over here just to tell us that?"

"Yeah, 'cause here's the thing. The car was stolen right here in the city."

"Congratulations on clearing the case," Mike said.

"Agent Kelly, you don't understand what I'm gettin' at, do you?" Dillon asked. "This ends it for the bureau. The only thing you had goin' for you was a car with Jersey plates. But since the car was stolen in New York City, whoever stole it didn't cross the state line. For the Bureau of Investigation, this case is over. You're out of it, Kelly."

"Not quite," Mike replied.

"What do you mean, 'not quite'?"

"I now have reason to believe that the person who killed LaRosa and Bendetti might be the same one who killed Agent Tim Clark, Carmine D'Angelo, and the two New Orleans police officers."

"What?" Dillon asked. "Are you trying to tell me that some New Orleans punk came up here just to rob one of our movie houses?"

"You are the one who is trying to make this into a simple robbery," Mike reminded the captain. "I believe it was a gangland murder and I believe it is connected with what happened in New Orleans."

"Have you got some reason for thinkin' this? Or did this just come out of your ass?" Captain Dillon asked disdainfully.

"No, I have a reason," Mike said. "We found one of the shotgun shells used in the Bendetti killing. It matches the shells we picked up down in New Orleans."

"You found one of the shells used in this killing? Where?"

"At the scene of the crime. Your boys were a little sloppy. They overlooked it."

"Agent Kelly, I would strongly advise you to turn that evidence over to me. You've got no right to it."

"Oh, but I do," Mike said. "As long as I have this shell, I have the link I need to the New Orleans killing."

"You got nothin'," Captain Dillon snorted. "So it's the same kind of shell. So what? There must be millions of shotgun shells sold...that same brand and gauge."

"Uh-huh. But not loaded with nail heads. Tell me, Dillon, why didn't it say in the coroner's report that the victim was killed by a blast of nail heads?"

"What makes you think he was?"

"The empty shotgun shell," Mike said. "It had the same markings and damage as the ones used in New Orleans. And the shotgun shells in New Orleans were filled with cutoff nail heads. That was what killed Tim Clark and Carmine D'Angelo, and that was what killed Bendetti. Now, back to my question. Why didn't it say in the coroner's report that the missiles were cutoff nail heads?"

"Why should it? What difference does it make? You sure can't run a ballistics test with nail heads."

"No," Mike said. "But I can compare these nail heads to some of those we got from New Orleans and determine if the nails were bought in the same lot."

"So what if you do? What good will that do you?"

"If the nail heads came from the same lot then we could definitely establish a link between the killing here and the killing in New Orleans," Mike said. He smiled at Dillon. "And that would mean that this is our case."

"Yeah? Well let me tell you something, Mr. Federal Agent Kelly," Dillon said angrily. "You stay the hell out of the way of the NYPD, you hear me? You do anything to interfere with our investigation of this case and I'll have you up on charges for obstruction. And that includes holding back any more evidence like that shotgun shell."

"Oh, I brought the shotgun shell with me," Mike said, pulling an envelope from his jacket pocket and holding it out. "I'll be glad to turn it over to anyone you say."

"I'll take it," Dillon said, reaching for it.

"On one condition," Mike said, pulling the envelope back.

"Yeah? What's that?"

"I want some of the nail heads and photos of finger-prints from the knife and car."

"We already matched the prints on the knife with prints from the car."

"Good. But I'd like all the prints."

Dillon hesitated.

"I could get a court order very easily," Mike said. He smiled without mirth. "And your threat of obstructing an investigation can cut both ways. Why don't you try your local charges against my federal charges and we'll see how it all comes out?"

Dillon growled, then picked up the phone and snapped the hook up and down several times. "Yeah," he said, when the precinct operator came on the line. "I'm sendin' Agent Kelly down to see you. Give him every-thing he asks for." He hung up the phone and looked over at Mike. "Satisfied?"

"Quite," Mike said, handing the envelope containing the expended shotgun shell to the police captain.

IN ANOTHER PART OF THE CITY...

*Mama Tantinni's Restaurant on West Forty-eighth, just off*Eighth Avenue, was, as usual, crowded with tables and diners. The six big rooms were filled with statues of the Madonna, splashing fountains, figures of birds, potted plants, oversized paintings and hanging tapestries. The restaurant was also festooned with Christmas decorations, even though it was not the Christmas season.

Mama Tantinni's was the preferred eating spot for New York's large population of Italian-Americans because of the quality and quantity of the food the restaurant served. As soon as a diner was seated he would be brought a big hunk of cheese and a loaf of Italian bread, plus artichokes, tomatoes and peppers. That would be followed by steaming plates of pasta, followed by the entree of veal parmigiana, or chicken cacciatore, or roast chicken or filet of sole. After that would come the deep-fried bugie, sugar-dipped and crunchy, and if one was still hungry, there was also an entire assortment of pies, cakes and ice creams.

Mama Tantinni's was a very popular tourist attraction, so that on any given night, its clientele would be divided about half and half between its regular trade and tourists from middle America. What very few of the Italian-American customers and none of the outsiders knew was that by tradition and practice, Mama Tantinni's was also the "Switzerland" of the Mafia. On the very night a farming family from Kansas might be celebrating the birthday of one of their children, at another table, in a private room, might be the most powerful and dangerous people in the underworld. Mama Tantinni's was used not only by the Five Families of New York but sometimes by other Mafia families from all over the United States.

If one family felt the need to have a "sit-down" with

another family, they could arrange it between the two of them. If, however, something important required a meeting of all the families, such a meeting was much more difficult to arrange. The Tantinni brothers sometimes acted as go-betweens to bring all the families to the table. For these services the Tantinnis were paid very handsomely. The heavy fees were justified in two ways. First, the lucrative fees kept the Tantinni brothers honest. They had no incentive to get into any of the other "businesses" and therefore would never have a vested interest in the outcome of any meeting. The other reason the fees were heavy was so that meetings would not be called frivolously. If someone wanted to call a meeting, he must be willing to pay the price.

When another one of his theaters was burned and a valuable shipment of film was destroyed by acid, Johnny decided that the price was worth paying. He asked the Tantinnis to set up a meeting of all the families.

Because Johnny had called and paid for the meeting, he was already there as the others arrived. Al Provenzano, Johnny's consigliore, was sitting beside him. The other family heads also brought their own counselors with them. Except for these counselors, however, no one but the family heads themselves were present, not even their chief lieutenants, for this was a meeting of the very highest order. Both Vaglichio brothers were present, a concession Johnny had agreed to in order to get them to come to the meeting. In fact, though the Vaglichios didn't realize it, Johnny had actually wanted both of them present, for he strongly suspected they might be behind his troubles.

As usual, Johnny had asked Don Pietro Nicolo to act as chairman for the meeting. Nicolo would hear all the evidence offered by both sides, consider the facts carefully, then offer his suggestion. It was a suggestion only, for, of course, Nicolo had no way of enforcing his decision. It was a measure of the respect everyone had for him that his suggestions were, invariably, carried out.

Enrico Nicolo greeted each man and shook him down for weapons, then allowed him to pass. As each visitor arrived in the room he went to Don Nicolo and embraced him, then nodded perfunctorily at Johnny, then at the Vaglichios and finally at the others. There was a quiet buzz of conversation among the men as they waited for Don Nicolo to start the meeting. Finally, when the last guest had arrived and was in place, Don Nicolo nodded to Enrico. Enrico, who was not qualified to be present for the hearing of the evidence or the rendering of the decision, closed the door behind him and stepped outside. That left the family heads and their consigliore alone. Only fifty feet away, on the other side of the walls around their private dining room, ordinary citizens laughed and dined, unaware of their proximity to such a meeting.

As Johnny popped a lemon drop into his mouth, he looked around at the other men, thinking they could very well be considered as captains of industry. In a way, they were, for surely they accounted for a significant percentage of the total gross product of the city of New York. These were men who were bigger than life and they lost none of their mystique by being seen in person. They were generally corpulent men, with large noses, generous mouths and heavy cheeks. They were men who were listened to. They were also men who had grown accustomed to power. For the moment each found himself in the unusual position of being present at a meeting but not in charge. They all were, however, more curious about how this was going to work than they were jealous of their positions of authority. They waited patiently for Don Nicolo to speak.

"Gentlemen, I want to thank all of you for coming,"

Don Nicolo said, speaking Italian in a Sicilian dialect. "Is there anyone among you who feels you might make a better peacemaker than me? If so, speak now."

Don Nicolo looked around the table at each man in turn and all acquiesced to his authority with silent nods of their heads.

"Thank you for your vote of confidence," Don Nicolo said. He took a deep breath and stroked his chin, then looked over at Johnny. "Don Sangremano, you have requested this meeting," he said. "You may speak now about what is troubling you."

"Thank you, Don Nicolo," Johnny said. "And I thank each of you for coming." He folded his hands on the table in front of him and looked earnestly into the faces of them all. Johnny was by far the youngest man in the room and he knew that his youth troubled some of the others, so he addressed that first.

"I should not be here like this," he said. "My father built the family for my oldest brother, Tony, to run. Tony was the businessman, and my brother Vinnie and I both knew that one day Tony would take over. That was as it should be, and Vinnie was prepared to serve Tony in whatever way Tony asked. I, being the youngest in the family, was prepared to do what the youngest son of a successful father does best...to spend the rest of my days chasing after fast cars and faster women."

The others around the table laughed.

Johnny paused for a moment before he continued. "But that wasn't to be," he said. "Man proposes, God disposes. When my father died a natural death Tony took over, just as planned. But all of you know what happened next. There was a short but bloody war that killed not only Tony but Vinnie as well. That same war also killed Don Vaglichio." Johnny looked across the table into the faces of the Vaglichio brothers. They had been responsible for the deaths of his own brothers and he in turn had killed their father, then the head of the Vaglichio family. Under normal circumstances, he would not bring up such painful memories but he did so for a reason. He wanted to see their reaction to it and though they gave no outward sign, the cold glint in their eyes told him all he wanted to know. They had not forgiven him.

"Of course my brothers and Don Vaglichio were not the only ones to die in that war. Many good men on both sides were also killed, leaving behind grieving wives and children. Since those terrible days, however, we have enjoyed several years of peace. And as a result of that peace, there are no grieving widows nor fatherless orphans. All have profited. Now, however, that has all changed."

Johnny told of the deaths of two of his best men, the burning of many of his theaters, and the destruction, by acid, of some of his motion picture film. He went on to say that many of the theater owners were frightened, and some had told him they would not be able to handle his films anymore.

"Don Sangremano," Don Nicolo said when, at last, Johnny was through with his litany. "We have listened to your problems and we offer you our sympathy. But what has that to do with us? Are you accusing one of the families of making war on you? And if you are, which family?"

"Which family stands to gain the most by bringing me down?" Johnny asked.

"Now, see here!" Luca Vaglichio shouted, pointing across the table at Johnny. "Are you accusing us?"

"He isn't accusing you of anything," Don Nicolo said, speaking calmly.

"The hell he isn't," Luca said.

"Did you have anything to do with it?" Johnny asked.

"No!"

"What about the man who did the actual killing?" one of the others asked. "Who was he? Who did he work for?"

Johnny sighed and shook his head slowly. "This, I have not been able to discover," he admitted.

"He was not one of our men," Luca put in quickly.

"You would be willing to swear to that?" Nicolo asked.

"Yes, of course I would."

"Then I ask each of you, on your honor, to answer this question truthfully," Nicolo continued. "Did the man who killed Mr. Bendetti and Mr. LaRosa work for you?"

One by one, Don Nicolo went around the table, posing the question to the others present. To a man, they denied any knowledge of who the killer was.

"Don Sangremano," Don Nicolo said, "I'm afraid you have called this meeting in vain. It would appear that none of the families represented here have anything to do with your killer. Perhaps he was an individual, working on his own."

"Yeah," Luca said. "Did you ever consider that? Besides, who wants anything to do with the theaters? You know what I'm after and it isn't theaters."

"Yes, I know what you are after."

"Don Nicolo, I would like to discuss the fact that Don Sangremano refuses to allow us to do any business with marijuana, cocaine and heroin."

"Do all the business you want in your territory," Johnny said. "Just leave me and my people out of it I don't like dope, or anyone who has anything to do with it."

"Dope is no different from liquor," Luca insisted. "But then of course, the Sangremanos had to be convinced to go into the liquor business too. Don Nicolo, I would like to propose that—"

"Excuse me," Johnny interrupted, "but I am the one who paid to have this meeting called. That means we will discuss what I want to discuss and nothing else."

"But I just wanted to get everyone else's opinion on..." Luca started to say, but this time Don Nicolo held up his hand.

"I'm sorry, Don Vaglichio," he said. "But Don Sangremano is right. He did call the meeting." He looked at Johnny. "Have you anything else to discuss?" he asked.

"No," Johnny said. "Nothing else."

Don Nicolo sighed. "I have heard the evidence presented by you, Don Sangremano. I speak for the other families when I offer you our sympathies for what has been happening. But you have to admit yourself, you have given us nothing to go on. The Vaglichios deny that they are behind your troubles and there is nothing to prove that they are."

"So, what are you going to do?" Johnny asked.

"Nothing," Don Nicolo said. "There is nothing I can do, except declare this meeting adjourned."

CHAPTER 6

When Clara awoke she stretched luxuriously on silken sheets and looked around the large bedroom she shared with her husband. She had been Mrs. Johnny Sangremano for over a month now and she still couldn't get used to living in such luxury. She was happier than she had ever been in her life, but it wasn't only the luxury of her surroundings that made her happy. She was happy with her husband because she loved him and she had discovered, quite unexpectedly, that she liked sex. No, she thought, like doesn't describe it. She loved sex.

Clara had been a virgin when she married because her mother had insisted it would be the only way she could win a man like Johnny Sangremano.

"He is a man of great power," Clara's mother explained. "He would not wish to take for his wife a woman who had been used and discarded by other men."

"But if I keep saying no to him, won't he go away and find someone else?" Clara asked her mother.

"Yes," her mother had answered with a mysterious

smile. "He will find another and he will make love to her. But, after he has used her he will discard her and come back to you...and always he will come back to you until, one day, he will be driven mad with want. After that, he will offer you a ring, because he will know that marriage is the only way he can have you."

Clara had to admit that her mother's plan had worked. She got out of bed and went into the bathroom to draw her bath. As the steam rolled up from the hot water she slipped out of her nightgown, then sat, nude, on the edge of the tub. Johnny had been particularly attentive to her last night, and she had enjoyed it immensely.

Clara had been innocent to the extent that she was still a virgin when she married, but she already a secret about herself. She knew she was a woman with a passionate nature. She came to that conclusion because unbidden erotic thoughts often played their temptations in her mind. As she had been completely without experience there was no form or substance to those fantasies, but there had been an insistent longing for something more.

Then she had married. All her erotic dreams were fulfilled and now, with her salaciousness unbound, she intended that there would be no more repression of her passionate spirit.

The bath was long and sensual, and as Clara lay in the tub allowing the water to change from hot to tepid, she recalled the pleasurable sensations of last night marveling that there could still be as much excitement after a month of marriage as there had been on the very first night. But then, Johnny had told her it would be so.

"Believe me, the more you learn, the better it gets," Johnny said.

Of course, Johnny should know, because Johnny was

a man of experience. It didn't bother Clara that Johnny had been with a lot of women before they were married. It did bother her to think that he might be with other women now.

"Men like Johnny," her mother had warned her before they were married, "are powerful men, with powerful needs...needs much too strong for one woman to supply. You must expect that he will be with other women after you are married. You must expect this and you must accept it."

"But Mama, I don't want him to be with other women," Clara had complained.

"Hush, child," Clara's mother had told her. "What does it matter how many women's beds he visits? As long as you do not become a fishwife who makes his life miserable, you will always be the one he will come home to."

That had been her mother's warning but, as far as Clara could tell, Johnny had not been with any other woman since they were married. Maybe Clara's mother was right, maybe it was impossible to maintain such a condition where the husband is satisfied to be only with his wife, but Clara certainly intended to try.

Clara stepped out of the bathtub and began patting herself dry with a big, soft towel when she heard the door open in the bedroom. She felt a small tingle of excitement "Johnny?" she called. "Johnny, is that you? Don't go away, darling, I have a surprise for you."

Clara dropped the towel to the floor, then caught her image in the bathroom mirror. Full-breasted, with a tiny waist and flaring hips, she was, as her mother liked to say, "built for having babies."

"If I'm not pregnant yet, it isn't for lack of trying," Clara said under her breath. She smiled and thought of

Johnny, waiting for her in the bedroom. "And I'm about to try again."

Clara didn't see him when she first stepped into the bedroom. Then she sensed, more than saw, something in the shadows in the corner of the room.

"Johnny?" she said. The anticipation and sexual excitement she had felt a moment earlier suddenly drained away, to be replaced by a deep, cold, numbing fear. She could not explain exactly why she was afraid, only that she was more terrified than she had ever been in her life.

She started toward the bedroom door, not caring that she was naked, interested only in getting away. Then her worst nightmare was realized as something came out of the shadows toward her. She tried to scream but, before she could, a hand was clamped down over her mouth so that the scream burst in her own brain like the wail of a thousand banshees, yet was absolutely silenced. The last images her eyes ever recorded were the pink eyes and chalk-white face of her assailant.

———

Johnny had had a difficult day. Many of the theater owners were frightened and some of them were becoming openly rebellious about continuing their relationship with him. He had to convince them they were better off staying with him than they would be with anyone else or trying to go it alone. He found, however, that it was getting increasingly difficult to convince the theater owners of this fact. He wished Weasel were back from California. Weasel had a way of handling things like this.

When Johnny got home he saw Clara's yellow Duesenberg convertible still sitting in the circular driveway. She had told him this morning that she planned to go into town to visit her mother, so he had brought the car around for her before he left. The car was unmoved, so he figured Clara must have changed her mind. Maybe she was afraid to try it by herself.

Johnny laughed. The Duesenberg had been his wedding present to her, and it wasn't until after he handed her the keys that he learned she didn't even know how to drive. He taught her, but most of the time she still preferred to have someone else drive her, especially if she were going to go into New York, like today. Maybe she couldn't find anyone to take her into the city and she didn't feel up to driving herself. No matter. Actually, Johnny was glad. He needed to get away from the business for a few hours. If she still wanted to go see her folks, he would take her.

Johnny saw one of the armed guards patrolling the grounds, and he exchanged waves with him as he climbed the steps to the front porch, then went on into the house.

"Clara!" he called. "Clara, are you here?" He bounded up the stairs to the bedroom.

Marriage had been a big surprise to Johnny. One of his first surprises was in learning that Clara was an exceptionally passionate woman. She had fought him off so forcefully throughout their courtship that he was beginning to wonder if she might be a cold fish. He was very pleased to discover just how wrong an assumption that was!

The other surprise was the fact that he felt no need, nor desire, to play around on her. He remembered his remarks at the bachelor party his friends had given him, when he had laughed and said, "I might be getting married, but who said anything about settling down?"

Contrary to his bravado at the party that night, he had settled down.

Clara wasn't upstairs either. He looked into the bathroom and saw that the tub was full. He thought it rather strange that she hadn't drained the water, so he pulled the plug himself.

Johnny searched the entire house without finding her, then decided she must have found someone to take her to her mother's in a car other than the Duesenberg. Johnny was glad. It was good that she could go for a visit. Such trips into town were the only time Clara got to see her mother because her mother didn't like to come out here. Clara's mother made the excuse that such a big, fancy house made her nervous. Johnny wasn't sure that was the reason, but he didn't want to make his mother-in-law any more uncomfortable than she already was, so he didn't question her. Besides, he loved Clara...really loved her. And when Clara's mother realized that, she wouldn't be uncomfortable anymore.

Johnny was hot and sticky from his trip into the city, so he decided to take a swim. He put on his swimsuit, then went downstairs and outside. The bright blue pool flashed with sunbursts from the surface of the gently undulating water. It was so inviting that he ran through the grass, dashed across the tile coping and dove right into the cool, refreshing pool.

Johnny plummeted down through the water, then opened his eyes as he flattened out his dive to glide just above the blue tiles, far beneath the surface. That was when he passed over the cold, unblinking stare of Clara, lying nude at the bottom of the pool. Tiny bubbles of blood were still rising from the slit in her throat.

One thousand, five hundred dollars in twenty-dollar bills was counted out and placed in neat little stacks on the table.

"It was a good, clean job," the payee said, complimenting the man who reached for the money.

"Yeah, well, killin' a woman is no different from killin' a man, far as I'm concerned," the small, neat man replied. "Dead is dead."

"That's right. But some people would have made it messy. I don't like messy jobs."

"You mean like raping the woman?"

"Yes, that's what I mean."

"You don't have to worry about me doing something like that. That kind of man has no business in our profession."

NEW YORK

It rained the day of Clara's funeral. The rain didn't stop the funeral, of course, nor did it lower the number of mourners who attended. Though Clara's parents would have preferred that she be buried in a cemetery in the city, Johnny wanted her buried out on Long Island, very close to where they lived.

The white gravel road of the cemetery was filled with a double line of cars. Hundreds of mourners poured out of the cars, then walked through the mud and stood in the downpour as they fanned out around the freshly dug grave for the final part of the service. Clara's brother, who was a priest, was too upset to conduct the funeral mass, so the priest in charge of the burial service was the same one who had assisted Clara's brother and the bishop in the wedding, just six weeks earlier.

A canopy had been erected beside the open grave and, on a carpet of fake grass, chars had been put in place for Johnny and Clara's parents. Johnny's mother sat in the second row, along with Clara's brother and a few more of Clara's relatives.

The hem of the priest's cassock was spattered with mud, and Johnny stared at it as he listened, with only half an ear, to the lengthy prayers in English and Latin.

> *O Lord Jesus Christ, the king of glory, deliver the soul of your faithful departed, Clara, from the pains of hell and from the deep pit; deliver her from the lion's mouth, that hell engulf her not, that she fell not into the darkness; but let Michael, the holy standard-bearer, bring her into the holy light which Thou didst promise of old to Abraham and his seed. We offer Thee sacrifices and prayers of praise, O Lord; do Thou accept them for this soul of whom we this day make commemoration; cause her, O Lord, to pass from death to the life which of old Thou didst promise to Abraham and his seed.*
>
> *Suscipe, sancte Pater, omnipotens aeterne Deus, hanc immaculatam hostiam, quam ego indignus famulus tuus offero tibi, Deo meo vivo et vero, pro innumerabilibus peccatis, et offensionibus, et negligentiis meis, et pro omnibus circum-stantibus, sed et pro omnibus fidelibus christianis vivis atque defunctis: ut mihi et illis proficiat ad salutem in vitam aeter-nam. Amen.*

Johnny lifted his eyes from the mud-splattered cassock of the priest and began looking into the faces of the mourners. The priest's prayers and supplications faded into the background, and Johnny could almost feel himself leave his body. A part of him was there, sitting in the chair beside the open grave and the shining casket, but another part of him was wandering around the graveyard, touching on the face of this mourner and that, looking into the eyes, delving into the soul.

Clara's murderer was here, today. Johnny knew that as well as he knew his own name. Perhaps the person who actually wielded the knife wasn't here, but the person who ordered it done, was.

Every family from the city was represented. Don Pietro Nicolo was present, as were Don Vincent Barbutti of the Barbutti Family and Don Carmine Lombardi of the Lombardi Family. The Vaglichio brothers were here also. "Johnny? Johnny?"

It wasn't until Johnny's mother had leaned forward to whisper his name that Johnny realized the priest was standing in front of him. Johnny nodded, then took a rose and lay it on top of Clara's casket. After that, four men, using ropes, began to lower the coffin slowly into the ground.

With the funeral over, the mourners began to file by slowly. Many were friends and relatives of Clara's family and they embraced Mr. and Mrs. Ricco. Most just nodded sadly at Johnny as they walked by. The godfathers of the other families also filed by.

"This is a terrible thing, Johnny," Don Nicolo said sadly. "It is not right, a young, beautiful girl should die like that."

"I will find out who murdered her, Don Nicolo," Johnny vowed. "I will find out and I will make him pay."

"Johnny, Johnny, I agree you should find out who did this terrible thing and make him pay," Don Nicolo said. "But I beg of you: do not let your thirst for vengeance lead into a war. This, you do not want. This, no one wants."

Don Barbutti and Don Lombardi echoed Don Nicolo's sentiments. They also thought it was a terrible thing and agreed that whoever was responsible should pay for his crime. But they too did not want to see another war.

"I am very sorry," Luca Vaglichio said when he and Mario came through the line. "To think that such a short time ago I was at your wedding and now I should come to your bride's funeral."

"I want you Vaglichios to know that I will not let this go unavenged," Johnny said coldly.

"What do you mean by that?"

"You know what I mean."

"Sangremano, you accusing us of this?" Mario asked indignantly.

"I am accusing no one," Johnny replied.

"I hope you don't think we did it," Luca said. "If we did, do you think we would come to the funeral?"

"If you did it, you could not afford not to come to the funeral," Johnny replied.

"You are right," Mario said. "Whoever did this would have to come. But I swear to you, we are not responsible."

"I know. We are old friends of long standing," Johnny said sarcastically.

"Come along, Mario," Luca said. "Our expression of sympathy is wasted on him."

"Johnny, my son, you don't mean these threats you make," Father Ricco said, coming over to stand beside him. Father Ricco had overheard the conversation between Johnny and the other godfathers and between Johnny and the Vaglichios.

Johnny looked into the face of the young priest who was Clara's brother. The priest's face was streaked with tears, for he had been particularly close to his sister.

"Yes, I do mean them."

"But, surely you cannot mean that. You would dishonor your wife's...my sister's...memory if you carried out those threats. The way of the vendetta is not the way of the Lord," Father Ricco said, passionately.

"Well, I'll tell you, Father," Johnny said coldly. "The Lord has his way and I have mine."

"Please don't say such things, Johnny. That's blasphemous."

"Is it? Well, I think God was blasphemous to allow someone as young and sweet and good as Clara was, to die. Where was your God then, priest? Where was he when Clara needed his protection? You know she prayed for mercy. Why didn't he answer her? Why didn't he help? Was he asleep on watch?"

"I...I will give you time to be alone with your grief," Father Ricco said, unable to deal with Johnny's agonized inquiries, perhaps because, secretly, he had already asked the same questions himself.

As Father Ricco walked out to the road, the car doors of the many mourners were now beginning to slam shut. Soon scores of engines were running, and the automobiles began moving away, slipping and sliding through the rain and the mud.

Johnny walked back to the canopy and sat in the chair as everyone else left. The priest who had conducted the service was still at the graveside. Now he kissed his stole and came over to speak with Johnny.

"You were a little hard on Father Ricco, weren't you, my son?"

"Was I?" Johnny asked.

"I know your sorrow is great, but so is his. It does not ease your grief to add to his."

"No, I guess not," Johnny admitted.

The priest reached out and put his hand on Johnny's shoulder. "You shouldn't stay here any longer," he said. "You should leave now and let these men do their work. They must close the grave."

"They can close it with me here," Johnny said.

"You don't mean that," the priest said. "That isn't done. It simply isn't done."

"I'm staying," Johnny said resolutely.

The priest looked at Johnny for a moment. Finally he sighed in defeat. "Very well. Have it your own way, Mr. Sangremano." The priest hurried through the rain to the car the Riccos had ridden in, then got into the backseat and left with them. Within fifteen more minutes, all the cars were gone and no one was left except Johnny and the two gravediggers. Though the two mud-spattered men had been in the cemetery during the funeral they hadn't actually been present, for they had remained discreetly out of sight behind a nearby crypt until now. They approached the open grave tentatively.

"Excuse me, sir," one of them said. "We must close the grave now."

"Go ahead," Johnny said.

"But you…"

"Go ahead," Johnny said again.

"Yes, sir."

Johnny remained sitting as the two men began shoveling dirt down into the hole. He heard the thumping sound of the first several turns of dirt hitting the coffin. Finally the coffin itself was covered so that there was only dirt falling upon dirt and the sound grew more muffled. The men worked quickly and quietly; within fifteen minutes the grave was completely covered. After that, the flowers were arranged over and around the mound. Then, with one final nod at Johnny, the two men picked up their shovels and walked away, leaving him alone.

The rain continued to fall, and Johnny could hear its drumming rhythm on the canvas over his head. He looked out through the rain, at the forest of tombstones, crosses and obelisks that made up the graveyard. Just a few feet away was the rather large and ornate marker of the grave of a man who had been an important general in the Civil War. And now there was no difference between that general and Clara.

That didn't seem right. Graveyards were for old people, for people from another time, not for a beautiful young woman who, just a few nights before, had shared his bed.

About fifty feet away from the canopy, standing near the crypt of a former state legislator, Mike Kelly watched Johnny as his onetime friend sat quiet and alone in the chair near the grave. This was the first time Mike had seen Johnny in over three years, and he couldn't help but feel a sadness for the way things had turned out between them. Mike had been here throughout the funeral, thinking of how things turned out. He remembered a happier time between them when they left New York for their great adventure.

After fixing up an old airplane, Mike and Johnny barnstormed all across the country, just as they planned. They flew airshows in Ohio, gave rides in Indiana, took aerial photos in Illinois, doing anything and everything that would earn enough money to keep them going. Finally, they wound up in St. Louis, where they were about to take a job with Robertson Aircraft Company, flying the U.S. Air Mail. It was there, on the front page of the St. Louis Globe-Democrat, that Johnny saw the article about his brothers getting killed and decided then to return to New York.

Because Mike didn't want to continue the barnstorming without Johnny, they sold the airplane and took the train back. Standing outside Grand Central Station, Mike learned that he hadn't known his friend nearly as well as he thought he did.

Johnny took out a sack of lemon drops, gave one to Mike, then stuck one in his own mouth. "We had fun, didn't we?"

"The most fun I ever had in my life," Mike agreed. Johnny shoved an envelope toward Mike. "Listen, Mike, we have two hundred eighty dollars left from the sale of the airplane," he said. "I want you to have it."

"No, not all of it," Mike replied. "I'll take a hundred and forty, that's my share."

"Take it all," Johnny insisted.

"No," Mike said, laughing in protest as he shoved it away. "Why would you try and give all of it to me?"

"The money doesn't mean anything to me. I don't need it. You might."

Mike laughed again. "The money doesn't mean anything to you? Do you know who you're talking to, Johnny? Don't forget, I've watched you squabble with a farmer for half an hour over half-a-dollar's difference in what he was charging us to park our plane overnight in his field."

Johnny laughed with him. "Yeah, I did put up some pretty good fights, didn't I? But, that was then, this is now," he finally said. "I guess I'm about ready for a few changes to be made in my life."

"A few changes? What do you mean?" Mike asked, still smiling.

"The truth is, I've been giving it a lot of thought on the way back." Johnny sighed. "Mike, I've decided what I'm going to do. I'm going into the business."

"The business? What business?"

"You know what business I'm talking about."

"No, I..." Mike stopped in midsentence and looked at Johnny. The smile fell away from his face, to be replaced by a look of disbelief and disappointment "Johnny, no. You don't mean you are joining the Mafia?"

"Mike!" Johnny said sharply, his eyes flashing a warning. He raised a warning finger. "I told you, never say that word. Goddamnit, that can get you killed!"

"Listen to yourself," Mike said, stung by the severity of the reprimand. "It sounds like you are threatening me.

Is that what you intended, Johnny? Are you threatening me?"

"No, of course not," Johnny replied. "But I did warn you. Take the warning seriously, Mike. Be careful, that's all I'm saying."

"Why are you doing this, Johnny? You know what kind of business your family is involved with."

"Yes, I do know. But with Papa and Tony both dead, I have no choice. This is the only right thing to do."

"Right? How can you use that word with what your family does? I would think the word right would stick in your throat."

"Wait a minute, here. Listen to the righteous one. Just who the hell are you to judge me?" Johnny asked sharply. "And who are you to tell me about my family? Are there no skeletons in your closet? Correct me if I'm wrong, Mike, old friend, but aren't you the same person who confessed to me that your father was the very kind of policeman that my father so easily corrupted?"

"We aren't talking about my father or yours. We are talking about right and wrong," Mike said.

"Listen, there is right and there is honor, and sometimes right is one thing and honor is another," Johnny answered.

Mike looked confused. "What the hell is that supposed to mean? That statement doesn't make any sense. But then, that's understandable because you aren't making any sense," he accused.

"Maybe not. But I know what I'm going to do. My mind is made up."

"You don't really want to do this, do you?"

"I told you, I have no choice. I am destined for this. It's in my blood."

"Johnny, didn't you once tell me that I'm not my father and you aren't yours?"

"Maybe I did say that," Johnny admitted. "But if I did, I was just kidding myself. It wasn't real when I said that," he went on. "Where were we? In a farmer's field somewhere on some other planet?" A nearby car honked angrily at a pedestrian, who shouted back at the driver of the car. "That wasn't real. This is," he added, taking in the busy street with a wave of his hand. He tried again to pass the envelope over to Mike. "Now take the money, Mike. It will help you get started in whatever it is you are going to do." Mike felt a chill pass over his body and, resolutely, he reached out to push the envelope back once again.

"You may be like your father, Johnny, but I am not like mine. I will not take one cent more than is due me, don't you see? Not from you, not from anyone."

A screen rose over Johnny's eyes. It was the kind of screen a person would put up when he wanted to separate himself from whoever he was talking to. Mike had seen the same protective screen in others, but he had never seen it in Johnny. At that precise moment a gulf opened up between them, and Mike didn't know if either of them would ever be able to reach the other again.

"Okay," Johnny finally said. "I understand."

"I don't want to make you mad," Mike said as Johnny counted out one hundred and forty dollars.

"That's all right," Johnny replied, coolly. "I guess there are some lines that even friendship can't cross." He counted out the exact amount due Mike, then handed the bills to him.

"Thanks," Mike said. He put the money in his billfold, then reached out to shake Johnny's hand again. "I'll see you around," he said.

"Good-bye, Mike," Johnny replied pointedly.

The two men held their handshake and, for a moment, the screen covering Johnny's eyes almost came down. It was as if this conversation had never taken place. They weren't in New York, they were in Ohio, or Indiana, or Illinois, bound together on their quest for adventure. But, almost as quickly as the screen came down, it went up again, and Johnny turned and walked over to get into a waiting taxi. Johnny looked back as the taxi drove away, but he didn't wave. His eyes were sad and distant, and Mike wasn't at all sure that Johnny even saw him.

Mike blinked several times, to force those memories away. He walked over to stand just outside the canopy.

"Hello, Johnny."

Johnny was startled to hear his name called, and when he turned, he was even more startled to see who had spoken to him.

"Mike!" Johnny said, and for a moment there was genuine joy in his expression. Then, as if remembering where he was and why he was here, the sadness returned. He held out his hand. "It's good to see you, old friend," he said. "Please, come in out of the rain."

Mike accepted Johnny's invitation, taking his hat off as he stepped under the canvas awning. He poured water from the crown and brim of his hat.

"I'm so glad you came," Johnny said.

"I wasn't going to," Mike answered. "I mean"—he made a gesture with his hat—"we aren't exactly running in the same circles nowadays."

"No," Johnny agreed. "I guess we aren't. Nevertheless, I'm glad."

"I never got the chance to meet her," Mike said. He gestured, toward the flower-bedecked mound.

"It's too bad you didn't. You would've liked her," Johnny said. "She wasn't like me. Then again, none of our women ever are. They are saints, these women," he said. "They put up with…" Johnny let the sentence hang, as if afraid he was about to say more than he intended. "Well, you know as well as anyone what they put up with," he said.

"Yes," Mike said. "I know."

"That's why It's so hard for me to understand why she…" Again, Johnny paused in midsentence. This time, however, it was because he couldn't go on. He blinked his eyes several times, and Mike could see that he was fighting back the tears.

"Johnny, do you know who did it?"

Johnny shook his head. "No," he said. "But I'm going to find out."

"If you would let me, I would like to help."

"Thanks, but I don't need it," Johnny said. "And I don't want it," he added.

"Do you think it has anything to do with your men who were murdered last week?"

"What men are those?" Johnny asked.

"Bendetti and LaRosa," Mike said. "You know who I'm talking about."

"I may have read something in the papers," Johnny said evasively.

"Goddamnit!" Mike swore. "Look, Johnny, I know all about the code of omerta. I know you can't tell me…or at least, you think you can't tell me anything. But I'm trying to help!"

"If you know that, you already know too much," Johnny said.

"Yes, maybe I do," Mike replied. "But then we both know where I got it, don't we?"

Johnny glared at him. "Mike, your big mouth could get us both in serious trouble, do you know that?" he asked.

"From the death soldiers?"

This time Johnny really did look surprised and Mike noted his expression with interest

"I don't know what you are talking about," Johnny said.

"You've never heard the term death soldiers?"

"No."

"That's too bad," Mike said. "I was hoping you might know. I was also hoping you might be able to tell me what connection there could be between a murder in New Orleans, a murder in Chicago and the murder of your two men."

"I know of no connection."

"Neither do I," Mike replied. "Except that the prints we took off the knife that killed one of your men match a set of prints taken off the getaway car that was used in New Orleans. And the shotgun shells were loaded with nail heads there, just as they were here. In addition, one of the New Orleans gunmen was also involved in a Chicago killing."

"What does all that have to do with me?"

"I was hoping you would know," Mike said.

"I don't."

Mike sighed, then put his hat back on. "Yeah, well, I thought it might be worth a try." He turned to leave, then he looked back at Johnny. "I really am sorry about your wife," he said.

"Thanks," Johnny replied. As Mike left, Johnny called out to him.

"Mike?"

"Yes?" Mike turned toward him, hoping Johnny was about to tell him something...anything he could use.

"Take care of yourself, Mike," Johnny said. "I mean it."

"Yeah, I will," Mike replied.

When Mike returned to his office he was surprised to see that J. Edgar Hoover was there.

"Mr. Director," Mike said, extending his hand in welcome. "What a pleasant surprise! I had no idea you were in the city."

"Hello, Agent Kelly," Hoover said. "It's good to see you up and moving around after your, uh, problem. How are you doing?"

"I'm doing fine, Mr. Director," Mike said. He moved his arms up and down several times to demonstrate his mobility. "As you can see, I'm as good as I ever was."

"Well, that's pretty self-limiting, isn't it?" Jason asked, and the others laughed.

"What gets you away from the Potomac?" Mike asked.

"I came to see you," Hoover replied.

"Me?" Mike replied, surprised by the director's statement "You came all the way up here, just to see me?"

"Yes," Hoover replied. "I want to talk to you. Actually, I want to talk to all four of you. But what I have to say, I need to say in person. I hope you don't mind my just dropping in like this."

"Mind? We're honored, Mr. Director."

Hoover glanced over toward the door and nodded at Joe. "Please close that door, would you, Agent Provenzano?"

"Yes sir," Joe replied, complying with the director's request. A moment later all four were sitting around the long table that served as conference, work and sometimes dining table. Hoover removed an envelope from his inside jacket pocket.

"Before I begin, I have some information that you might find interesting," he said. He opened the envelope and pulled out a piece of paper.

"What is that?" Mike asked.

"It's a report on the nail heads that were used in the murders in New Orleans and here in New York," Hoover said. Then after a moment, he added, "And Cleveland."

"And Cleveland?" Mike asked.

"Cleveland," Hoover replied.

"I haven't heard about that one yet. When did it happen?" Mike asked.

"Last year," Hoover answered. "And there was no reason you should have heard of it. It was a local case, still is as far as I'm concerned. But when I heard that nail heads had been used in New Orleans and again in New York, I got curious. I was wondering if the use of nail heads was something new, something that was going to spread around the country. I got curious about it so I had some research done. It turns out all these nail heads came from the same lot."

"That's very interesting," Joe said.

"It gets even more interesting," Hoover added. "We've been able to trace the lot from the manufacturer to the wholesaler."

"And where did they all wind up?" Mike asked.

"Steubenville, Ohio," Hoover said. "At a place called Home Materials Incorporated."

"So whoever did the killing bought their nails there," Jason said.

"That's how it looks," Hoover agreed.

"Joe, any Mafia families in Steubenville that you know of?"

"I can find out," Joe replied.

"Mike, wait a minute," Hoover said. As it was most unusual for Hoover to call Mike anything but Agent Kelly, Mike looked at him with more than average curiosity. Hoover stroked his bulldog chin for a moment before he went on.

"As you know," he said, "I don't really believe there is

a national organization of criminals." Before Mike could reply, Hoover waved his hand. "I will confess that, from time to time they may, well, unite for a common purpose, but such a union would be temporary. In the final analysis, by the very nature of the criminal psyche, it would be every man for himself."

"In other words, you don't believe the Mafia exists," Mike said.

"No," Hoover replied. "Oh, I'm sure the Italians have romanticized their criminal involvement by creating the myth of the Mafia, but as a functioning organization, I won't give them the respect of believing that it exists at all."

"I see," Mike said.

"People are always using that argument to get me to declare the bureau as a national police force," Hoover went on. "And I must admit that there are several tempting reasons to form a national police force, but in the long run, I think it would be difficult to prevent such a force from infringing upon the rights of the people. That's why I am against a national police force. Instead, I would prefer to see the solidarity and linking up of all law enforcement agencies. However..." he let the word hang for a long time, so long that Mike finally decided that some response was required.

"However, sir?"

"There are times when it is difficult for me to sustain my position. At such times, I need the maximum flexibility in interpreting both the law and the charter under which the bureau operates."

"And this is such a time?" Mike suggested.

"Yes," Hoover said. "Agent Tim Clark was one of our own, Mike. He was one of our own and they killed him. I do not intend to let that crime go unpunished. And the fact that these cutoff nail heads have been used in three murders, in three different states, gives us all the justification we need to make this into a federal case."

"Yes, sir, that's what I thought as well," Mike said. "Who else in the bureau is working on this case?"

"Just you," Hoover replied. He looked around to make certain the door was still closed. "And that's why I wanted to come talk to you men, personally. I want you to make this the number one priority, but I want you to form an ad hoc task force to deal with it. I don't want it to be perceived publicly as a Bureau of Investigation operation."

"You don't want the Bureau involved?" Mike asked, surprised by the director's comment "Why not?"

"For the reasons I told you. Mike, we simply cannot afford to have the Bureau perceived as a national police force. That is why I want you to form a small task force," Hoover said. "Now, that is not to say that you will be operating outside the law. On the contrary, you will have all the authority of the Bureau, and you will, of course, be able to draw from its resources. But no one else in the Bureau, except me, is to know of the existence of such a force."

"Such a force already exists," Mike said.

"It already exists? What do you mean?" Hoover asked. "I know of no such organization."

Mike smiled. "Mr. Director," he said, "allow me to introduce you to the members of the Blood Oath Society."

"The what?" Hoover asked, looking at the other three men.

"The Blood Oath Society," Mike explained. "You see, Mr. Hoover, we have an organization as secret as the organization of those we fight and dedicated to the eradication of the Mafia. Only ours is even more secret, for while we know of their existence, no one but the four of us—now five, counting you—knows that we exist."

"What, exactly, is this group?" Hoover asked, warily.

"As I explained, sir, it is dedicated to the eradication of the Mafia."

"And as I explained to you, there is no Mafia."

"But you will admit, Mr. Director, that there is a criminal element who wishes us to believe in the Mafia."

"Yes," Hoover said, stroking his chin as he wondered where Mike's reasoning was taking them.

Mike smiled. "Then you might say that our group exists in order to destroy the myth of the Mafia."

"All right, I'll accept that as a valid objective. But tell me, what made you decide to form such a group in the first place?"

"We wanted something that would bind us together even more closely than the oath of office we took when we joined the bureau."

"I see. You mean like belonging to KA?"

"I beg your pardon?"

Hoover smiled. "That was the fraternal brotherhood I belonged to in college," he explained.

"I see. Well, to answer your question, I would have to say no, sir. What we have is far beyond fraternal," he said. "It's more like a sacred order. We have sworn an oath, a blood oath, pledging our very lives, if need be, to each other and to honor, loyalty and secrecy."

"And you four are its only members?" Hoover asked.

"Yes, sir. We are, for now," Mike answered.

"You say, 'for now.' Does that mean you anticipate more members?"

"There will eventually be other members," Mike answered. "Though as we have developed it, we believe membership should be granted only to the select few who might meet the ideals that we have set."

"We have already established high standards and

ideals for membership in the Bureau," Hoover admonished.

"Yes sir, I agree," Mike replied. "Think what a wonderful pool that gives us to draw from. What we have done is create a group whereby only the best of the best can be considered for membership. It is our hope that the group we have created will outlive its creators and its future members will take up the journey we started."

"What do you mean, the journey you started?" Hoover asked. "Do you not plan to finish the job?"

Mike smiled. "There will be victories for us, yes," he said. "I feel confident that we will be victorious over the Sangremanos, the Vaglichios and the other families within the Mafia. But wrongdoing will certainly survive us as individuals. We will therefore have to pass the torch on to those who follow us if there is to be an ultimate victory."

"Gentlemen, when you took your oath to serve in the Bureau, you vowed to serve the best interests of the bureau and the United States. I hope that this, this blood oath that you take, does not bind you to anything that may be in violation of your original oath."

"Absolutely not, sir," Joe said. "If anything, the blood oath binds us more tightly to the oath we already took."

"In fact, Mr. Director," Mike said, "we have discussed this before and I think I'm not speaking out of turn when I say we would like you to become a member of our society."

"Me?"

"Yes, sir," Mike replied. "If the director belonged, it would legitimize our operation, without having to compromise it by having anything about it on paper."

"You have nothing on paper?"

"No, sir,"

"What about the oath?"

"We have it committed to memory," Bill said. "We'll write it out for you. Then, after you take it, we'll prick your finger to seal the oath with a drop of blood. After that, we'll burn the paper so that its elements become a permanent part of the gases of the atmosphere, as ours is now. That way, a thousand years from now, though dispersed by wind and time, these atoms will still exist."

Hoover chuckled, self-consciously. "It all sounds very mystical," he said.

"Yes, sir, I suppose it does," Jason admitted. "But we are very bound by it."

"And, we have now taken you into our confidence," Mike added. "Do you wish to join?"

Hoover looked at the four young men for a long moment then his pugnacious face spread into a wide, easy grin.

"I would be very honored," he said.

"I'll write out the oath," Jason offered.

A few moments later, after studying the oath Jason had written for him, Hoover agreed to having the end of his finger pricked. He let a drop of his blood fall on the paper, then he held up his right hand and repeated the oath. The others took the oath with him.

I, in agreeing to become one of the Brethren of the Blood Oath Society, do hereby solemnly swear allegiance to the Society, loyalty to the Brethren, and fidelity to the principles upon which the Society was founded.

As Brethren of the Blood Oath Society we are sworn enemies to the Mafia and we are the true stewards of justice. We vow never to betray these ideals by any act of dishonesty or compromise. We further swear to hold sacred the mystic rites of the Blood Oath Society, keeping secret even its very existence except to those deemed worthy of induction into its mysteries.

After the oath, Mike put the piece of paper upon

which it had been written into an ashtray. He set fire to it then he, Bill, Joe and Jason shook hands with the director, welcoming him into the society.

"Use this society of yours—" Hoover started to speak, but Mike interrupted him.

"Ours," he corrected.

Hoover smiled. "Ours," he said. "Use it to get to the bottom of these murders. Whether it is part of an overall criminal organization as you contend, or merely coincidentally linked, these men murdered one of our own, and I want them brought to justice."

"They will be," Mike promised.

"We won't let you down, Mr. Director," Bill added.

"I know you won't," Hoover replied. He looked at the tiny pinprick in the end of his finger, then held it up. "Make me proud, boys. Make me proud that I belong."

CHAPTER 7

STEUBENVILLE, OHIO

When Joe got off the train in Steubenville, people who knew him well would have had to look twice to recognize him. Not only was his hair a little longer than he normally wore it, he also had it combed straight back and slicked down with a heavy hair oil. A pencil-thin moustache was over his lip. He was wearing a dark pin-striped suit, a black shirt and a white tie. A tiny red feather was stuck in the rather wide band of his hat. It wasn't just his physical appearance that was altered; there was a change in his entire demeanor. He walked with a challenging, swaggering gait and he looked at people through insolent eyes that were half closed.

Joe lit a cigarette by snapping the match head with his thumbnail. With the cigarette lit, he blew out the fire, then flipped the match away. He walked over to one of the several taxis standing in line at the taxi stand. Many had brought passengers to the departing train, and now they, like the others, were waiting for arriving passengers.

"Where to?" the driver asked as Joe slid into the back-seat of the closest cab.

"I don't know," Joe said. "Someplace where I can relax, you know what I mean?"

"We have several nice hotels in town," the driver said. "Take your pick."

"What are you, some kind of wise guy?" Joe snarled. "When I say relax, I'm not talkin' about sleepin'. Where's the action in this town?"

"I could maybe take you to a pool hall."

"Yeah, a pool hall," Joe agreed.

"Murphy's or Lambretta's. Take your pick."

The side of Joe's mouth curled into what might have been a smile. "Lambretta's," he said. "What the hell I look like, a goddamn mick?"

Lambretta's may have been in Steubenville, Ohio, but as far as Joe was concerned it could have come right out of Little Italy in New York. A smell of spices pervaded the place: oregano, thyme and garlic. The smells weren't over-powering, they were just enough to be familiar. A dozen or more ceiling fans hummed and rattled as they twirled from long suspended stalks. The fan blades cut through the overhead lights to create flickering effects on the green felt-covered tables. The flyblown walls were plastered with price lists and admonishments. (No Spitting On The Floor; No Gambling; No Cursing), a calendar and adver-tisements for half a dozen products, many of them Italian. There was also a large framed picture of Benito Mussolini over which were crossed a pair of Italian national flags.

Joe racked up the balls on an empty table and shot a few games by himself. When someone asked him, in Ital-ian, if he wanted a game, Joe answered in the same language. "The name is Carlo. Carlo Lambretta. What's yours?"

"Joe," Joe answered. He didn't give a last name. "Nice place you got here." They continued to speak in Italian.

"I got the same last name, but this here place don't belong to me," Carlo said. "It belongs to my uncle. So, where you from?"

Joe was about to make a shot, but he paused long enough to fix Carlo with a blunt stare.

"What the hell you doin', writin' a book?" Joe asked.

"No," Carlo answered. "I was just wonderin'. I mean I ain't seen you around before and there ain't that many Italians in Steubenville."

"I ain't from Steubenville," Joe said. He thrust the cue stick forward. There was a loud clack, and the four-ball clattered into the corner pocket, while the cue ball spun in place on the green felt.

"Say, you're pretty good," Carlo said.

"Thanks," Joe replied. "Want to play for a little money?"

"You kiddin'? I wouldn't play you."

"That's too bad, I could use a few bucks," Joe said. "Know anyone who might give me a game?"

"Not if they get a look at you with that cue," Carlo replied. "Listen, you need a few bucks, I'll lend you a few bucks."

"No," Joe said.

"No? What do you mean, no? I thought you said you need money."

"I mean no. I don't know you."

Carlo laughed. "Hey, I'm the one offerin' to lend money to you, it ain't the other way around."

"That don't matter none. I don't know you, I won't borrow from you."

"You was goin' to take it off me if I lost at pool."

"That's different," Joe said. "I would'a won that and I wouldn't be beholden to you." He ran the last ball, then racked them up and returned his cue stick to the rack on the wall. "Listen, how does a fella make a little money in this town?"

"They may be hirin' over at the mill," Carlo replied.

"I ain't interested in that kind of job," Joe said.

"What kind of job are you interested in?"

Joe snorted. "Forget it. You have to ask, you aren't the one I need to be talkin' to."

The expression on Carlo's face changed. "What can you do?" he asked.

"Whatever has to be done."

Carlo stared at Joe as if measuring him. For a moment, Joe thought he might have scored, then he saw by the expression in Carlo's eyes that he had not. It wasn't that Carlo distrusted him, it was that Carlo was afraid to make any kind of a decision on his own.

"I hear anybody lookin' for somebody, I'll give 'em your name," Carlo said. "Joe what?"

"Joe's all anyone needs to know," Joe said. "If they want to know anything other than that, they can ask the goddamn cops."

Carlo chuckled. "Yeah," he said. "Yeah, I know what you mean. Listen, I got to go outta town a few days. I got somethin' to do. You goin' to be here? I'll see you around."

"Yeah, sure," Joe replied. "I'll see you around."

Carlo started to leave, then he turned back. "You got a place to stay?"

"Haven't got around to it yet."

"There's an extra room upstairs, over this place," he said. "I'll talk to my uncle. He'll let you have it real cheap."

"It'll have to be cheap," Joe said.

"He'll wait till you've got somethin'," Carlo promised.

"Faggio," Joe said.

"Beg pardon?"

"Faggio. That's my last name."

"Faggio. Okay," Carlo said. He smiled. "So, listen, you goin' to be here when I get back?"

"Never can tell," Joe answered.

"If you are, I'll look you up. Maybe I can do you some good."

"See you," Joe said, waving at Carlo as he left the pool hall.

————

Mike rolled the Bellanca cabin monoplane out of a tight left turn and found himself perfectly lined up with the runway at the Steubenville airport. He pulled back on the throttle and the airplane settled into a steady thousand-feet-per-minute rate of descent. It was a wonderful feeling to be back in the air again, even if for a short time and even if under false pretenses. Jason was riding in the right front seat beside him. Mike was dressed like an aviator in a leather flying jacket, riding pants and high boots. Jason, on the other hand, was wearing a suit and tie.

Mike needn't have worried about being rusty. He greased the Bellanca in as cleanly as if there had been no interruption whatever to his flying days. When he taxied up to the apron, one of the airport line boys hurried out to meet the plane.

"Do you want gas, sir?" the line boy asked as he began shoving the yellow blocks of wood into place under the wheels.

"Yes," Mike said. "Check the oil too."

"You sure have a pretty airplane," the lineboy said appreciatively.

"Thanks," Mike replied.

"Are you two here to meet Mr. Adams, the banker?" the line boy asked.

"Yes, how did you know?" Jason replied.

The line boy smiled. "Easy," he said. "I even know your names. One of you is Jarvis, the other is Wodehouse. The reason I know is, Mr. Adams is in there waitin' for you."

"Well, then, we mustn't keep the gentleman waiting," Mike said. "Come along, Mr. Wodehouse."

Mike and Jason were role-playing. Mike had written to Eric Adams, passing himself off as an aeronautical engineer. Jason was using the name Wodehouse and the two men were supposedly coming to Steubenville to build an airplane manufacturing company.

As the line boy had stated, Eric Adams was in the airport administration office, waiting to meet them. Actually, there were two men waiting for them. One was Eric Adams, the other was a much younger man. Adams introduced the young man as Stewart Dempster, an attorney.

"I see," Mike said. "And are you the bank's attorney, Mr. Dempster?"

"No, sir," Stewart answered. "I represent Mr. Ignatzio Coppola."

"Coppola?" Mike said, raising his eyebrows and looking at Eric Adams fractiously. "Who is this Mr. Coppola and what does he have to do with our deal?"

"Uh, when you contacted me, Mr. Jarvis, you indicated that you were interested in locating your manufacturing facility here," Adams explained. "I took the liberty of getting in touch with Mr. Coppola. He is a very successful businessman who might be interested in providing you with whatever financing you might need."

"We don't need financing," Jason said, speaking for the first time. "That's my role."

"You?" the banker said. "You'll excuse the incredulity, but you hardly seem old enough to have the experience necessary to put together a deal of this magnitude."

Jason smiled. "Yes, the people I deal with often come to that same conclusion. Generally, it turns into a very costly mistake for them."

"Are you sure you have all the financing you need?" Stewart asked.

"I'm positive."

"Then why did you gentlemen contact a banker?"

"Who better to answer all the questions we might have?" Mike replied.

"Mr. Jarvis, Mr. Wodehouse, if you would allow a suggestion," Stewart said. "Why don't you let Mr. Coppola know just what you have in mind? I think you will find that he is a very astute businessman and, believe me, sir, he can be a powerful ally."

"What if I told you we don't need any allies."

"If you would pardon my saying so, you don't need any enemies either," Stewart said. "And Mr. Coppola can be every bit as powerful an enemy as he can an ally."

"Are you threatening us?" Mike asked.

"Not at all," Stewart replied, smiling easily. "I'm just trying to be helpful."

Mike glared at Adams. "I don't appreciate being put on the spot like this, Adams," he said. "I don't have to put my company in Steubenville, you know. There are half a dozen other places that would welcome me on my own terms."

"Yes, but you chose Steubenville," Stewart said. "We

didn't send for you. Therefore, it stands to reason that this is where you want to be."

"Maybe it is," Mike agreed.

"Of course it is," Stewart said, easily, smugly, confident in the way he was handling the situation and wishing that his boss could be here to see him. "And we want you here too. Now, why don't you just meet Mr. Coppola? If, after the three of you talk, there is nothing to be gained by working together, then you can both go your own way."

"What do you think, Wodehouse?" Mike asked.

"I suppose it can't hurt," Jason replied.

Mike sighed, as if the whole thing were an inconvenience to him. "All right," he said. "I'll meet with him. But I'm not making any promises that we will work together. Now, when can we meet?"

"I'm certain I can set up a meeting for you this very evening."

"Fine, fine. I'll be staying at the Biltmore Victoria. Tell your Mr. Coppola I will expect him for dinner. Now, if someone would tell me how to call a cab in this town?"

"You don't need a taxi," Stewart said. He handed Jason a set of car keys. "The blue Oldsmobile just outside. Use it with Mr. Coppola's compliments for as long as you are in town."

"Well, you must thank Mr. Coppola for us," Mike said as he took the keys.

Bill Carmack was also in Steubenville, so that now all four members of the Blood Oath Society were gathered. Unlike the other three, Bill had come as himself, an agent for the Bureau of Investigation. Even though he was being truthful as to his identity, he wasn't being completely straightforward as to why he was in town.

Bill had reported to the chief of the Steubenville police

department as soon as he arrived, to request the department's help on a case he was ostensibly working on.

"I'm looking for a man named Charles M. Boone," Bill said. "That may not be what he is calling himself now. He has gone under several aliases, including Charles Broome and Michael Bourne. We have reason to suspect that he may be here in Steubenville."

"I've never heard of him," the chief replied. "Not as Boone, Broome or Bourne."

"He's here, I'm sure of it," Bill said. "At least we know he was here, because he mailed a letter from here."

"What did this man Boone do?" the chief asked.

"He is a communist agent," Bill explained. "He belongs to a group of traitors who are advocating the overthrow of our government."

Bill wasn't lying: the Bureau did want a man named Charles Boone for questioning. Boone's name had come up as the possible associate of a communist agent who had been killed when a bomb he tried to plant went off prematurely. The Bureau wanted to find him, but finding him was not a particularly high priority. However, it did provide Bill with a perfect excuse for coming to Steubenville and nosing around in the police files.

"How long are you going to be here?" the chief asked.

"As long as it takes," Bill replied. He smiled. "We have a saying in the Bureau: The wheels of Bureau justice grind slowly, but they grind exceedingly fine. What that means is," he explained, "it may take us a while to find him, but when we do we'll have an ironclad case against him."

"Well, if you are going to stay here any length of time, you'll need a desk," the chief said. He walked over to the door and stuck his head through. "Jock! Jock, come here."

A powerfully built policeman with a square jaw and thinning red hair answered the chief's call.

"This is Captain Jock O'Connell," the chief said. "If you need any help on anything, see him. Jock, this is a federal agent for the Bureau of Investigation. I want you to find him a desk and offer him any help he may need."

"Fine. Who are you looking for?" O'Connell asked, and Bill provided him with the same information he had just given the chief.

"Communist, huh? Well, I don't know much about communists. Boyle," he called. "Officer Boyle."

A young uniformed policeman came over in answer to O'Connell's summons.

"This is Terry Boyle," O'Connell said. "I'm going to assign him as your liaison. If you need anything from us, anything at all, he'll take care of it. You got that Boyle?"

"Yes sir," Boyle replied.

"You can start by getting the man a desk," O'Connell said.

"There's an empty desk right across from mine, Mr. Carmack," Boyle suggested. "If that would be all right."

"That would be fine," Bill said.

"You'll have to see Officer Patterson for any supplies you might need. Also, he'll give you your own set of keys. That will let you into the squad room, even if no one else is in here."

"Thanks," Bill said.

A few minutes later Officer Patterson was sliding keys across his desk. "Outside door, bay door, desk, filing cabinets, and..." The officer held up the last key for a moment. "Are you supposed to get a key to the classified files?"

"I would think so," Bill answered. "I mean, I'm supposed to get full cooperation from the department."

"I don't know. Maybe I shouldn't give this one to you."

"Why don't you call the chief and find out?" Bill

asked. Officer Patterson reached for the phone, then hesitated. Bill had been on the force long enough to recognize the personality. Patterson was the kind of man who liked to stay out of everyone's way. He didn't want to be noticed by anyone, and certainly not by his superior officer. He sighed, then pulled his hand away.

"You're right," he said. "If you're supposed to have full cooperation from the police department, I'm sure that would include access to the classified files." He handed Bill the key. "Be careful with it," he instructed.

"What kind of business you plannin' on puttin' in here?" Coppola asked. Coppola and Eric Adams were Jason's guests for dinner that evening. The dinner had been brought up to Jason's suite, thus affording them complete privacy as they talked.

"An aircraft manufacturing plant," Mike replied.

"Really? Is there actually any money in makin' airplanes?" Coppola asked. "I mean, how many people do you think would buy one of those things?"

Mike laughed. "You tell him, Mr. Wodehouse."

"I'd be glad to. Mr. Coppola, we don't care whether we sell any airplanes or not. We plan to go public and capitalize for two million dollars. We'll sell half the stock and keep the other half ourselves."

"Well, I'll be," the banker said. "That's what you meant when you said you didn't need financing."

"Yes," Jason replied.

"But you do need me," Coppola said.

"Why do we need you?" Mike asked.

"I have a feeling that what you are plannin' isn't exactly legal," he said.

"It might be frowned on in some circles," Jason admitted. "But it isn't exactly like robbing a bank."

Coppola smiled. "No, it's better than robbin' a bank.

But, whether you build the first airplane or not, you are goin' to have to have a factory, am I right?"

"Yes. We can't sell stock to a company that doesn't even exist."

"Then you're goin' to need lumber, bricks, steel and workers. I can furnish all of them," Coppola said. "And you might also find that you will need the support of a friendly judge or legislator somewhere. I can take care of that too."

"Mr. Coppola, those judges and legislators who can be bought...can be bought by us as easily as by you," Mike said. "It's the other people who give us the difficulty."

"What other people?" Coppola asked.

"The people who can't be bought. The people who get in the way of progress."

"People who cause problems," Jason added.

Coppola pulled out a cigarette and lit it then studied Mike and Jason for a long moment frowning at them through the cloud of cigarette smoke. "I tell you what. These people who get in the way of progress," he said with a wave of his hand. "You leave them to me. I'll take care of them."

"How? We've already determined that they can't be bought off," Mike said.

"You don't worry about how," Coppola said. "You just get started on your plans. Like I said, I'll take care of them."

Much later that evening Mike, Bill, Joe and Jason had a meeting in the suite of rooms Jason had taken at the Biltmore. Mike was reporting on how the meeting had gone with Coppola, while Joe made himself a roast beef sandwich with leftovers from dinner. He spread a generous portion of horseradish on a pink piece of meat.

"Damn," Joe said. "Some of us have it a little better than the others. You should see the dump where I am.

Look at this. Good food, silk sheets, a radio, this is really something."

"I know," Mike said. "Living like this is a thankless job, but someone has to do it."

The others laughed.

"What about you, Bill? What have you found out?"

Bill explained about getting the key to the classified file room.

"Coppola does seem to be the head man around here," Bill said. "I found his name in a dozen or more reports, including a couple of times where he was a prime suspect for murder. They were gangland rub-outs, so there was never enough evidence to pin anything to him."

"Those gangland rub-outs," Mike said. "Were they shotgun killings?"

"No, I know what you're getting at," Bill replied. "But the answer is no, I didn't find anything about nail heads like the ones we had in New Orleans and New York. But he does own Home Materials. That's where the nail heads came from, if you remember."

"Yeah, I remember," Mike said. "Is he into booze?"

"He was," Bill said. "But from everything I've been able to find out, he gave it up a couple of years ago. Now he is the perfect citizen."

"What about you, Joe?"

"Nothing yet," Joe said around a large bite of his sandwich. "I met a guy named Carlo Lambretta and he hinted that he might be able to find a job for me if I was interested. I told him I was."

"What did he say?"

"He said he would get in touch."

"What's next?" Jason asked.

Mike sighed. "We'll just keep playing our roles a little longer," he said.

———

THE BRONX

Amerigo Sollozo was one of the top men in the Vaglichio Family organization. He was married to Angelina Vaglichio, Luca and Mario's younger sister but it wasn't one of those situations where a man made a good marriage then profited from it. Amerigo had worked his way into his present position years before, coming up under Luca and Mario's father. It was only after he had achieved the position of *capo de regime* that he felt worthy to begin calling on Angelina Vaglichio.

By now Amerigo had been married to Angelina for nine years and they had three children. Though the more successful of the Mafia leaders were now living in fashionable homes on Long Island, Amerigo continued to live in the Bronx. He had been invited out to Long Island; in fact, Luca even offered to allow him to build a house within the family compound. Amerigo refused, not from a lack of sociability, but from a genuine belief that he could do his work better if he stayed closer to the source.

Amerigo owned a laundry on Alexander and East 138th Street. It was a legitimate laundry that did legitimate laundry business, but only the naivest person would believe that was all that went on in the building.

The big back room was divided into two sections. One section had long tables for folding clothes and two dozen chattering women worked here every day. On the other side of the divider was the headquarters for the bookies, numbers and protection rackets. Here, too, Amerigo kept track of the bootlegging and dope business. His territory was the largest within the Vaglichio operation. He not only ran it efficiently, he was also honest, insofar as his dealings with the Vaglichios went.

There was quite a vast amount of money going through his laundry every day, so Amerigo never kept it overnight. He had three bookkeepers working fulltime to process the income from all the activities of the day, then he put the money in a canvas pouch and sent it by armed guard to the Vaglichio headquarters over on Long Island.

Because he had no money on the premises, Amerigo felt no sense of apprehension this particular evening when, after staying late, he saw a shadowy figure standing in the doorway that led from the front of the building.

"We're closed," he called out to the shadowy figure.

The visitor said nothing.

"Didn't you hear me? I said we're closed."

It was unlikely his visitor was actually here for laundry business. He was more likely a gambler who had bet heavily on the ponies and lost and hadn't yet pulled himself together to go home.

"What's the matter? Were you a big loser tonight?"

The visitor said nothing.

Amerigo sighed. "Look," he said. "I always say, if you can't afford to lose, don't play the ponies."

There was still no answer.

"All right," Amerigo said. "I don't want to send you home flat broke. You got to at least have some money for the groceries. What, are you married? You got kids?" He started toward the door, sticking his hand down in his pocket as he did so. "How much do you need?"

When Amerigo got within fifteen feet of the man, the silent figure stepped out of the shadows and raised a shotgun. Amerigo gasped, then stepped back and threw his hands out in front of him.

"No!" he said. "Don't shoot! Don't shoot! You can have it all!"

A two-foot-wide flame pattern erupted from the

barrel of the shotgun. Amerigo felt something slam against his chest, hitting him as hard as if he had been kicked by a horse. He wasn't aware of falling but the next thing he knew he could feel the concrete floor against his back. There was no pain and that surprised him because he could see his blood everywhere.

The man who shot him walked over to look down at him. Amerigo wanted to say something to him, wanted to ask him why, but he couldn't speak.

"Hey," the gunman said. "That was a nice thing you was goin' to do, givin' me money like that 'cause you thought I needed it. It was a nice thing and I appreciate it. I'm sorry about this. I don't have nothin' personal against you, you understand. It was just business, that's all. It was just business."

———

Enrico Nicolo was going over numbers receipts with his father. The money they made from numbers, policy and prostitution combined, equaled the money they made from the speakeasies and bootlegging operations they ran. And that was what troubled Enrico.

"What are we going to do, Pop, when Prohibition is repealed?" he asked.

"Don't you be worryin' about that. They ain't goin' to repeal Prohibition," Don Pietro said.

"Yeah, Pop, they are," Enrico insisted. "I read in the paper the other day where there was a petition delivered to Congress with seven million names on it, all of 'em askin' that Prohibition be repealed."

"Seven million? What's seven million? There's more'n a hundred million people in America."

"It doesn't matter," Enrico said. "For every one person who signed the petition, there were probably ten more who would have, if they had the chance. I'm tellin' you, Pop, Prohibition is goin' to be repealed, and when it is, we're goin' to be left high and dry, unless we have somethin' else."

"Somethin' like what?" Don Pietro asked.

"Well, like dope," Enrico replied. "I really think we ought to get into that, Pop. And since the Sangremanos don't want to get into dope, maybe we could make a deal with them to work their territory too."

"They're not goin' to let anyone else work their territory. That's the problem right now," Don Pietro said. "The Vaglichios want to sell dope in their territory and the Sangremanos won't let them."

"Yeah, well, maybe the Sangremanos won't let them because they have been enemies with the Vaglichios for too long," Enrico suggested. "Maybe if someone else asked them, someone like us, they might go along with it. Besides, you're always talkin' about how we are peacemakers," he added. "Wouldn't it help keep the peace if we were selling dope in the Sangremano territory? Maybe the Vaglichios would stop bothering them."

"You can't be a real peacemaker by turning someone else's war to your own advantage," Don Pietro said.

"Well, it wouldn't actually be a war," Enrico said. "Not if we—"

"Enough," Don Pietro said, holding out his hand. "We will not get into the business of selling dope and especially not in Sangremano's territory."

At that moment Gino Conti stepped through the door. "Excuse me, Don Pietro," he said. The counting of the take was, by tradition, a very private affair, conducted only by Don Pietro and his son. For anyone else to be there would be an expression of distrust in the Nicolos' accounting and disbursement. To express distrust would be to impugn their honor and that would be a very dangerous thing. Therefore, for Gino even to interrupt the count was highly unusual.

"Yes, Gino, what is it?" Don Pietro asked over his shoulder. "You have a telephone call from Don Carmine Lombardi," Gino said.

Don Pietro twisted around in his chair. "Lombardi?"

"Yes," Gino said. He cleared his throat. "Amerigo Sollozo was killed last night. I think Don Lombardi wants to talk about that."

"Amerigo Sollozo," Don Pietro said, looking at his son.

"Amerigo is married to the Vaglichios' sister," Enrico told his father. "He is very important to them." Enrico smiled. "I guess Johnny Sangremano has struck back for the killing of his wife."

"No, I don't think so," Don Pietro replied.

"What do you mean, you don't think so? Of course he has. He said he was going to get even with the Vaglichios and now he has done so. Let's face it Pop. This whole city is about to break out into war."

"A brother-in-law is not the same as a wife," Don Pietro replied. "No, I don't think Johnny Sangremano did this."

"You don't huh? Well, I'll bet the Vaglichios do."

"Yes," Don Pietro replied. "The Vaglichios will think that." He sighed. "And if that is what they think, it is just as bad as if the Sangremanos actually did it. I'd better talk to Don Lombardi to see if there is anything we can do to stop this war before it is too late."

———

STEUBENVILLE, OHIO, TWO DAYS LATER

When Carlo stepped into the pool hall, he saw Joe playing at the back table. Carlo went over to speak to his uncle.

"So, did you miss me?"

"Didn't know you was gone," his uncle answered in a gruff voice.

"You didn't know I was gone? You kiddin' me? I'm over here ever' day, I go three days without comin' by and you don't even notice it."

"I got other customers," his uncle replied.

"Yeah, maybe so. But they ain't kin." Carlo took a Coke out of the drink box. It was cold and dripping, and little pieces of ice clung to the side of the bottle. He pried off the cap, then took several swallows before he spoke again. He noticed that Joe was playing pool with Big Sal Prizzi. Carlo had wondered when the two men might meet. Big Sal made a living by hustling games. Big Sal was a pretty good pool player but he didn't depend on just his skills with the cue stick. Big Sal would take advantage of his opponent any way he could...including intimidating him by threats of bodily harm if everything else failed.

Carlo walked to the back of the parlor to watch the game. Big Sal was shooting. Joe was leaning against the wall with his arms folded across his chest. Half a dozen others were watching the game.

"How's it goin'?" Carlo asked.

"I'm a few bucks ahead," Joe replied.

'You ain't goin' to be for long," Sal said.

"I see you're back."

Carlo looked surprised. "How did you know I had gone anywhere?"

"You told me, remember? You said you had business

that was goin' to take you out of town. You said when you got back, you might have some ideas for me."

"Oh, yeah, I remember."

"Will you two shut the hell up," Big Sal growled. "You're makin' me break my concentration." He leaned over the table to get a better position, and when he did, his cue stick hit the cue ball. It rolled about six inches and Big Sal reached out to stop it, then he put it back.

"Hold it. What do you think you're doin'?" Joe asked.

"What's it look like, you dumb ass? I'm shooting pool."

"You just had your shot."

"The hell I did."

"The ball moved."

"So what? It was an accident."

"There's no such thing as an accident. It's my turn."

Big Sal smiled but, because of his ugly, twisted teeth and his low brows and huge jaw, the smile only made his features look more fearsome.

"It's your turn when I say it's your turn, asshole," Sal said. He leaned back over the table.

To the others watching the game, this was nothing new. One of them even turned away, figuring that what had started out to be a pretty good game had now deteriorated, like all the others, into another example of Big Sal's intimidation.

Big Sal was leaning over the table with his legs slightly spread. Joe stepped up behind him, then put his fist between Big Sal's legs and brought it up to the junction.

"What the hell are you doing? You gone queer or somethin'?" Big Sal growled.

"Better be careful," Joe warned. "You feel something sharp sticking into your balls?"

"What?"

"I've got a knife," Joe said calmly. To emphasize his statement, he jabbed upward a little.

"Holy shit!" Big Sal shouted. "Watch it! Watch what you're doin'!"

"Oh, good. I see I've got your attention."

"You dumb son of a bitch!" Big Sal snarled. "Who the hell do you think you are?"

"I think I'm the man that's goin' to cut off your cock," Joe replied calmly.

"No, no!" Big Sal shouted. He started to jerk away, but Joe gave him another jab.

"You'd better be careful," Joe said menacingly.

"What do you want?"

"I want you to get the hell out of here," Joe replied.

"All right, all right, I'm goin'! Only watch what you're doin' there," Big Sal snapped. He started to reach for the pile of money lying on the rail, but Joe jabbed his hand upward again.

"Leave the money here, Sal," Joe said easily.

"Leave it here? What the hell for? That's my money."

"Let's just say that's what I'm chargin' you for not cuttin' off your pecker."

"You crazy son of a bitch!" Big Sal shouted angrily. "You know who you're dealin' with here?"

"A big dumb ox," Joe said.

"You won't have that knife on me all the time. What do you think is going to happen next time I see you?"

Joe stepped back away from him. "Well, I don't know," he answered. "I'm not holding the knife at your crotch now. Why don't we just find out?"

Big Sal turned toward him, then raised his arms menacingly.

"You little shit. I'm goin' to tear you apart, piece by piece," he growled.

"No, I don't think so," Joe said, raising his other hand

and pointing a pistol at Sal's face. The pistol stopped Sal in his tracks. "Come any closer and I'm going to spray your brains all over the wall."

Sal stood his ground for a moment, purpling in impotent rage. Finally he pointed at Joe. "I'm goin' to get you for that," he said. "One of these days, I'm goin' to get you." He spun on his heel, then left, followed by the laughter of a dozen or more of the patrons who were delighted to see that he had, at last, gotten his comeuppance.

Carlo joined in the laughter. "Hey, I gotta hand it to you," he said. "You got balls."

"Balls I got," Joe said as he counted the money Big Sal had left behind. It amounted to eleven dollars. Joe held up the money. "Money, I don't got. I had to risk my life for eleven lousy dollars. I thought you said you were goin' to find somethin' for me to do."

"Yeah, I have found somethin' for you," Carlo said. "Why don't you come along with me? I've got someone I want you to meet."

"Faggio," Coppola said. He poured bourbon into a glass and handed it to Joe. "Joe Faggio. That's your name?"

"Yes," Joe said.

"You any kin to Jimmy Faggio, outta Kansas City?"

"No," Joe said. "I'm from New York."

"New York, huh. Let me see, what Faggios do I know up there?"

"Did you know Billy Faggio?" Joe asked.

"Ice Pick Billy? Yeah. Yeah, I knew him," Coppola said. "You kin to him?"

"He was my older brother," Joe said.

Joe hadn't chosen the name Faggio out of the blue. William Faggio, or Ice Pick Billy, had been an enforcer for the Tolino Family. Ice Pick Billy was dead now and the

Tolino Family no longer existed, having been assimilated by other families when the old don died. Joe knew that Ice Pick had a younger brother named Joe. He knew also that the real Joe Faggio, who had no interest in the rackets, had changed his name and joined the merchant marine. With the assimilation of the Tolino Family into other families and Joe Faggio's disappearance, it was unlikely that any unpleasant surprises would result from Joe's using someone else's name.

Coppola smiled broadly.

"No shit," he said. "You're Ice Pick's younger brother. You as good as he was?"

"Who was Ice Pick?" Carlo asked.

"Ice Pick was the best there was at what he did," Coppola said.

"I hope I'm better," Joe said.

"Better?"

"Yeah." Joe smiled. "Ice Pick got hisself killed. I don't plan to."

Coppola laughed out loud, "You're all right, kid," he said. "Carlo told me how you handled Big Sal and in my book, that makes you all right. So, you want to work for me?"

"Yes."

Coppola laughed again. "You didn't ask what I wanted you to do."

Joe looked around the richly appointed library slowly and deliberately.

"I don't care what you want me to do," he said. "As long as I get paid good, I'll do it. And from what I can see around here, you can afford to pay good."

Coppola laughed again, long and hard. "Yeah," he finally said. "Yeah, I can afford it. I provide a service, a very special service, for my customers. And you want to know the best part? We don't do none of it around here.

You take me, for instance. Here in Steubenville, I'm a model citizen, you know what I mean? I could probably even get elected to the school board. I'm the kind of guy they give the key to the city to." Coppola pulled a fresh cigar from a box, bit the end off and lit it. He examined Joe through the cloud of blue smoke his cigar raised.

"You ever killed anybody, Joe?" he asked.

"What do you mean?"

Coppola pulled the end of the cigar from his mouth and spit out a little piece of the leaf. "What do you mean, what do I mean? It seems like a pretty easy question. What is it, you don't understand?"

"Yeah, well, I understand all right," Joe said. "I just don't know why you would ask me such a thing. I mean, who the hell are you to ask a question like that?"

"Who the hell am I? I'm the person that's going to pay you a lot of money."

"How much money is a lot of money?"

"Fifteen hundred dollars per job," Coppola said.

"Fifteen hundred? That is a lot."

"I thought you might like that. Now, I'm goin' to ask the question again. Have you ever killed anybody, Joe?"

"Yeah," Joe finally said. "I have."

"Think you can handle a few special jobs for me?"

"What kind of special jobs?"

"I thought you said a few minutes ago that you didn't care."

"I don't care."

"Then you'll find out about the special jobs when they come up," Coppola said. "So, are you interested or not?"

"I'm interested."

"Good. When Vinnie Letto gets back, I'm goin' to have Carlo introduce you," Coppola said. He smiled at Joe. "Vinnie is sort of my vice-president, if you know what I mean. He's the man you'll answer to. Whenever he tells you something, I want you to figure it just like it came from me, direct. Will you have any problems with that?"

"No problems," Joe said. "Where is Vinnie now?"

"I'll tell you where the lucky stiff is," Carlo said. "Right now he's prob'ly layin' around in the sun, eatin' oranges and lookin' at gorgeous dames."

Coppola glared at Carlo, then at Joe. "I had better tell you now, Joe, you'll go much farther in this business if you don't ask unnecessary questions," he said.

"Yeah, sure. I didn't mean anything by it I was just wonderin' when he'd get back, that's all. I'm real anxious to get started. I could sure use the money."

Coppola pulled out a large wad of money, peeled off five one-hundred-dollar bills and handed them to Joe. "You'll get started soon enough," Coppola said. "And you'll go to work as soon as we need you. In the meantime, here's a little advance."

"Didn't I tell you, Joe?" Carlo beamed. "Didn't I tell you I could get you set up? Mr. Coppola is an all-right guy to work for."

"Yeah, I'd say so," Joe said. "Thanks, Mr. Coppola. Thanks a lot."

Coppola picked up his glass of bourbon. "Now, what do you say we seal this bargain with a little toast?" he suggested.

"Good idea," Joe answered, raising his own glass.

"Salud," Coppola said.

"Salud," Joe answered. The glasses rang as they touched them together.

CHAPTER 8

THE BRONX

t was the size of the funeral that surprised everyone. Amerigo Sollozo was married to a Vaglichio and he was very popular with all his people, but he wasn't a don and he never would have been. Nevertheless, the funeral the Vaglichios' threw for their slain underboss was as elaborate as it would have been had either Luca or Mario been the victim.

The funeral turned into a parade, led by two policemen mounted on motorcycles, followed by a young man carrying a crucifix. Behind the crucifer marched two drummers who, like the cross-bearer, were wearing vestments. Their drums were draped with black crepe and muffled for the funereal beat. Behind the drummers came the hearse, a highly polished Cadillac that glistened and sparkled in the afternoon sun. Through the windows of the back of the hearse, the thousands who lined the streets could see the coffin, piled high with flowers.

A closed-body Lincoln followed the hearse. Inside the Lincoln, Mrs. Angelina Sollozo, dressed in black and with her face covered by a black veil, sat between her two loving brothers. The three Sollozo children, who were too young to fully comprehend what was going on, sat on the jumpseats, looking through the windows and waving at the huge crowd.

The cars of the mourners stretched on behind the widow's car for another six blocks. Each car was filled with dark-suited, somber-faced men and black-clad women. Most of the women were crying. Though they would admit it to no one, not even to themselves, the tears they shed were as much in fear for their own husbands, as in sorrow for Amerigo Sollozo and his family.

"The dirty bastard," Luca muttered as he held his sister's hand, patting it gently. "Sangremano did this. I know he did."

"Of course he did," Mario replied. "The question is, what are we going to do about it?"

"We're going to make him pay," Luca said. "That's what we're going to do."

"In front of the children, I do not wish to hear such talk," Angelina said.

"You don't want revenge for your husband?"

"Will it bring him back?"

"No, of course not."

"Then what is the good?"

"The good is that the man who is responsible for this will be punished so that he cannot do it again."

"Amerigo is already dead," she said. "How can he be killed again?"

"I meant so that he doesn't do it to anyone else," Luca explained.

"I don't care about anyone else," Angelina replied in a cold, flat voice.

"You can't let something like this go unpunished," Luca insisted.

"What do you care?" Angelina wailed. "Did you love him like I do? No. Is your heart broken? No. The only thing you feel now is anger."

"It is not a bad thing to feel anger," Luca insisted. "That is as good a reason to kill someone as grief."

When the car stopped in the graveyard a few moments later, Luca and Mario got out, then walked with their sister over to the open grave. They sat quietly beside her throughout the entire graveside service and held her hand while she wept as the coffin was lowered into the hole.

After the funeral, as the mourners filed by to pay their final respects and to say a few words of comfort to the widow, Luca and Mario stood to one side, out of the way, giving Angelina the center stage as was her due. Don Pietro Nicolo, Don Vincent Barbutti and Don Carmine Lombardi were all expressing their sorrow to the widow and family of Amerigo Sollozo.

Enrico Nicolo stepped away from his father and came over to speak with the Vaglichio brothers. "I suppose now you will be wanting to go after Johnny Sangremano."

"Who said anything about us going after Sangremano?" Luca asked.

"You said nothing, of course. But I must confess that if I were in your shoes, I would want to go after Sangremano," Enrico replied.

"Enrico, are you saying that you take our side in this?" Mario asked.

"I haven't exactly taken sides yet. In my position as a neutral, I can also see why Johnny Sangremano felt it was necessary to seek revenge for the death of his wife."

"We had nothing to do with the death of his wife," Luca said.

"Perhaps you didn't. But Johnny believes that you did, doesn't he?" Enrico asked.

"Yes."

"Well, then, what difference does it make whether you had anything to do with her getting killed or not? Johnny Sangremano believes you were responsible; therefore he is going to exact his revenge."

"That kind of leaves us between the rock and the hard place," Mario complained. "On the one hand, we have you and your father, as well as the Barbuttis and the Lombardis, telling us we must not pay Sangremano back for this evil he has done to us. On the other hand if we don't stand up for ourselves, who is to say that he won't find some other reason to attack us again?"

"Yes," Enrico agreed. "You are in a difficult position. However, I feel you must know that, while I am my father's son, we do not always agree on everything. My father is concerned that a war might break out between your family and the Sangremanos. I agree with him that a war is a terrible thing, but I also know that, sometimes, one must do things for honor. Do what you feel you must do. You will have a friend in the Nicolo Family." Enrico shook Luca's hand, at the same time placing his left hand on Luca's shoulder.

"Thank you, Enrico," Luca said. "I appreciate that. I really do."

Enrico looked around and saw that his father was now leaving Amerigo's wife and children, and was coming over to speak with the Vaglichio brothers.

"Oh, here comes my father," Enrico said quietly. "I think it would best for all concerned if, for now at least, he doesn't know how I feel about this."

"We understand," Luca said softly, then, looking up at

Don Pietro, Luca smiled. "Don Pietro, you honor us by paying your respects," he said.

"I wish we could be meeting on a happier note," Don Pietro said. "It is a terrible thing, all this killing. A terrible thing."

"Yes."

"It is nice, what you are doing for Amerigo, though," Enrico said, taking in the funeral with a sweep of his hand. "You have given him the funeral of a don."

"He was our dear sister's husband," Luca explained. "That made him family."

"Yes, I can see that," Don Pietro said.

"That is what makes his murder all the more intolerable. Johnny Sangremano knew how we felt about Amerigo, how we loved him like a brother."

"You believe Johnny Sangremano is responsible?"

"Yes, of course. Don't you?"

"I don't know," Don Pietro replied. "But even if he is, all things considered, don't you think you have come out ahead now?" he asked. "You lost your brother-in-law but he lost his wife."

"We didn't have anything to do with that," Luca insisted. "I'm not the one you must convince," Don Pietro replied. "You must convince Johnny Sangremano. Also, do not forget that, before his poor wife was murdered, two of his own men were killed."

"We had nothing to do with that, either."

Don Pietro smiled sadly. "I told you, I am not the one you must convince. You must convince Johnny Sangremano."

"No," Luca said coldly, buoyed by the earlier conversation he had with Enrico. "We don't have to convince that sonofabitch of anything. We know what Johnny Sangremano did to us and we know what we must do to him."

Don Pietro's face, which had alternated between expressions of grief and sincere attempts at persuasion, now grew hard.

"I have told you before and I will tell you again: the other families will not sit by and watch the Sangremanos and the Vaglichios go to war again. I suggest that you curb your appetite for revenge."

"I beg your pardon, Don Pietro," Luca replied. "I have the utmost respect for you, but you are not strong enough to tell us what we can and cannot do."

"Perhaps not," Nicolo agreed. "But if you insist on making in New York, I will join with the Sangremanos and so will all the other families. Are you so strong that you can fight us all?"

"Goddamn you!" Luca shouted, so loudly that the mourners who were waiting in the long line to speak with Angelina looked over in surprise. Luca, realizing he was attracting unwanted attention, lowered his voice before he continued. "How dare you tell us that we must accept these crimes committed against us, but we can do nothing to avenge them!" he hissed.

"I know it is hard," Don Pietro said.

"Hard? It is impossible."

Don Pietro sighed, then put his hand out, comfortingly, on Luca's wrist He looked into Luca's, then Mario's eyes. "I'll tell you what I will do," he said. "I will talk to the others...we will investigate. If we find that Johnny Sangremano is responsible for this, we will do something about it."

"What?"

"I don't know," Nicolo admitted. "Something." He held up his finger and waved it. "But before I start this, be sure it is what you want. For if I find that you two are responsible for killing Johnny's wife, then it is you who must face the sanction of the others."

"We've got nothing to hide," Luca insisted. "Do it." Luca looked over toward Enrico to see how the don's son had taken this conversation. If he hoped to be able to read Enrico's face, though, he was frustrated, because Enrico had already walked away, putting as much distance between himself and his father as he could.

HOLLYWOOD, CALIFORNIA

After Clara was killed, Johnny made a long-distance telephone call to Weasel and Katherine, telling them that under no circumstances were they to come to New York for Clara's funeral.

"But Johnny, how would it look?" Katie asked. "She was my sister-in-law. I can't just stay out here as if nothing has happened."

"Don't you understand, Katherine? I'm afraid for you," Johnny said. "I know you want to do the right thing but, believe me, this is the right thing. Now, put Weasel on. I want to talk to him."

Johnny told Weasel that he was to stay in California until he specifically sent for him.

"How long is that to be?" Weasel asked.

"As long as it takes," Johnny answered. "If it's a year, then it's a year. But I'm holding you personally responsible for her."

"I will guard her with my life, Padrone," Weasel said.

"I know you will, kid," Johnny replied softly. "I know you will." It made Weasel feel very proud.

Weasel stayed on in California with Katherine, keeping an eye on her just as the don had ordered. Katherine, or Katie as she preferred to be called out here, had introduced Weasel to everyone as a cousin who was staying with her while he visited Hollywood on vacation. When it became obvious that he was going to stay even longer than the lengthiest vacation, he suggested that they might not believe her story anymore. She chuckled.

"They didn't believe it in the first place," she said. "Everyone thinks you are my lover."

"No! What if the don hears that? You must tell them the truth!"

"The truth? I can't tell them the truth. I can't tell people you are my bodyguard," she explained. "They wouldn't understand someone like you."

"They wouldn't understand someone like me?" Weasel replied. "Did you get a load of those two who were over here the other day? I don't understand them!"

"You must be talking about Paul and Gareth."

"Paul and Gareth, yeah, that's them. Only if you ask me, their names should be Pauline and Geraldine or something. Didn't they seem a little strange to you?"

"Oh, they're okay. They are very artistic. Paul is a hairdresser and Gareth is the most sought-after costume designer in Hollywood."

"Are they queer?"

Katie laughed. "Now why would you think that? Was it just because they were sitting over on the sofa, feeling each other up?"

Weasel gasped. "I didn't see that," he said. "My God, you mean to say they was doin' that right here, in front of everybody?"

"Yes, but no one thought anything about it. Everyone knows that Paul and Gareth are lovers. It's pretty much live and let live out here. At least as far as that sort of thing is concerned."

"Is there much of that kind of stuff goin' on out here?"

"Why, Weasel, you sound as if you might be interested," Katie teased.

"What?" Weasel sputtered. "See here, I'm not like that!"

Katie laughed easily, then put her hand on his wrist to calm him down. "Take it easy," she said. "I'm just teasing, that's all."

"Yeah? Well, I don't like that kind of teasin'," Weasel said.

"If you are going to live out here, I think perhaps you had better learn to be a bit more open-minded about such things," Katie warned him. She put her finger to her cheek and smiled at him. "You are actually quite a good-looking young man, you know. Someone is likely to make a pass at you."

"Someone? You mean one of them?"

"Perhaps," Katie said.

"I'd kill him."

"See, that's what I'm talking about. You can't go around killing everyone who makes a homosexual pass at you. Heavens, if that's the case, I would have already killed a dozen or so."

"I don't understand," Weasel said. "How can one of them queers make a homosexual pass at you? I mean if he did, it wouldn't be homosexual, would it?"

Katie laughed easily. "I'm not talking about a 'he,' I'm talking about a 'she.' And if a woman makes a sexual pass at another woman, then it is definitely homosexual."

Weasel's eyes grew wide. "Why, I've never heard of such a thing. Women?" he said. "You mean to tell me that some women like other women?"

"Sure. We're no different from men. We have our homosexuals just as you have yours."

Weasel stared at Katie for a long moment, so long in fact, that Katie laughed, nervously. "What is it?" she asked. "Why are you looking at me like that?"

"Did you, uh, did you do it?" Weasel asked.

Katie laughed again, this time a heartier, more throaty laugh.

"Well, Jimmy Pallota. If I didn't know better, I'd think the thought of me with another woman was turning you on."

"What? No, I, uh, was just curious, that's all."

"Curious? Or horny?"

"Katherine, you shouldn't talk like that," Weasel cautioned. "The don wouldn't like it."

"Well, what Johnny doesn't know won't hurt him, will it?" Katie said. "And I asked you to call me Katie when we're out here." Katie stepped up to Johnny and lay her finger on his lips. "You can remember that, can't you?"

A line of perspiration broke out on Weasel's upper lip. From the moment he had seen her with Vic, Weasel had been aware of a sexual tension while he was around her. Now, with the conversation as frank as this had become, the tension was growing unbearable. Weasel knew he wanted her. In fact, he wanted her more than he had ever wanted any other woman. But she was the don's sister, the very person he was out here to protect. It would be a violation of the don's trust if Weasel gave in to those desires. It would be a violation of his own honor. It could also be very dangerous, for if Johnny Sangremano ever found out, he would have Weasel killed without the slightest hesitation.

"Oh, my," Katie said, smiling at him. "You seem to have suddenly become quite warm. Perhaps you should go outside and take a swim."

"Yeah," Weasel mumbled. "Yeah, that might be a good idea."

"I might even join you in a few moments," Katie said. "That is, if you aren't afraid," she added, as if reading his every thought "No, I..."

"No? You mean you don't want me to join you?" Katie asked with a disappointed pout.

"No, I mean, no, I ain't afraid," Weasel said.

"Good. You go ahead, I'll be out in a few minutes." Weasel went into his room and put on his bathing suit Katie had laughed at the suit when she first saw it and she had taken the top off and thrown it away, explaining to him that here in California, men didn't wear the tops to their bathing suits.

"Do women?" Weasel had wanted to know.

"Yes, silly." Katie had laughed. "We haven't come that far, yet."

"Too bad," Weasel had answered.

Weasel was splashing around in the pool a few minutes later when Katie came outside. She was wearing a long yellow dressing gown and she walked over to the edge of the pool and stuck her toe down into the water.

"How is it?" she asked.

"The water's fine," Weasel answered. "Listen, what did you say they called this pool? I mean the way it's shaped?"

"Kidney-shaped."

"Kidney-shaped," Weasel repeated. "Yeah, that's what I thought you said. Is this what a kidney is shaped like?"

Katie giggled. "I don't know," she said. "I've never seen a kidney."

"Me neither," Weasel admitted. He turned and began swimming to the opposite end of the pool. When he turned away from her, Katie took off her dressing gown, then moved quickly down into the water. She walked out until it was up to her armpits. Weasel swam back to her.

"You swim well for an Italian boy from the Lower East Side," she said.

"Yeah, well, I used to sneak into the Y and..." Weasel started to explain, then he stopped and stared at Katie with his mouth open wide. "You...you ain't wearin' no bathin' suit!" he said.

"I know. The question is, why are you?"

"Katie, we ought not…"

"Who are you afraid of, Weasel? My brother? Or me?" Katie smiled, seductively, challengingly.

Weasel stood for a moment longer, as if trying to make up his mind. Then he smiled an answer to her challenge and ducked underwater. When he came up a moment later he was holding his swimming trunks in his hand. He threw them out onto the coping.

"Does this answer your question?" he asked.

"I guess it does," Katie replied.

Weasel moved through the water toward her, then stopped and pointed to Katie's naked breasts. "I'll be damned," he said. "They're floating."

Katie laughed a low, throaty laugh. "Of course they float."

"Ain't that the damnedest thing though?" Weasel asked.

"Now, Jimmy Pallota, are you going to try and tell me that you've never experimented with another girl's titties? I know you're younger than I am, but surely mine aren't the first you've ever seen in water?"

"Oh, I've seen lots of titties," Weasel said. He giggled. "I just ain't never seen none of them in a swimmin' pool before."

"Oh. Then that means you've never had sex in a swimming pool," Katie said easily.

"Damn, girl, what would Johnny say if he knew you talked like that?"

"Johnny's never going to know, is he?" Katie asked. Weasel sighed. "Not from me, he ain't."

"So, have you?"

"Have I what?"

"Ever done it in a swimming pool."

"No."

"Well, I have," Katie said. "And the best place to do it is down by the steps. That way we're still in the water, but it's not so deep that you're likely to drown if we get carried away." She gave Weasel a seductive smile. "And, honey, I intend for us to get carried away," she added, squeezing him to emphasize her words.

With Katie leading him, they walked toward the steps. When they reached them, Weasel started to maneuver Katie into position, but she stopped him.

"No," she said. "No, you sit there. I'll do all the work. You just lean back and enjoy it."

Just a few minutes earlier, Vinnie Letto had been moving through the rocks on a small hill behind Katie's house, trying to find a position that would afford him an unobstructed view of the property. Finally he found a place, and he looked out over the backyard at the large, shimmering blue swimming pool. To one side of the pool was a shelter constructed of lath to block out the more intense rays of the sun. Hanging from the slats were baskets of begonias. Elsewhere, in bright counterpoint, were large pots of red-orange geraniums. The flowers, the stucco walls and the red tiles made a pretty scene, and it reminded Vinnie of pictures he had seen of Sicily.

There was someone in the pool, a man, swimming quietly. The French doors leading into the back of the house opened, and a woman came out, wearing a yellow dressing gown. Vinnie looked down at her through his binoculars just to make certain she was the right one. It was Katie Starr, all right. He couldn't miss her; he had certainly seen her in enough movies.

Vinnie had been surprised when he learned who she really was. He had no idea Katie Starr was actually

Katherine Sangremano. In a way, it seemed a shame. She was such a beautiful girl. And she was Italian too. There weren't enough Italian women in pictures. Someone should do something about that. And now, the one beautiful Italian girl there was, Vinnie was going to have to get rid of. He hated to do it but it was business. And in his profession, business always had to be business. There was no room for anything like personal feelings.

Suddenly Katie Starr took off her dressing gown, and when she did, Vinnie gasped. She was naked underneath!

"Oh, you beautiful thing you," he said under his breath. "Yeah, stay there, just like that." He continued to stare at her, enjoying the unexpected pleasure of the scene. He didn't get to appreciate it for very long, however, because once the dressing gown was dropped, Katie stepped quickly down into the water.

"What the hell?" Vinnie asked under his breath. "What'd you go and do that for? Now I can't see shit."

Vinnie wondered who the man in the pool was. He was short, thin and dark complexioned. From here, he didn't look much older than a boy. Maybe he worked for her. Maybe he was the pool boy or the yard man. Vinnie heard that rich Hollywood movie stars sometimes liked to ball their servants. Maybe that's what this was.

Vinnie watched as Katie and the other swimmer talked for a few moments, then moved over to the edge of the pool.

"What? What are you going to do now?" he asked under his breath.

The question was answered when he saw them begin to make love on the steps at the edge of the pool.

"Goddamn," he breathed. "Goddamn, people out here really know how to live. Tearin' off a piece of ass in the swimmin' pool like that. Who would've thought such a thing?"

"Hey, you little shit, what are you doin' on the bottom?" he asked, chastising the man in the pool. "Why ain't you on top like you're supposed to? Hell, you don't even know how to do it. I should be down there and you should be up here. I could give it to her. Yes sir, I could give her what she wants

Vinnie broke open the breech of his gun and checked the load. There were two shells in the chamber, each shell a twelve-gauge with sufficient powder load for double-aught buckshot. The buckshot had been removed, however, to be replaced with cut-off nail heads.

Vinnie snapped the breech shut, then moved down the hill and through a loose board in the fence

"You got no right," he mumbled. "You got no right to do a thing like that. You're nothin' but a goddamn whore, to do it outside like that. And a pool boy. You wasted it all on a goddamn pool boy. Whores like you got no right to even live."

Vinnie crossed the backyard, moving quickly and in a slight crouch. He passed the pool, smelling the sharp aroma of chlorine and as he glanced over toward the steps at the shallow end of the pool, he thought about what he had seen there a few moments earlier.

"No," he said under his breath, forcing the image out of his mind. He had a job to do and he didn't want to be distracted by anything.

"No, I ain't goin' to think about that now." Vinnie tried the French door at the back of the house. It was locked, but the lock was small and easily forced. It only took a few seconds and he was inside.

The house was spacious and full of light from dozens of windows. He didn't like California houses. They weren't at all like normal houses. If this had been a normal house, he would know exactly where to go. But this house had long hallways going off in two different directions and windows and doors in unexpected places. He stopped for a moment and listened carefully. He heard a radio playing and started toward that sound, then he heard Katie's voice from a totally different direction.

"Jimmy, would you like to go out for lunch?" she called.

"Yeah, sure," a man's voice answered. The man was in the same room as the radio.

"I'll just take a quick shower, then I'll be ready."

"A shower? You just got out of the pool. What do you need a shower for?"

The woman laughed. "You're funny," she said.

Vinnie began creeping down the hallway toward the sound of the woman's voice. She was in the opposite end of the house from Jimmy, whoever Jimmy was. With any luck, he could take care of his business and be out of the house before the kid could even get down there. That would be better for the kid too. If the kid showed up, Vinnie would have to kill him. Otherwise, the kid would live. That was because Vinnie was being paid only to take care of the woman, and he didn't believe in working for free. Killing Jimmy would be working for free.

Weasel found some music, then walked over to the closet to look for something to wear. Katherine had been teasing him about the clothes he chose to wear—the dark pin-striped suits and dark shirts. At first he didn't take too kindly to her teasing. As a kid on the streets of New York, hustling just to stay alive, he had dreamed of being able to wear dark pin-striped suits like these someday. He had bought these suits from the finest tailor in little Italy and now she was telling him people were laughing at him. She bought him a tan suit and a lime green shirt, but so far he hadn't worn them. When she first showed them to him, he suggested that people might take him for a fruit if he wore such an outfit. These were the kind of clothes Paul or Gareth would wear.

Now he looked at the clothes from a different perspective, and he chuckled.

"Let people think whatever they want to think. Paul or Gareth sure wouldn't have been able to do what I just did, would they?" he asked under his breath. Maybe he would wear them today. If Katherine liked these clothes, why not?

As Weasel reached for the suit, he thought about what he and Katherine had just done. What would the don think of that? Shit, he knew what the don would think. Johnny would be angry, because he would think Weasel had taken her virginity. Weasel knew that wasn't true, but he didn't know if he could, or should, tell the don.

Maybe he could marry her. Yeah, that would be good. That would be somethin', him bein' married to the don's sister.

The fact that it meant he would also be married to a movie star never entered his mind. To Jimmy Pallota, Katherine Sangremano's position as sister to the don was much more important than her position as Katie Starr, movie personality.

Weasel took the tan suit out of his closet and carried it over to the bed. As he did so, he happened to look through the window at the surface of the pool. The pool was reflecting the back of the house, including the French door. The door was standing open.

"That's funny," he said quietly. "I know I locked that damn thing."

Weasel laid the suit down and started back to check the door. Then, for some reason, a strange feeling overpowered him, and he knew someone was in the house. He reached over to the shoulder holster that lay on the top of the chifferobe, pulled out his pistol, slid the barrel back to chamber a round, then started down the long hall.

Katie turned the shower on, then stuck her hand in to check the temperature. When it felt right she took off her yellow dressing gown and caught the reflection of her nude body in the full-length, steamed-over mirror.

And she saw something else. Or at least she thought she did. She gasped and turned around. There, standing just outside her bedroom door, stood a man holding a shotgun.

"JIMMY!" Katie shrieked in an ear-piercing scream.

"Shut up, bitch!" the man with the gun shouted. He pulled the trigger just as Katie jumped behind the bathroom wall. The steamed-over mirror and the glass shower wall came crashing down. Katie was sprayed with tiny pieces of broken glass, but none of the charge hit her.

"Look this way, you sonofabitch!" Weasel demanded. Katie heard a second blast from the shotgun, while at the same time, almost on top of the shotgun blast, she heard the sound of another gun being fired. She screamed again, then sat down on the floor in the middle of the shards of glass, wrapped her arms around her knees and buried her head in her arms, waiting to be killed.

She heard footsteps coming across the bedroom floor, and she screamed again.

"No! No! Get away! Get away!"

The footsteps came down on pieces of glass and mirror, making a crunching sound. Katie shuddered and waited for the blast that would take her life.

"Katie. Katie, it's all right, he's dead."

"Oh, Jimmy, thank God," Katie replied. She raised her head to look at him, then she screamed again. Jimmy's face, neck and upper chest were covered with blood.

Pieces of flesh were hanging from his face, and she could see the white bone of his skull. "Jimmy!"

Weasel twisted around, then fell, pitching backward into the shower. The water cascaded down on his face and washed the blood away, causing it to swirl and gurgle as it rushed down the drain. Quickly Katie got up and turned off the water. Then she knelt beside Weasel and put her hand gently to his cheek. His eyes were open, but already they were beginning to grow opaque. She didn't have to be a doctor to know that he was dead.

"Oh, Jimmy," she whispered. Slowly she stood up; then, gasping, she remembered the other man. She looked around, half expecting to see him standing there. She was relieved when she saw him lying on the floor at the door, half of him inside her bedroom, the other half out in the hall. Cautiously she walked over to him and looked down. Unlike Weasel, his eyes were closed, and for just a moment she thought perhaps he was deformed, because he seemed to have one eye out of position. When she looked closer, she saw that it wasn't an eye. It was a bullet hole, right in the bridge of his nose. Weasel managed to get off only one shot, but he had made it count He hit the would-be murderer right between the eyes.

CHAPTER 9

NEW YORK

Although Maria Vaglichio lived with her mother and father in their large estate on Long Island, she often came into the city. Sometimes she came to shop, sometimes she came to visit friends and sometimes she came to meet Joe Provenzano. Of course, no one knew about her meetings with Joe, not even her best friend. It was bad enough that she, a young, unmarried Italian Catholic girl, would be sleeping with anyone. Add to that the fact that her lover was Joe Provenzano, and the problem was intensified. In the first place, Joe's uncle, Al, was consigliore to Johnny Sangremano, the archenemy of Maria's father, Mario. And if that wasn't enough, Joe was also a policeman, albeit a federal policeman.

Sometimes, though, Maria came into the city for no other reason than to visit the old neighborhood. Mario didn't like that either.

"Why do you think I've done all this?" he asked her

once, when one of his soldiers reported he had seen her working in the neighborhood soup kitchen. "It's so we wouldn't have to live there anymore and you wouldn't have to be there anymore."

"But Papa, I like the old neighborhood," Maria insisted. "I still have friends there. And I like the sounds and the sights and the smells of the street."

"The smells of the street? What the hell are you talking about? In that neighborhood, the street smells like shit, for chrissake!" Mario insisted.

"And I like to work in the soup kitchen," she added. "Yeah? Well, that's the worst of all. There's no one in that kitchen except a bunch of drunks, bums and degenerates. Why would you want to be there?"

"Because I like to help people."

Mario turned to his consigliore. "She likes to help people," he repeated in exasperation.

"She is a saint, your daughter," Ben Costaconti said. "What am I going to do with her?"

"Let her go," Costaconti suggested. "We have enough people down there. We can look out for her."

Finally, Mario shook his head in frustrated resignation.

"All right," he told her. "You can visit the old neighborhood if you want. But stay out of trouble and don't get any ideas about moving there."

"Thank you, Papa," Maria replied happily, embracing her father but feeling guilty about it even then, for this had guaranteed her the perfect excuse to visit Joe whenever the opportunity presented itself.

Whenever Maria came into town the first place she would visit would be the neighborhood church where she grew up and where she took her first communion. As she came into the church she dipped her fingers in the holy water, crossed herself, genuflected as she passed in front of the altar, then stepped into the confessional booth. She opened the little screen and heard the priest open the screen on his side of the wall.

"Bless me, Father, for I have sinned. It has been three weeks since my last confession."

"In the name of the Father, and the Son, and the Holy Ghost, amen," the priest intoned.

Maria was silent for a moment. She had confessed before to the sin of being with a man. The fact that she was about to confess it again was certainly proof that she had no intention to "go and sin no more" when she left here. She felt her cheeks burning with shame, but she had no choice. She could not receive absolution if she wasn't truthful in her confession.

"This is the sin I am most sorry for. I have been with a man, Father," she said. "I have confessed this same sin before, so now I fear the transgression is greater, for I have done it again."

"You are right to have such a fear, my daughter. So, tell me, do you think you will do it again?"

Maria was silent for a long moment before she answered, not because she was debating whether or not she would—she knew that she had to—but because she hated to have to admit it.

"Yes, Father," she said. "I'm sorry, but I will do it again."

"You do this, knowing that you are placing your soul in jeopardy?"

"Yes, Father."

"Then why do you do it?"

"Because I love him."

"If you love him, why don't you marry him? Then there would be no sin."

"You don't understand, I can't marry him."

"And why is this? Is he already married?"

"No, nothing like that."

"Is he of the faith?"

"Yes, Father. He is a good Catholic."

"Then I don't understand. Why can't you marry him?"

"You don't know who he is, Father. If I married him, Papa would be very displeased."

"And so, to please your earthly father, you would continue to sin against your heavenly father?" the priest asked.

"No," Maria said quickly. "I mean, yes. Oh, I don't know what I mean. I don't want to sin against Jesus and the church. But Father, you know what business Papa is in. You know who he is and what he does. The man I love is, uh, on the other side of the law. I'm afraid that someday one of them might kill the other."

"That is indeed a predicament," the priest said.

"Couldn't you help?" she asked.

"What would you have me do, child? Do you wish me to speak with your papa?"

"No, please, don't do that."

"Then what?"

"Couldn't you grant me special dispensation?"

"Special dispensation?"

"Yes. You know, could you say that, under the circumstances, I mean especially since I love him and he loves me, and since we can't get married, that it would be all right for me, that is, for us to...?" She let the incomplete question hang, realizing now how stupid it sounded even to her ears.

"No," the priest said. "No, I can't do that."

"I see. I understand. Forgive me for asking, Father."

"Have you any more sins to confess?"

"No, Father."

"Very well. Then make the act of perfect contrition," the priest ordered.

"O my God, I am heartily sorry and beg pardon for all my sins, not so much because these sins bring suffering and hell to me, but because they have crucified my loving savior, Jesus Christ and offended Thy infinite goodness. I firmly resolve, with the help of Thy grace, to confess my sins, to do penance and to amend my life."

"Your penance is fifteen Hail Marys and fifteen Our Fathers," the priest said. "Go, and sin no more."

When Maria left the chinch she felt better, uplifted and cleansed. She would work in the soup kitchen this afternoon and that would be a part of her penance as well. And besides, for today at least, there would be no chance of her repeating the sin. Joe was gone. He had gotten a message through to her that he would be out of town for a while. He didn't say where he was going or when he would be back and Maria knew not to ask. She knew he would let her know the moment he returned.

Maria had made plans to do some shopping with one of her girlfriends this afternoon, but they weren't supposed to meet until four. It was only two o'clock now, so that gave her two hours to work in the kitchen. She crossed the street, then went into the Daughters of Mercy. Sister Veronica was working in the kitchen today. Because Maria had worked here several times before, Sister Veronica recognized her immediately. She smiled and hurried over to welcome her young friend.

"Ah, Maria, I was told you would be in today. It is so good to see you," Sister Veronica said. "Come into the kitchen. You can help me with the pots and pans. I have saved some for you, because I know how much joy you receive from hard work." She laughed at her little joke.

When Maria saw the pile of pots and pans, she

laughed as well. "Yes, well, I can see that we are going to be very joyful," she said.

"This is a good time of day to clean up," Sister Veronica said. "We don't have many customers right now."

Sister Veronica was right. There were only six men out in the dining hall and three of them had their heads lying on the table, asleep.

"Those poor creatures," Maria said. "Look at them. They have no place to go and no one to turn to."

"Oh, but they do have someone to turn to," Sister Veronica said. "They have the Lord."

"Yes, of course," Maria replied. "They do have the Lord." The door to the street opened and a man came in. He stood just inside the door for a moment without taking off his hat.

"Oh, there is another one. I'll go see what he wants."

"I'm sure he'll be hungry," Sister Veronica said.

When he stepped into the Daughters of Mercy kitchen, it was almost like stepping back in time, as if he were twelve years old again. The only difference was, this was a kitchen, run by a bunch of nuns. What he had known as a twelve-year-old boy in Cincinnati was an orphanage, run by the city. He had grown up in an orphanage, not because he was truly an orphan, but because his parents didn't want him around, couldn't stand to look at the strange, freakish abomination they had brought into the world. He had once heard the expression, "A face only a mother could love."

That expression may have covered everyone else, but it didn't cover him. Not even his mother could love him enough to keep him at home.

This place wasn't an orphanage of course but it didn't really matter. This place, and the orphanage where he was raised, were both the same. They even smelled the same. They had the same fare, meal after meal—watery soup, stale bread and weak coffee. They also had the same type of people looking down their noses at you, trying to get you to change your ways, telling you to make yourself productive to society or to get right with God.

Someone might believe he should have been grateful that the orphanage had taken him in. But he wasn't grateful. He hated the humiliation of being rejected by his own parents, and he hated the people who, though they had been there to help, were, by their very presence, witnesses to his humiliation.

Today, he had a special job to do here. It called for someone who could get in and out quickly, quietly, and that meant using a knife. Normally, of course, he was sent only where there would be no witnesses since his appearance was so distinctive that a witness would be able to identify him at once. However, it had been decided that, since this was a flophouse, anything the witnesses might say would probably be discredited, since most of them were alcoholics anyway.

He looked around. The furniture consisted of eight long tables, each flanked by backless wooden benches. Typically, there was nothing on any of the tables, no condiments, no napkins, no silverware of any kind. There were six men inside, all derelicts. Three of them were asleep or passed out. The other three were eating their soup, either looking directly into their bowls or staring out with vacant eyes, lost in their own world. No one was looking at him and, despite his rather freakish appearance, no one even seemed to notice him. The only exception was the woman in the kitchen, and she was now coming out to greet him.

She was dark, slender and very pretty. She fit

perfectly the description of the woman he had come to kill.

"Are you hungry?" she asked. "Can I get you something to eat?"

"Do I have to say a prayer first?" he asked sullenly.

The woman smiled, knowingly. She had dealt with the sullen ones before.

"No," she said. "Not if you don't want to."

"I don't want to."

"Then you don't have to."

"Are you afraid of me?" he asked.

"No," she replied, smiling brightly. "Should I be?"

"Have you ever seen anyone who looks like this?"

"I've seen very light-skinned people before," she said, easily.

"Freaks."

"God's children," she corrected. "You wait here. I'll get your soup."

"Wait a minute," he called. She stopped. "Come here, please."

Maria came back toward him. Her eyes reflected her puzzlement as to why he called her, but she exhibited no fear whatever.

"Are you Maria Vaglichio?" he asked.

"Yes," Maria said. The curiosity in her face deepened. "I've never seen you before. How do you know me?"

"I have a message for you."

"From Joe?" she asked hopefully. She stepped up to him, close enough to allow him to whisper, if need be.

He put his left hand on her shoulder, as if drawing her to him in confidence.

"Nothing personal," he said. "But business is business." With that, he thrust his right hand forward quickly, like the strike of a serpent's head. The knife he held in his right hand, palm up, the blade flat, slipped in easily between the fourth and fifth ribs. She gasped once, and he felt her hot blood spurt from the wound and spill over his fingers. He watched as the hopeful curiosity in her eyes changed quickly to surprise, then fear, then acceptance, as she knew she was going to die. He twisted the knife and let her fall so that her weight pulled against the upturned blade, severing vital organs and tissue. Finally she was free of the knife and she fell to the floor. Sister Veronica, who was still busy with her pots and pans back in the kitchen, heard nothing and never even looked around. Of the three conscious customers, only one was looking toward them when it happened, and because of the strange, pale appearance of the killer, he thought, literally, that he was seeing a ghost.

———

Don Pietro Nicolo's greatest joy was his garden. His gardening clothes consisted of a pair of oversized khaki trousers, a red plaid shirt so faded and worn that his wife had thrown it away three times only to have to retrieve it and a stained brown fedora.

Don Pietro enjoyed putting on the old clothes, then puttering about in his garden, carefully and lovingly tending to each plant. He particularly loved the smell of tomatoes on the vine. It reminded him of his youth and his father's small vegetable farm in New Jersey. During the season, young Pietro and his six brothers would fill the horse-drawn wagons with fresh tomatoes, then transport the tomatoes to the freight trains that, daily, took enough food into the city to feed the hungry throngs of New York.

The vegetable farm had not been large enough to see to the needs of seven sons, so it passed on to the oldest. Pietro, as the youngest, was given a pair of his brother's shoes and forty dollars, then sent out into the world to make his own way. That he was now the head of his own family and one of the five most important mafia figures in the city of New York was, to him, a worthy accomplishment.

Don Pietro's son, Enrico, however, had been showing some signs lately of discontentment with their lot. Don Pietro could not understand his son's dissatisfaction. Perhaps the Nicolo Family was the smallest but it was also one of the most respected. And Don Pietro Nicolo now had two houses, three automobiles, several hundred thousand dollars in cash and more than a hundred men working for him, who called him godfather and paid him the respect due a don. He had come a long way for a young boy who started out with only forty dollars and a pair of hand-me-down shoes. And when he was ready to pass it on to Enrico, he could retire knowing he had started his own son out in a much better position.

Don Pietro heard the backdoor to the house open and close, but he was busy picking the dead leaves off the tomato plants, so he didn't look around. Not until he heard footsteps in his garden did he acknowledge his visitor's presence.

"Watch the pepper plants that you don't break them down," he said.

"I won't harm them," Enrico replied.

"What is it, Enrico? Have you come to help your father with the garden?"

"Pop, you know I don't like to do this kind of stuff," Enrico said.

"I know. I wish you would learn. A man should know what it feels like to grow his own things. Where would we be if no one raised vegetables? What would we eat?"

"We could go to the store," Enrico said.

"But someone has to..." Don Pietro sighed. "Never

mind. If you do not understand, you will not understand. What is it? Why have you disturbed me in my garden if you do not wish to work?"

"I have some news, Pop," Enrico said.

Don Pietro found a tomato with a very bad blemish and he pulled it, held it to his nose to inhale its fragrance for a moment, then tossed it out of the garden.

"What is the news?" he asked, not turning his attention away from his plants.

"It is Maria Vaglichio," Enrico said. "She has been murdered. You know what this means, Pop?"

Don Pietro looked at Enrico with a stricken expression on his face, then he raised his hand and pressed it against his forehead.

"Yes," he said, sadly. "I know what it means. It means that a lovely young girl has died."

"More than that," Enrico said. "First there was LaRosa and Bendetti, you know, a couple of soldiers who worked for Johnny Sangremano. Then there was Johnny Sangremano's wife, then the Vaglichio's brother-in-law, and now Mario Vaglichio's own daughter. This means war, Pop. The Vaglichios and the Sangremano Family are going to go after each other now, tooth and nail."

"Then we have failed," Don Pietro said.

"We have failed? What do you mean by that? Oh, wait, don't tell me. You're talking about this peace-keeping shit, aren't you?"

Don Pietro didn't answer. Instead, he returned to his tomato plants, now snapping off bad fruit and dead leaves with a pointed effort designed to tell his son he was through with the conversation.

"Listen, Pop, I know how you feel, how you think a war is bad for everyone. Maybe in the old days, it was. But things are different now, and if a person plays it smart, he can just stand out on the sidelines, keep out of the fighting and not be hurt. Think about it, Pop. This could be the opportunity we have been waiting for. When Sangremano and the Vaglichios are both out of the picture, we can move in and take what we want from each family, picking and choosing, like going through a vegetable garden." He laughed. "Hey, a vegetable garden," he said, pointing to the tomato plants. "Get it?"

"You are a fool, Enrico," Don Pietro said, shaking his head in disgust.

———

STEUBENVILLE, OHIO

It had been several days now since Joe last saw Maria. He missed her, much more than he thought he would, and several times he was tempted to try, in some way, to get in touch with her. But how? He couldn't write; there was too much risk that her father or someone in the Vaglichio Family, with the capital F as opposed to family with the small f would get hold of the letter. He couldn't telephone either, for if she didn't answer the phone personally, he would never get to speak to her.

At least he had managed to get word to her, before he left, that he was going to be out of town for a while. That was something, anyway. Their entire relationship, satisfying as it was when they were together, was built upon such tenuous ground that, if he had not been able to inform her he was going to be away, she might very well think he had just decided unilaterally to break it off.

In the meantime, Joe would just have to put her out of his mind and concentrate on the business at hand: infiltrating Coppola's organization. From the time of his initial contact, Joe's best chance for doing that seemed to be through Carlo Lambretta. Joe went all out to be friendly with him. It soon paid off, because Carlo asked Joe if he would like to attend the Wednesday night fights with him. Joe accepted the invitation, then got word through to Mike, telling him where he would be.

The fight between Tiger Boyd and Kid Galvano promised to be a pretty good match, but the fight bill was filled with a lot of ham-and-eggers for the prelims. However, Joe and Carlo had excellent ringside seats. In fact, their seats were so close to the ring that when the knockout blow was delivered for one of the earlier events, the defeated fighter's mouthpiece flew out of his mouth and landed right in Carlo's lap. Carlo held the little piece of rubber up for all to see, mimed putting it into his own mouth, to the appreciative laughter of the crowd, then tossed it back to one of the hapless boxer's handlers.

"That was Billy Boston," Carlo said of the groggy pugilist. 'Two, three years ago, he showed some promise. He's got a strong right hand. Problem is, he has a glass jaw. He never could stay on his feet long enough to get in a good punch. I lost a lot of money on that bum."

"You must come here often," Joe said.

"Are you kiddin? I'm here so much I could move my clothes down here," Carlo said. "Some people like the ponies, but me, I'll take the fights anytime. Hey, you ever done any boxin?"

Joe had, in fact, won the citywide amateur championships when he was seventeen. Several promoters had approached him then, trying to get him to turn pro. He turned them all down because, even then, his heart was set on being a policeman.

"Uh, no," Joe said. He put his hand to his jaw. "I always been too fond of my pretty face," he teased.

Carlo laughed. "Yeah, I know what you mean," he said. "But I was just wonderin'. I mean, you sorta act like a boxer. You got that way about you, like the way you handled Big Sal."

Now it was Joe's time to laugh. "If you remember, I used a knife and a gun to handle Big Sal," he said. "I doubt there's any boxing commission anywhere that would let me in the ring using a knife and a gun."

Carlo laughed again. "No, I guess not," he agreed.

The timekeeper hit the bell several times to get the attention of the crowd, then the ring announcer walked into center ring carrying a microphone.

"The time, two minutes and thirty-seven seconds of the third round. The winner, by knockout, Louie La Grand!" The crowd applauded and whistled as Louis La Grand held his hands over his head.

"He looked pretty good," Joe said.

"Yeah," Carlo answered. "We goin' to let him win three, maybe four more fights, then, when we get the odds where we want them, he's goin' to take a dive."

Joe looked at Carlo in surprise.

"Why you look at me like that? You never heard of such a thing?"

"Of course I have," Joe admitted. "But I never heard it talked out loud at the fights before."

"Yeah, yeah, I know," Carlo said. "Vinnie's always tellin' me I got too big a mouth. But you one of us now, I figure I can tell you. You got any money on the main event?"

"Twenty dollars on Kid Galvano," Joe said.

Carlo laughed. "Twenty dollars on Kid Galvano. Don't tell me—it's 'cause he's got a good Italian name, right?"

"If I didn't know any other reason, that would be reason enough," Joe admitted. "But I've heard of Kid Galvano, and I know he's a pretty good fighter. I've never heard of Tiger Boyd."

"Give me fifty bucks."

"What?"

"Give me fifty bucks. I already put it on Tiger Boyd for you. Galvano's goin' down in the fifth."

Joe took out fifty dollars and gave it to Carlo. The bell rang again, and Joe looked up to see two more fighters climbing into the ring.

"Ladies and gentlemen," the ring announcer said. "The fifth and final bout before the main event. In this corner, wearing yellow trunks and weighing one hundred forty- eight and a half pounds, from Baltimore, Maryland, Jack Turner. Jack Turner."

There were some cheers, mixed with a few boos.

"And in this corner, wearing red trunks and weighing one hundred forty-seven pounds, from Cleveland, Ohio, Sailor Moran. Sailor Moran!"

This time the cheers were thunderous and it was obvious that Sailor Moran was a local favorite.

"This'll prob'ly be the Sailor's last prelim," Carlo said. "He'll be movin' up to main events after tonight."

Joe smiled. "Meaning he's going to win tonight."

"You got my word on it," Carlo replied.

"Yeah, well, listen, hold my seat, will you? I'm goin' to go take a leak."

"And miss the fight?"

"I'll be back in time for the main event," Joe said. "Anyway, you already told me how this one's goin' to come out...it sort of spoils it for me."

"It spoils it? You're crazy, man. I like knowin' how things are goin' to turn out."

Joe smiled, then gestured toward the ring. "Then enjoy the fight," he said.

Joe started up the aisle toward the rear of the gym. There were better than two thousand people here for the fight. At least three-fourths of the audience was made up of men and nearly all of them were smoking. As a result, a huge blue cloud of smoke rose to the ceiling, then spread out, eventually sinking back down to blanket the entire auditorium. Every light in the house was diffused by the thick smoke, from the high-powered pencil beams shining down on the ring, to the dim dome lights to the red Exit signs over each of the doorways. As if he were groping his way through a heavy fog, Joe followed one of the visible beams to the men's room.

Joe wasn't actually visiting the men's room on a sudden call of nature. He was going to keep an appointment. He had gotten word through to Mike to meet him at the fights tonight and they arranged to meet in the men's room at the beginning of the last preliminary bout.

Joe heard the clanging bell signaling the first round as he stepped into the restroom. He saw Mike standing at one of the urinals. In addition to the urinals, there were two toilet stalls, and when Joe glanced under the doors, he saw feet positioned in each one. He looked over at Mike, then nodded toward the feet.

Mike chuckled, then walked over and opened the two doors. Jason was in one of the stalls, Bill was in the other.

"We figured if we would keep the stalls busy, it would help keep the other people out," he explained. "What have you got?"

'To begin with, a good tip on tonight's fight," Joe said. "Kid Galvano is going down in the fifth."

"Son of a bitch," Bill said. "You mean they've got the fight fixed?"

"Not just the main event—this one too," Joe replied. "But we're after something bigger than fight fixing, and I think we've found it, Mike, it isn't just a coincidence that the murders in New Orleans, Chicago and New York all point here. This is where it all starts."

"I figured as much," Mike replied.

"You mean Coppola's enemies are spread that far apart? Not only does he really get around, he must be very hard to get along with," Jason suggested.

"I'm afraid Mr. Coppola's personality has nothing to do with it," Mike said. "I doubt he even knows his victims. In fact, I'm sure it would be better if he didn't."

"What are you talking about?" Jason asked. "Why would he kill someone he doesn't know? I mean, what would be the motive?"

"Oh, that's the whole point, you see," Mike said. "Take away the motive for killing and you eliminate at least half the possibility of ever being caught."

"What are you talking about?" Bill asked. "What's going on here, Joe?"

"From the way he's talking, Mike already has it figured out, don't you, Mike?" Joe said.

"Yes, I think so," Mike answered. "Unless I miss my guess, Coppola is running a murder-for-hire racket."

"You've got it," Joe replied. "That's the only thing it can be."

"Murder for hire? I've never heard of such a thing," Bill said. "Why would anyone do that?"

"Well, when you stop to think about it, it's a pretty sweet deal," Mike explained. "Say you live in New York and you want to bump someone off. You can't do it yourself—for one thing, whoever you are after probably knows you and they would be leery of you if you come around. And, for another thing, if they are known enemies of yours, you would be the first person the police would suspect. So, all you have to do is bring someone in to take care of your problem. I said New York, but it could just as easily be Chicago, or Kansas City or New Orleans."

"Yes," Bill said, now understanding what Mike and Joe were telling him. "Yes, I see now. That's why the New

Orleans police couldn't connect Matranga with D'Angelo's killers. And that's why we couldn't connect the killing in Chicago with the one in New Orleans."

"Right. It's like trying to make a connection between two men who just happen to ride in the same cab at different times on the same day. There is no connection at all, other than the fact that the same cabbie carried them both," Mike explained. "It was a business operation. Matranga ordered the murder from Coppola just the way he would order a suit from a tailor. Coppola sent in the muscle, did the job and collected the money. And, since there was no local tie-in, the police didn't have a clue."

"Death soldiers," Jason said. "Remember, that's what D'Angelo shouted in New Orleans, and it's what Nino said in New York."

"Joe, have you heard Coppola or anyone else use that term yet?" Mike asked.

"Not yet," Joe said. "As a matter of fact, no one has come right out and said, 'we are killers for hire,' but it's pretty obvious that's what they do. I've been invited to join them."

"Good, good," Mike said. "When do you start?"

"As soon as their top man gets back from a job. His name is Vinnie Letto, and unless I miss my guess, you would recognize him if you saw him."

"You say he's on a job now?" Mike asked. "Who is he after?"

"I don't know."

"Well, where is he? Maybe we can alert the local police before it happens."

"I think he's in Florida," Joe replied.

"Florida? Florida is a big state. Where in Florida?"

"I don't know that either," Joe admitted. "In fact, I don't even know for sure that he is in Florida. Carlo just said that Vinnie was lying around in the sun, eating oranges and looking at gorgeous dames."

"Yeah, that could be Florida," Mike agreed. "Probably Miami. Okay, we'll get word to the Miami Police Department to be on the alert."

"On the alert for what?" Jason asked. "What are we going to tell them to look for?"

Mike ran his hand through his hair. "I don't know," he admitted. "We don't know who he's after, so we don't know who to tell the Miami police to guard. I'm not sure which of the men I saw in New Orleans would be Vinnie Letto, so right now I couldn't give them a description of the suspect that would be any closer than describing Joe. And we're not even certain Letto is in Florida, let alone Miami."

"So what are we going to do?" Bill asked.

Mike sighed in frustration. "At this point, I guess we can do nothing." He looked at Joe. "You're doing a good job, Joe. Keep up the good work. We'll try and cover your ass as much as we can from out here. If you need us, you're going to have to find some way of getting word to us."

Outside, in the gym, there was a sudden roar from the crowd.

"I'd better get back," Joe said. "It sounds to me like Jack Turner just took his nosedive."

"Shit, now you tell us," Bill said. "Why didn't you tell us that this afternoon? I could've put down a little money."

"And lay a little on the side for Mr. Hoover, no doubt?" Mike teased.

"Why, sure, I wouldn't want to be hoggish about it," Bill said, laughing.

Joe started back toward the auditorium, but Mike called to him.

"Joe?"

"Yeah?"

"Be careful," Mike said.

Joe smiled and held his thumb up. "Got you," he said.

"Mike," Jason suggested as Joe left, "there is one thing we could do."

"What's that?"

"We could hire Coppola."

Mike stroked his chin. "Yeah," he said. "That might not be a bad idea."

"We'd have to be very careful, though," Jason said. "I mean, when you hire someone to commit a murder for you, you need to be in a position to keep a good watch on them so it doesn't really happen."

Well, all we have to do is hire him to kill someone who doesn't exist," Mike said.

"Or make sure he kills someone who really needs killing," Bill quipped. When the other two looked at him sharply, he laughed. "Just kidding, fellas, just kidding," he said.

As Joe worked his way back down the aisle to his seat, the crowd were still on their feet, cheering. Sailor Moran, covered with sweat, was bouncing around in the middle of the ring, smiling proudly as he hit his gloves together. Jack Turner was sitting on the stool in his corner with his head slumped forward and a towel draped across his shoulders. The announcer gave the official time, and the two fighters left the ring. At that same moment, the crowd broke into a loud roar and Joe saw that the two boxers for the main event were now coming toward the ring.

"Geez, where you been?" Carlo asked as Joe took his seat "You missed it."

"It's a long way up there and back," Joe said. "Anyway, what difference does it make? I'm back in time for the main event and that's all that matters."

The timekeeper slapped on the bell several times and the flat clang finally managed to quiet the crowd. They roared again as the announcer introduced both fighters. Joe studied them. Kid Galvano was short and square, with a receding hairline and a protruding brow. He was anything but a kid. Joe was telling the truth when he said he knew of him. Galvano had fought for the middleweight championship twice and was defeated both times, once by a knockout and once by a decision. The decision was split and some insisted that the Kid actually won. But that was four years ago. Though he was still a contender, his rank had fallen to about ninth or tenth, and he had long since given up any hope of ever fighting for the championship again, or even meeting one of the leading contenders. He was, however, still good enough to be a main eventer.

Tiger Boyd was a muscular young man with good shoulder and arm conformation. He had blond hair, blue eyes and the confident smile of the athlete who is young, healthy and has an unshakable faith in his own immortality. There was also something about him that was hauntingly familiar, but Joe couldn't place it.

The fighters returned to their corners, the buzzer gave the ten-second warning, then the bell called them out. Kid Galvano danced to the middle of the ring and Tiger Boyd rushed out to meet him.

The fighters slugged it out for five rounds. Joe was close enough to the ring that he could hear the pop of leather as the punches connected and after each blow, he could see the halo effect of sprays of sweat, illuminated by the lights. The punches were fast and furious and the fighters gave the crowd their money's worth. For a moment or two Joe almost got caught up in the fight himself, and he began to wonder if Carlo's information was wrong, or if Kid Galvano had taken it upon himself to cross them up. Several times Tiger Boyd was staggered by sledgehammer rights. One of Boyd's eyes was swollen shut, his nose was broken, his left ear was torn away from the side of his head and his lips were turned into hamburger meat. Then, between the fourth and fifth rounds, Joe saw something in Kid Galvano's eyes, and he knew the Kid was going to take the dive, as he was supposed to. This had just been his way of making Tiger Boyd pay a little extra.

In the fifth round, just as Carlo said he would, Kid Galvano went down.

"Come on," Carlo said, standing up and grabbing Joe's arm after the fight.

"Where are we going?"

"To the locker room. I want you to meet Tiger Boyd."

"Will they let us in?"

Carlo laughed. "Sure they'll let us in. Mr. Coppola owns him."

Several people were already in the locker room. Most of them were reporters and they bombarded Tiger Boyd with questions not only about this fight, but about the next fight with Mauler McElwain. McElwain was the number-one contender. Boyd would have to get through him to get to the champion.

"I'm goin' after McElwain and then the championship," Boyd said. "Tiger Boyd, champion of the world. How does that sound?" Boyd laughed. "I'll tell you one thing. It sounds a hell of a lot better than Bernie Bauman, doesn't it? That's why I changed my name. And don't none of you guys print my real name, either. If you do, you're goin' to answer to me."

"Far as I'm concerned, Tiger Boyd is your real name,"

one of the reporters said. "That's how your fans know you, that's how my readers know you."

"Mine too," another said.

"Same here."

Joe had been paying attention only half-heartedly until he heard Boyd say his real name. After that, he began studying him more closely. Now he knew why there had been something hauntingly familiar about him when he was first introduced.

Boyd clasped his hands over his head, and everyone laughed and applauded. As Boyd looked around at the reporters and fans, he saw Joe studying him intently from the back of the room. The smile left Boyd's face and he pointed at Joe.

"You," he said. "Do I know you?"

"No," Joe said, shaking his head and cursing himself silently for getting caught staring.

"Yeah, I do. I seen you somewhere. Hey, wait a minute, you're one of McElwain's trainers, ain't you."

"No, I'm not."

"Get this guy outta here," Boyd shouted. "He's a spy for McElwain."

"He's all right, Tiger," Carlo spoke quickly. "He's with me.

"Yeah? Well, there's somethin' about that guy. Somethin' that bothers me. You sure he's all right?"

"He's all right," Carlo said.

"Come on, Carlo," Joe said. "I'm making your fighter nervous."

As Joe and Carlo left the gym and walked through the dark parking lot toward the car, Joe snorted. "Can you imagine that guy thinkin' I was one of McElwain's trainers? McElwain's a bum. I don't know how he got this far."

"Don't you?" Carlo asked, then he chuckled.

"Yeah," Joe replied, laughing. "Yeah, I guess I do at that."

"Don't worry, he ain't goin' to last. Boyd will get him too."

The question Joe really wanted to ask was how Tiger Boyd had gotten this far. Eight years ago, Joe had defeated Bernie Bauman for the amateur championship of New York City. He knew that if he stayed around any longer, "Boyd" would recognize him as well. That wouldn't do. If Coppola found out Joe's real name, he could also find out that he was an agent for the Bureau of Investigation.

When Carlo and Joe returned to the pool hall, they had a message waiting. Coppola wanted to see them, right away.

"Maybe we've got a job," Carlo said. "Are you ready?"

"Yeah, sure," Joe replied. "Let me just run upstairs and change clothes real quick." What he really wanted to do was get to a telephone and tell Mike that something was up.

"No, don't worry about that. You don't have time for it," Carlo said. "When the Hammer sends for us, he means for us to get there right away. I hope he ain't too upset 'cause we're late gettin' back from the fights."

"Did you get a whiff of these clothes? Cigarette smoke, sweat, beer. They smell like shit." Joe complained.

Carlo laughed. "He ain't callin' us 'cause he wants us to smell good," he said. "Now, come on."

Joe smiled. "Okay. But if he starts holdin' his nose, it's your fault."

"I have some unfortunate news to share with you," Coppola said when they reached his house half an hour later. "Vinnie is dead."

"Vinnie? Shit, I didn't think anyone could ever get him," Carlo said. "How'd it happen?"

"There was a…a complication," Coppola said. He sighed. "And, to make matters worse, he didn't get the job done. So, you know what that means."

"Yeah," Carlo said.

"I don't," Joe said. "What does it mean?"

"I'm afraid it means we're going to have to make it right," Coppola said. "I'm going to send the two of you, together."

"All right," Carlo said, smiling broadly.

"Carlo, you will be in charge. Joe, I trust you will have no problem taking orders from Carlo?"

"No problem."

"Good. You two can get underway immediately."

"I need to run back to…" Joe started to say, but Coppola interrupted him.

"When I say immediately, Mr. Faggio, I mean immediately," he said. "You are going from here to the train, with no stops. You will not leave the train for any reason until it arrives at its destination."

"Why is that?"

"This way there are no slipups, no inadvertent word dropped here or careless clue left there. I want nothing to break your concentration on what you must do. Believe me, it is best for all concerned," Coppola explained.

"Listen to him, Joe. He's got this all worked out," Carlo said. "It's safest this way, it really is."

"Yeah, okay," Joe said easily. "No problem. I'm ready whenever you say."

"Whenever I say is now, Mr. Faggio," Coppola said. "Carlo, The Albino is waiting outside."

"He is? I didn't even know he was back. How did it go in New York?"

Coppola glared at him. "Carlo, you must learn to keep your mouth shut," he said.

"What's the problem? Joe's one of us now," Carlo said, defending himself.

"We have invited Joe to be one of us," Coppola said. "But until he has actually participated in one of our operations so that he has the same incentive to remain quiet that we do, he isn't one of us."

"Oh, yeah, I see what you mean," Carlo said contritely. "Yeah, I'm sorry, boss."

"One of these days, Carlo, sorry might not be enough," Coppola said. He sighed. "But, to answer your question, The Albino's part went fine. Now he's going to take the two of you to the depot. He has your train tickets ready for you. The train leaves in"—Coppola pulled out his pocket watch and examined it—"exactly seventeen minutes. So you had better get a move on. You've no time to waste."

"We're on our way," Carlo said, starting for the door and hustling Joe along with him.

"Oh, and Carlo," Coppola called. Carlo and Joe stopped and looked back toward him. "Please, no slipups this time. We've already been paid for this job once. I can't afford to keep doing it over and over again."

"We'll take care of it," Carlo said. "You can count on it."

"Oh, I am counting on it," Coppola said easily.

It was the first time Joe had ever met The Albino. He had seen albinos before, but never "The Albino." As he stood near the pale man he felt something, a presence of some sort. For some reason, Joe suddenly remembered a very unpleasant incident from his days as a policeman, before he joined the bureau. During the construction of a highway, a grave had been discovered and opened. As a young rookie, Joe had been called upon to make certain there was no vandalism while the body was moved and reburied. The coffin had been in the ground for over forty years, and because the box had stayed intact and the body had been pumped full of embalming fluid, both were still whole. However, a strange, chalk white mold completely covered the body. The bizarre image stayed with Joe for a long time. Now, meeting The Albino for the first time, he had an impression of foreboding, an overpowering sense that he was in the presence of those ancient spores of death. Involuntarily, he shivered.

"What, are you cold?" Carlo asked.

"No," Joe replied. "I'm all right."

"Don't worry 'bout The Albino none. He always affects people like that. He's okay, he does his job and everything. Just don't touch him. He don't like to be touched."

"That's okay," Joe said. "I don't plan to touch him."

Carlo laughed. "Yeah, that's what I say. I'd as soon touch a maggot."

————

ON BOARD THE TRANSCONTINENTAL TRAIN

Johnny Sangremano stuck his hand up to the window of his compartment, pulled the curtains aside and looked out over the station platform. He read the sign at the end of the depot: Steubenville. He let the curtain slide back and returned to his newspaper.

The article he was reading, about a congressional hearing on the Volstead Act, claimed Prohibition was having just the opposite effect of its intention. "Witnesses told the congressional committee that Prohibition is responsible for a great increase in crime and insanity in the United States," the article stated.

There was a light knock on Johnny's door.

"Yes, who is it?" Johnny called.

"Porter, sir."

Johnny took out his pistol and folded the newspaper over it, then stood and opened the door. A black man, wearing a white coat, was just on the other side. Johnny looked out beyond him to make certain no one else was waiting for him. When he was satisfied that the porter was not only who he said he was but was also alone, he stepped back to let him come in.

"I'm just checkin' to see if you would like me to make your bed, sir?"

"Yeah," Johnny said. When the porter turned to pull the seat out so he could make it into a bed, Johnny put his pistol away, then folded the newspaper and laid it aside. The way the paper was folded allowed the front-page picture of his sister to be in full view. When the porter turned around he noticed it and pointed to the picture.

"That pretty movie star sure had a close call, didn't she?" he said. "Those two men fightin' over her like they was. I guess they didn't either one of them stop to think that while they was shootin' each other, she could'a been shot too. Sure glad she wasn't hurt."

Johnny looked at the porter inquisitively. "Why?" he asked.

"Beg your pardon?"

"Why do you care whether she was hurt or not? You don't know her, do you?"

"No sir. That is, not personally. But I know her. Why, don't you know who that beautiful woman is?" the porter asked. "She's Katie Starr, the movie star. Killin' her would be just like pickin' a beautiful flower from a flower garden. Ever'one would be the less for it."

All the time the porter was talking, he was letting out the bed and adjusting the covers. Now he fluffed up the pillow and smoothed the bedsheets, then stood up. "There you go, sir. Your bed is all ready. You crawl in there tonight, I guarantee you, you'll have a good sleep all the way to St Louis."

"Thank you," Johnny said, giving the porter a generous tip.

"Yes, sir," the porter said, beaming happily at the size of his tip. "You want anything else tonight, you just let me know."

"I don't want to be disturbed," Johnny said. "Just keep everyone away from my door."

"I'll guard your room like it was the U.S. Mint," the porter said, smiling broadly.

Johnny was in bed by the time the train pulled out of Steubenville. His first thought, when he heard that Weasel had been killed protecting Katherine, was to hit back at the Vaglichios. The only reason he hadn't was because he wanted to get Katherine back safely under his control. To his surprise, however, Katherine didn't want to come back to New York. She told him that her life was in California now. "Besides," she added, "I owe it to my fans to stay out here."

Johnny had thought that was a rather vain, even pretentious, statement when she said it. Now, after hearing the porter talk about her as he did, he was having second thoughts. Maybe there was a legitimate reason for Katherine to stay in California, but that wasn't reason enough for her to get herself killed.

Johnny would take care of it when he got to California. He would make her understand why she must go to New York, that he was only looking out for her. After the Vaglichios were taken care of, she could return to California. In the meantime, she could just tell everyone she was taking a vacation.

Johnny tried to read a little longer, but his eyes grew heavy and, finally, he reached up and snapped off the light. Had he turned one more page, he would have read the story of a volunteer worker, a young woman named Maria Vaglichio, being killed by a crazed transient while she was working in a soup kitchen.

In another car on the same train, Joe Provenzano leaned back in the seat of the compartment he was sharing with Carlo and looked out through the window. It was dark outside, while a light burned inside the compartment. As a result, the glass was more like a mirror than a window, and Joe saw very little.

"Upper or lower?" Carlo asked.

"It doesn't matter," Joe replied.

"Good, I'm glad you don't care. I'll take the lower. I never did like sleeping in one of those pull-down things. Makes me feel like a can of beans or something, stuck away on some shelf." Carlo took a deck of cards from his pocket

"How about a little blackjack?" he invited.

"I'm not much for cards," Joe admitted.

"No? Too bad. You're goin' to get pretty bored before we reach California."

"No, I won't. I'll just get something to read."

"Huh-uh," Carlo said, shaking his head. "Mr. Coppola, he don't like for us to have any contact with anyone or anything till after the job is done. That means he don't want us talkin' to anyone or readin' anything."

"Well, what am I supposed to do?" Joe asked. "Sit here and twiddle my thumbs?"

Carlo chuckled. "If you aren't plannin' on playin' any cards, that's about all you can do," he said. "You sure you don't want to play?"

"I'm sure."

"Okay, suit yourself. I'll just see if I can beat 'Ole Sol' here."

Joe watched as Carlo dealt out the cards for a game of solitaire. If he couldn't get out even to buy a newspaper, how was he ever going to get word to the others? The answer, he knew, was that he wasn't going to get word to the others. Whatever this trip was for, he was going to have to make his own decisions and act on his own.

"Shit," Carlo said as he dealt out the first three cards of his run. "I need that red ten." Carlo studied the board for a moment, then shrugged his shoulders. "Oh well," he said. "What the hell." He took the red ten, even though it was the second card down, and put it on a black jack.

CHAPTER 10

STEUBENVILLE AIRPORT

" own all the land you see here, from the end of that hangar all the way out to the fence," Coppola said to Mike and Jason. He took in the property in question with a broad sweep of his arm. "Just the thing you need for your factory. If you want it, I can offer you a good price."

"You own the property?" Jason said. "How can that be? When the realtor showed it to us yesterday, he told us it belonged to a man named"—he pulled a piece of paper from his pocket and looked at the name—"Fielding Montgomery. Was he lying to me, or what?"

Coppola smiled smugly and looked at his young attorney. "Tell them, Stewart," he ordered.

Stewart Dempster cleared his throat.

"No sir, he wasn't lying," Dempster said. "At the time the realtor showed it to you, it did belong to Fielding Montgomery," Coppola said.

"So, as soon as you saw us looking at the property, you went out and bought it. Is that it?"

"Bought it? No, why would I want to do that?" Coppola replied. "When you have a smart young attorney working for you, you don't have to buy it."

"To be precise," Dempster elaborated, "Mr. Coppola does not own the property. However, he does have an ironclad option and, as far as you are concerned, it amounts to the same thing."

"I see," Jason said. "It would seem, Mr. Coppola, that if we are going to do business in this town, there is no way we can avoid you."

"So it would seem," Coppola agreed. He took out two cigars and offered them to Jason and Mike. "Have a cigar," he said. "Havana."

Mike accepted, Jason declined. The young attorney wasn't offered one. An airplane took off then, its engine roaring loudly as it passed by, not more than 150 feet overhead.

Mike waited until the noise of the ascending airplane had receded. "You know, Mr. Wodehouse," he said, using the name Jason had assumed, "perhaps Mr. Coppola can be of some assistance to us after all." Mike bit the end off his cigar and lit it.

"You mean in buying the land?" Jason asked.

"No," Mike replied. "We knew we weren't going to be able to do any business locally without involving him, didn't we?"

"That's what we figured," Jason said.

"No, I'm talking about another problem we are having back in New York."

"Are you sure you want to bring Mr. Coppola in on this? I thought we were going to try and solve that one ourselves," Jason said, picking up Mike's lead.

When Jason and Mike had discussed the possibility of hiring Coppola to commit a "murder" for them, they had made no precise plans but had decided to improvise the deal whenever the opportunity presented itself. That opportunity was now, so they were going to have to depend upon their creativity and ad-libbing ability to carry it off. However, that was a talent which both not only excelled at but also thoroughly enjoyed.

"What problem is that?" Coppola asked, lighting his own cigar.

"It's nothing you can help us with, I'm afraid," Jason said. Jason's dismissal had just the right effect, for Coppola's eyes narrowed in interest.

"Try me," he said.

"Yes, Mr. Wodehouse, I don't think we should be so quick to discard Mr. Coppola as a solution to our problem," Mike said. "Tell him what we're talking about."

"When we first came up with this plan, we contacted a lawyer in New York who was going to help us. But when he found out what our real scheme was, how we had no intention of ever manufacturing airplanes but were just going to sell stock, he became very difficult."

"Got too greedy, huh?" Coppola asked. "No problem. I've dealt with greedy people before."

"No," Mike said. "Greed, we can handle. He got honest. Honesty, we can't handle."

"He was going to expose us as frauds," Jason added.

"And if he learns what we are doing here, he might still try," Mike said. "And that could kill the golden goose for all of us...you included."

Stewart Dempster cleared his throat nervously. "Mr. Coppola, if you will excuse me, I have to get back to the office now."

"No, stay around," Mike said. "A smart young man like you may have some ideas we could use."

"No," Dempster said, shaking his head. "I'd really rather not be a party to this conversation."

Coppola chuckled. "You go ahead, sonny," he said. "I know that you have to keep your hands clean."

"Mr. Coppola, please," Dempster said, holding up his hands. "It would be best if you didn't even make a veiled reference to the fact that I am 'keeping my hands clean,' as you say. Even that suggestion implies that I may be aware of something that could 'soil' my hands. And if I knew for sure that what you are about to discuss now would be a violation of the law, that could leave me open to a charge of conspiracy. If I am to do the best job for you that I can, I must be like Caesar's wife. There can be no hint of a scandal."

"All right, all right, run along," Coppola said. "These gentlemen and I have some business to discuss."

"Yes sir," Dempster said. "And I want it well understood by everyone that I am leaving before any word pertaining to that business was ever mentioned. Therefore, I have no idea what it concerns." He looked at Mike and Jason. "I'm sure you will excuse me," he said.

Another airplane took off, its engine roaring as loudly as the one before. Dempster used that opportunity to walk back to his car. Coppola watched him until he started it and pulled away. Then Coppola spit out the end of his cigar and turned to look at Mike and Jason. "That's a smart kid," he said.

"Yes," Mike agreed. "I can see why you have him."

The laugh lines around Coppola's eyes were still there, but now, with his eyes narrowed and hard looking, they took on a more sinister cast.

"All right," he said. "The kid's gone now, so I want you to spell it out for me. What are we talking about here?"

Mike and Jason looked at each other. By expression, Jason asked Mike to take over.

"We're talking about a solution to our problem," Mike said.

"Uh-huh," Coppola grunted. "How permanent do you want this solution?"

Mike knew Coppola was trying to force him to commit by actually saying the words that he wanted someone killed. It was, he supposed, dictated by Coppola's sense of security. If someone asked him to commit murder, then that someone was equally as guilty and would be unlikely to give evidence against him if the murder case ever came to trial. However, as there was no real potential victim, Mike didn't feel constrained to mince words.

"We don't want any chance of him messing things up for us," he said. "How permanent can you make it?"

Coppola took a puff from his cigar and examined Mike through the cloud of smoke. "Like I said, how permanent do you want it?"

Mike exhaled audibly, as if being forced into saying the words. "Very permanent," he said. "We want the sonofabitch dead."

Coppola smiled. "Now you are talking a language I can understand," he said.

'Yes, well, the question is, can you handle it?" Mike asked.

"Oh, I can handle it all right," Coppola answered. "But that kind of permanent solution to your problem will cost you five thousand dollars."

"Let me get this straight," Jason said. "You are telling us we can have him killed for five thousand dollars? Just like going to a tailor and ordering a suit?"

Coppola chuckled and pulled the cigar from his mouth, causing a line of spittle to trail out, then snap in two. "Yeah," he said. "Yeah, I like that like ordering a suit. So," he continued, using the analogy, "when do you want this suit?"

"How soon can you do it?" Mike asked.

"As soon as I can get someone up there," he said. "What's the name of the man you want bumped off?"

"His name is Gatsby," Mike said. Jason surreptitiously looked at Mike in surprise.

"You have a telephone number and address?" Coppola asked, writing the name in his book.

"Not here. Not with me. I'll have to get it for you."

Coppola wrote the name in the notebook, spelling it out loud, one letter at a time, then he closed it and put it back in his jacket pocket "Yeah, do that. And bring the money with you too. All five thousand dollars."

"Before the job is done?" Mike asked.

"This isn't the kind of thing you can do on credit," Coppola said. "If you don't pay off, I can't very well undo the work." He laughed at his own joke and continued to laugh until he broke out in a wheezing cough.

"All right," Mike said. "We'll bring the money tomorrow."

"See you tomorrow, then," Coppola said as he took his departure.

Another airplane took off, this time a tri-motored Fokker. The combined roar of its three engines dwarfed the earlier sounds. Not until the noise subsided did Jason speak. "Gatsby?" he asked, laughing. "You have to be kidding."

Mike laughed with him. "Well, I couldn't think of anything that quick. I had to come up with something."

"But why 'Gatsby'?"

I'm a fan of F. Scott Fitzgerald," Mike said.

"Let's hope Coppola isn't."

Jason chuckled. "He doesn't exactly strike me as the

type. So, now that we have a murder planned, what's next? I mean, since there is no Mr. Gatsby except in F. Scott Fitzgerald's imagination, there won't be a murder, so what have we accomplished?"

"It's a little like putting tracer dye in the system," Mike said. "Tonight, when we see Joe, we'll tell him what we've done. Since he is on the inside, he might be able to follow the 'dye' from start to finish and, with the knowledge of how it works, we might be able to come up with the evidence we need for a conviction."

"A tracer dye," Jason said. He chuckled. "I wonder what Joe will say about that."

Joe didn't have anything to say about it that evening, because Joe didn't show up for the meeting. Mike, Jason and Bill sat around in the hotel for two hours waiting for him.

"Damn," Jason said, nervously grinding his fist into the palm of his hand. "I wish there was some way we could reach him."

"Aw, don't worry," Mike said. "Joe's pretty resilient. Maybe he'll find some way to reach us."

"Yeah, I guess you're right," Jason said. He sat down. "Say, is that this morning's paper? Toss it over, I want to see if Ruth got any home runs yesterday."

"See how the Dodgers did too, will you?" Mike asked.

"The Dodgers? I don't even have to look, they lost," Jason teased. "They always...hey, wait a minute. Mike, isn't Katie Starr Sangremano's sister?"

"Yes," Mike said. "Why?"

"Look at this headline: 'Jealous Suitors Shoot Each Other in Fight Over Movie Star,'" Jason read. "The movie star was Katie Starr. Oh, and this is getting more interesting," he said, looking up from the story. "One of those killed was Jimmy Pallota."

"Jimmy Pallota. You mean Weasel?" Bill asked.

"One and the same."

"That's funny. I can't see Weasel as a suitor for Katherine Sangremano. Who was the other man killed?" Mike asked.

"According to the paper, there's been no identification. Ah-ha! I think you'll find this interesting."

"What's that?" Mike asked.

Jason looked up from the story. "The unknown assailant died with a single pistol bullet between his eyes, but Weasel was shot with a shotgun—"

"Don't tell me. It was loaded with cutoff nail heads," Mike interrupted.

"Give the man a cigar," Jason said.

Mike smiled at the others. "Gentlemen, that's the man Joe was talking about, one Vinnie Letto. The sun, beach, oranges and good-looking women weren't in Florida," he added. "They were in California."

"You know, what amazes me is the scope of his operation," Bill said. "I mean, when you stop to think about it, he has sent his death soldiers to Chicago, New York, New Orleans and Los Angeles."

"Yeah," Jason said. "And now he's going to send one of them into the land of The Great Gatsby."

"Where?" Bill asked.

Mike and Jason laughed, then Mike explained to Bill the arrangement he and Jason had made.

"Of course, this all depends on Joe," Jason concluded. "I wish he would show up."

"Who did you say wants to see me?" Coppola asked his butler.

"Mr. Boyd, sir," the butler replied. "Mr. Tiger Boyd, the prizefighter."

"What does he want?"

"I don't know, sir. He didn't volunteer and I didn't ask."

Coppola sighed, then waved his hand. "All right, all right, bring him in."

"Very good, sir," the butler replied in his haughty manner.

A moment later the butler returned, leading Tiger Boyd. Boyd's left eye was black and swollen, his lips were fat and his ear was puffed up. He was carrying what appeared to be a scrapbook under his arm.

"So, Mr. Coppola, did you hear about my fight last night?" he asked.

"I heard about it," Coppola said. He stared at the pugilist for a long, critical moment. "The only thing is, I thought you won."

Boyd looked surprised. "Why, yes sir, I did win," he said.

"Did you? Well, you can't prove it by looking at you," Coppola said. "He must have beat up on you pretty good. You look like death warmed over."

"You don't need to worry none about that part," Boyd said. "The important thing is I won."

"And is that why you came to see me?"

"What?" Boyd asked, his face a study in confusion.

"Why are you here, Boyd? What do you want?"

"Oh!" the fighter said, as if suddenly remembering why he was here. "I remember now. Where is Joe Provenzano?"

"Where is who?" Coppola asked.

"Joe Provenzano," Boyd said. "You know, the new guy you got workin' for you?"

"I have no one working for me by that name," Coppola said.

"Sure you do," Boyd insisted. "He come by the dressing room after the fights last night. He was hangin' around with Carlo."

"Oh, that Joe. Well, I'm afraid you've got him

confused with somebody else," Coppola said. "That was Joe Faggio. He's Ice Pick Billy's brother."

Tiger Boyd tried to chuckle, only his nose was as badly damaged as the rest of his face, so his chuckle came out as a series of whistles and grunts. "Maybe old Joe's changed his name, like I did," he said. "But I know who he is. I ought to know. I knew when he come by last night I had seen him before, only I couldn't remember where or when. You know how that is, don't you? I mean, when you see someone in a place that's different from where you are used to seeing them? That's the way it was with me when I first seen Provenzano. Then, it clicked, you know what I mean?" Boyd snapped his fingers and pointed to his temple.

"Mr. Boyd, would you please tell me what you're gettin' at?" Coppola asked, obviously beginning to lose patience with the fighter.

"Well, I'm gettin' to where I seen Joe Provenzano before," Boyd explained. "I just couldn't place him, so, I went back to my place and I took out my scrapbook. And I found him, too." He opened the book. "Look here. This here is the first man I ever lost a fight to. This here is Joe Provenzano."

"I'll be damned," Coppola said, staring at the picture. "It is him."

"Yeah, that's what I said," Tiger Boyd said. "So the thing is, he's workin' for you now and I'd sure like to fight him again. You know, to make up for the one I lost? You think you can arrange it, Mr. Coppola? You think you could set up another fight between us?"

Coppola continued to stare at the newspaper photograph of the "Amateur Champion of the City of New York" until he was certain it was the man he knew as Joe Faggio.

"Now, why would he tell me he is someone he isn't?" Coppola mused. "Unless he's trying to hide something."

NEW YORK

Vito Patrizzi was the youngest underboss in the Sangremano Family. It was ironic that everyone considered him a very young man, almost too young to hold the lofty position he now occupied, when, in truth, he was no younger than Johnny had been when Johnny took over the entire family.

Of course, Johnny had assumed his position by right of inheritance, whereas Vito reached his position by hard work and loyalty. The loyalty went both ways, for Vito was very loyal to those people who were over him, and was the object of extreme loyalty from those who worked for him.

Vito rewarded the loyalty of his men in many ways. If their work was particularly good, he would give them a bonus, even if it meant that the extra money came from his own cut. He also saw to it that they were mentioned favorably to the don, so that those who showed potential for advancement within the organization were duly recognized.

Tito also liked to give a special dinner once a week, and every Saturday night as regular as clockwork, he and his top men would gather for pasta and sausages at Luigi's Restaurant. They always sat at the long table by the front window, laughing, eating, passing straw-covered bottles of wine around in clear view, secure in the knowledge that no one was going to say anything to them for violating the law.

Al Provenzano, the consigliore, and Guido Santini, Johnny's chief enforcer, had both recommended to Vito that he be particularly careful now.

"The don is gone," Provenzano had told Vito that very afternoon. "And someone bumped off Mario Vaglichio's daughter. We didn't have anything to do with that, of course, but I doubt the Vaglichios will believe us. I'm afraid they are going to try something…soon."

"Let 'em try," Vito said. "In fact, I wish they would try. I figure my men and me can take care of the entire Vaglichio Family, all by ourselves. We could just go ahead and get it all over with. Then, when the don came back he wouldn't have anything to worry about anymore."

"Just be more careful" Al Provenzano cautioned.

If, by "be more careful," Provenzano meant for Vito to change some of his habits, his admonition was no good. By nine-thirty that Saturday night, Vito Patrizzi and six of his top lieutenants were sitting around the table as usual, putting away great quantities of food and drink. Because they were laughing and telling stories, they didn't even notice two closed-body touring cars pull to a stop on the street, just in front of the restaurant.

A waiter taking another serving of pasta to the table happened to look through the big front window just as half a dozen tommy guns poked out over the sides of the two cars. He knew at once what was about to happen.

"Look out!" he shouted, and he tossed the tray to one side, then dived to the floor. Other diners in the restaurant, hearing the waiter's shouted warning, also dived to the floor, as women screamed and men shouted in alarm.

"What the hell?" Vito asked, though even as he shouted, he was already reaching inside his jacket for his pistol.

Outside, the machine guns opened fire. The first fusillade brought the great window crashing down. One of the men at the table was hit and pitched forward, falling across the windowsill, half in and half out of the restaurant. Another went over backwards.

Vito got his gun out and managed to get off two or three shots even as the bullets were plunging into his flesh, spilling blood over his white shirt and opening holes to his lungs.

The two carloads of assassins kept firing, knowing that a heavy volume of fire was their best protection. Their reasoning proved accurate, because Vito was the only one inside the restaurant who managed to return any shots at all and all of his went wild.

Finally, when the last bullet was fired and there was nothing left of Luigi's but shattered windows, splintered tables and sprawling corpses, the guns grew silent.

"Good shootin', Mr. Vaglichio," one of the men in one of the cars said. "I didn't know you could shoot that good."

"It's been a long time since I had to," Mario answered. "But this was for Maria," he added, barely able to choke the words out. He took a deep breath. "I just wish it had been Johnny Sangremano sitting at that table."

"We'll get the sonofabitch," one of the others said. "Don't you worry none about that. We'll get him."

A crowd was already beginning to gather in front of the restaurant. Some of the more morbidly curious were getting close enough to examine the corpses.

"Come on, let's get the hell out of here!" Mario ordered. The driver put the car in gear and roared off, with the other car just behind.

ABOARD THE TRANSCONTINENTAL TRAIN

When the train stopped in Phoenix, Johnny was completely unaware that Vito and his men had been attacked. The porter told Johnny that there would be at least three hours to kill here before the train would continue on to Los Angeles. Johnny decided to take the opportunity to walk around and see a little of this city he had only read about, but never visited. Also, he wanted to find a telephone and call Al Provenzano in New York. He had left Al in charge, and though Al was quite capable of running things in his absence, Johnny had been out of touch for nearly four days now, and he didn't like that. He felt he should at least find out what was going on back home.

It was unbelievably hot when Johnny stepped off the train. He took his jacket off and tossed it across his shoulder, then braced himself to walk from the shade of the car shed out into the bright Arizona sun.

An old Mexican woman was operating a taco stand right across the street from the station. She didn't have any teeth and she kept her mouth closed so tightly that her chin and nose nearly touched. A swarm of flies buzzed around the steaming kettles, drawn by the pungent aromas of meat and sauces. The old woman worked with quick, deft fingers, spooning the spicy ingredients into tortillas, then wrapping them up in newspaper as she handed them to her customers.

When she saw Johnny watching her, she smiled a toothless smile and held one out toward him. Johnny shook his head no, then walked on down the street, taking in the sights and sounds of Phoenix. The city was undergoing a transition from a sleepy cow town of the Old West to a bustling city of the future. Trolleys whirred down the dual set of tracks in the center of the street, and cars honked impatiently at the horses and wagons with which they shared the road. The sound of jackhammers and other power equipment filled the streets with noise, and Johnny saw at least two ten-story buildings going up.

After he walked several blocks, Johnny saw a bar with

a picture of a frosty mug of "near beer" on a sign out front. He thought how good a cold beer would be, even if it was only near beer. The bar was named Saguaro House, and the sign insisted it was Arizona's finest "parlor of relaxation."

It was much darker inside and a little cooler, because several rows of overhead fans turned briskly, keeping up a steady breeze. There weren't many people inside, since it was still early afternoon. Behind several round tables covered with green felt sat the dealers, waiting for the evening games to start. Most of the dealers were counting their chips, and the bright red, white and blue stacks caught the dim light vividly, contrasting sharply with the light-absorbing felt. Some of the dealers were dealing hands methodically, flipping them over to look at them, then pulling them back to deal again. The bar was made of burnished mahogany, with a highly polished brass footrail. Crisp, clean white towels hung from hooks on the customers' side of the bar, spaced every four feet. The mirror behind the bar was flanked on each side by a small statue of a nude woman, set back in a special niche. A bartender with slicked-back black hair and a handlebar moustache stood behind the bar, polishing glasses industriously.

"What can I do for you?" the bartender asked.

"I'd like a beer and a telephone."

"What kind of beer?"

Johnny shrugged his shoulders. "I don't know your local brands," he said. "And if it's all near beer, what difference does it make?"

"A quarter will get you a real beer," the bartender suggested.

"Really? You mean, you people haven't heard of the Volstead Act out here?"

"Are you telling me you can't get real beer where you come from?"

"Well, you can," Johnny said. "But not quite this openly."

"Maybe we're a little more independent-minded out here," he said. "So, what's it goin' to be? You want a real beer or not?"

"Yes," Johnny said, slapping a quarter on the bar.

The bartender pulled the handle on one of the barrels and drew Johnny a big mug of beer. As soon as Johnny tasted it he knew it was the real thing, and he smiled. There's a telephone booth over there," the bartender said.

"Thanks," Johnny said, taking the beer with him.

Johnny gave the operator the information for the long-distance call, asked that the charges be reversed, then hung up the phone and leaned against the wall while he waited for the operator to complete the call. A few minutes later the phone rang, and he picked it up.

"I have your call to New York, sir," the operator said. "Go ahead."

"Hello?" It was Al's voice.

"Al, it's me, Johnny."

"Johnny, you've got to come back here," Al said.

"Why? What's wrong?"

"The Vaglichios hit us last night."

"Where?"

"At Luigi's," Al said. "Vito was killed, and three more besides."

"Damn," Johnny said. "What the hell do you suppose set them off?"

"I know what set them off," Al replied. "Mario Vaglichio's daughter was killed the other day. In fact, it was the same day that Weasel was killed. Someone stabbed her."

"Mario's daughter. You mean Maria?" Johnny asked,

surprised by the announcement "Al, what's going on back there? Who would do such a thing?"

"The Vaglichios think we did it," Al said.

"What? Why, that's crazy," Johnny said. "Get hold of them, Al. Get hold of them and tell them we had nothing to do with killing Maria Vaglichio."

"I've tried, but I can't get through to them," Al said. "I can't even get Ben Costaconti to talk to me, let alone either of the Vaglichios. This is getting out of hand, Johnny. I don't know how much longer I can hold Vito's boys back. They are pretty upset. They want to hit the Vaglichios hard."

"No," Johnny said. "Not yet. You've got to tell them not to do anything until I get back."

"I'll try," Al said. "But what about puttin' our people on the mattresses? How would that be? That way we would be on the defensive in case anything else happened. It wouldn't satisfy Vito's people, but it might keep anyone else from getting hurt."

"Yeah," Johnny agreed. "Yeah, go ahead."

"When will you be back?" Al asked, anxiously.

"Look," Johnny said, I'm in Phoenix now. The train isn't due into Los Angeles until tomorrow morning around eleven, but I'm sure there's an airport in this town. If there is, I'll get a plane and fly the rest of the way. Soon as I'm sure Katherine is all right I'll come on back home. I think it's time we got the Vaglichios to listen to reason."

"Hurry back, Don Sangremano," Al said. "The Family needs you."

———

STEUBENVILLE POLICE DEPARTMENT

"Coffee, Mr. Carmack?" Officer Boyle asked, holding up the pot in invitation.

"Yes, thank you, Terry," Bill replied, looking up from the papers he was studying.

"I never have asked: what do they call you guys?" Boyle wanted to know as he poured a stream of steaming coffee into Bill's cup. "I mean, do they call you Officer Carmack, Mister Carmack, or what?"

"Agent," Bill said. "I am Agent Carmack."

Boyle poured himself a cup of coffee as well, then sat at his desk, which butted up against the one they had given Bill to use.

"Agent Carmack," Boyle said. He chuckled. "Sounds like someone who sells train tickets. Do you like your job?"

"Yes, sure," Bill said. "Why do you ask—don't you like yours?"

"Oh, yeah, I suppose so," the policeman answered. "I mean, I wouldn't do it if I didn't like it. Sometimes, though, it can be a pain in the ass. Like, take this afternoon, for instance. It's supposed to be my afternoon off. I had it all set up to take this certain young lady I know out for a drive. I been trying to get this girl to step out with me for two weeks and she finally says yes, but what happens? Captain O'Connell comes up with some job that's going to take all afternoon. Now I got to call her and tell her I can't make it."

Bill chuckled. "That's the way of it sometimes," he said. "What's O'Connell got you doing?"

"He wants me to find out all the information I can about somebody," Boyle said. "And what pisses me off is I don't even think it's genuine police work. I think it's just because he wants to make a big impression on that big shot, Coppola."

That caught Bill's attention, and he looked up from what he was doing. "You're looking up somebody for Coppola?"

"Well, not officially," Boyle said. "Officially I'm looking up the information for Captain O'Connell, not for Mr. Coppola. But, like I said, I know where it's going."

"Who is the person you are supposed to be finding out about?" Bill asked.

"His name is Joe something. Wait a minute, I've got it written right here. Yeah, here it is: Joe Provenzano."

Bill managed to show absolutely no reaction to the name. Instead, he smiled and held out his hand for the piece of paper the policeman was holding. "Listen, Terry, would you like me to take care of that job for you?" he asked.

"You'd do that for me?"

"Sure, why not? O'Connell assigned us to each other, didn't he? And so far, you've been doing all the work for me and I haven't had the opportunity to pay you back," Bill said. "Besides, one of the things the bureau does best is find missing people. Is this guy missing, or what?"

"Missing? I don't know. All I know is Captain O'Connell gave me the name about an hour ago and asked me to find out what I could about him. Oh, he did give me this to go on: the guy was once the amateur boxing champion for New York City."

"Well, that ought to give me a place to start, anyway," Bill said.

"Say, this is sure swell of you, Agent Carmack," Boyle said. He walked over to the hat rack to retrieve his hat. "If you really are going to take care of this for me, I guess there's nothing to stand in the way of my taking my afternoon off, is there? I can take that young lady out after all."

"Sure thing," Bill said easily. "I hope you and your girl have a very nice time."

"She's not my girl yet," the policeman admitted. He squared his hat on his head, then smiled broadly at Bill. "But, with any luck, she's going to be."

————

LOS ANGELES

The airplane Johnny was flying was an experimental model, built by an aircraft engineer in Phoenix. The engineer had hoped to get enough backers interested in his plane to secure the financing he needed to go into production, but no one came through. As a result, of the failed project, the engineer lost everything—his money, his house and his family. Finally he even lost the airplane when it was repossessed by a local bank. The engineer left Phoenix for what he hoped were the friendlier climes of Australia and the bank put his airplane up for sale.

Because it was a one-of-a-kind airplane, no one wanted to buy it. As a result, Johnny was able to pick it up for a few hundred dollars. It was a steal, especially as it was faster, roomier and more stable than anything Johnny had ever flown before.

The airplane was a high-winged monoplane with an enclosed cabin large enough to hold four. The wheels were covered with teardrop fairings, and the wings were fully cantilevered. The cantilevered wings frightened off would-be backers and buyers alike. The sight of those smooth, sleek wings sticking out from each side of the fuselage, unsupported by any external strut or brace, was quite unnerving to the uninitiated. To Johnny, it just added to the overall appeal of the airplane.

The fabric of the airplane had been hand-rubbed to a super smooth finish, then painted white with a bright blue stripe right down the middle. The propeller had a large spinner, painted the same shade of blue as the center stripe. It was, Johnny had to admit, a beautiful airplane, and though he had bought it specifically to allow him to get to Los Angeles faster, he was already thinking about keeping it and flying it all the way back to New York.

As Johnny cleared the mountains and started letting down into the Los Angeles basin, he checked the eight-day clock on the instrument panel. He had taken off less than three hours ago, and he was already in Los Angeles. It made him feel good to know that the train he had been on was just now leaving Phoenix.

Johnny greased it in for a perfect three-point landing, then taxied up to the parking apron, where he was met by a curious line-boy.

"What kind of plane is this, mister?" the line-boy asked as Johnny stepped down onto the tarmac, then stretched.

"What kind of plane?"

"Yes, sir. I've never seen one like this," the line-boy said, patting the plane's smooth skin gingerly.

"Why it's a...a Weasel," Johnny said, smiling at the idea of naming the plane for his friend. "It's a Pallota Weasel."

"A Pallota Weasel. I never heard of it, but it sure is beautiful."

"Yes, it is, isn't it?" Johnny agreed. "Listen, can you have it fully serviced and ready to go before I come back?"

"Yes sir. When will you be back?"

"Well, that's just it. I don't know exactly when I'll be back," Johnny replied. "But when I do come back, I don't want to have to wait around to leave." Johnny gave the boy a twenty-dollar bill. "Take care of it for me, will you? You can keep whatever is left over," he said, knowing that even if the lineboy filled both wing tanks to their combined total of forty gallons of gas, it would still cost him less than ten dollars.

"Gee, mister, thanks!" the line-boy said, his eyes wide in excitement over his windfall.

"Now, where can I get a cab?" Johnny asked.

"Don't you worry about that. That's easy enough took care of. You just go on in there and have a seat and be comfortable," the youth said, pointing to the small shack that served as the administration building. "I'll have the cab come to you."

Johnny reached into the backseat of the plane for his bag. The bag was a little heavier than usual, its additional weight due to the fully loaded .45 caliber automatic that rested in its shoulder holster, just on top of all the clothes.

STEUBENVILLE, OHIO

"Joe's in trouble," Bill said to Mike and Jason when he saw them in their room at the Biltmore Victoria a little later. "Coppola knows his real name. We've got to get him out of there. I'm afraid it's not going to take long for Coppola to put two and two together."

Mike sighed. "That's not the only thing going badly for Joe," he said. "I just talked to the New York office: Maria Vaglichio has been killed."

"Oh, damn," Bill said. "She is...she was Joe's girlfriend."

"Yeah, I know," Mike said.

"How did it happen?"

"Officially, she was murdered by a crazed derelict in the soup kitchen where she was doing volunteer work," Mike explained. "But the Vaglichios believe that Johnny Sangremano had it done."

"I don't believe that," Bill said. "Mike, you know Johnny Sangremano."

"No," Mike said. "I used to know a Johnny Sangremano. But the man who is the head of the Sangremano Family today bears no resemblance to the man I once knew."

"Maybe not, but not even the Sangremano we know today could do something like that. Anyway, what would it get him? What would be his motive for killing an innocent girl like Maria Vaglichio?" Bill asked.

"Revenge, maybe?" Jason suggested. "Don't forget, the Vaglichios tried to kill his sister."

Bill shook his head. "That might sound plausible, but it won't wash."

"Why not?"

"Maria Vaglichio was killed one hour before the attack on Katie Starr," Bill explained. "The truth is, I don't think they were related at all."

"Do you think it really was some deranged customer of the soup kitchen?"

"It could be," Bill said.

"What do you think, Mike?"

"I don't know," Mike answered. "Things like that have happened before, but..."

"But you don't think that's what happened this time?"

"No," Mike replied. "It's too much of a coincidence."

"Then somehow it all has to be related," Jason suggested. "It makes no sense, otherwise. But that does get us back to Bill's question. Why would Sangremano kill Maria Vaglichio? If he did, which I don't believe for a minute."

"I guess it doesn't matter much whether we believe it or not," Mike said. "The thing is, the Vaglichios believe it. There's already been a raid against Vito Patrizzi, one of Sangremano's capo de regimes." He sighed. "I'm afraid that by the time we get back to New York, we're going to be right in the middle of a full-scale gang war."

"Speaking of which, when do we go back?" Bill asked.

"We can't go back," Mike answered. "Not yet, anyway. Not until we find out what's happened to Joe. Especially now that we know he is in danger."

"I'll go back and give O'Connell a phony report of some sort," Bill said. "What are you guys going to do?"

"Well, we made an arrangement with Coppola to kill a fictitious man named Gatsby. Just to keep that going for now, we're going to give him the five thousand dollars he asked for," Mike said.

Bill looked surprised. "Where did you come up with that much money?"

Mike chuckled, then nodded toward Jason. "One of the advantages of having a rich partner is to have access to funds that would not otherwise be available."

"Jason, you're using your own money? What if you don't get it back?" Bill asked.

"It's only money," Jason replied. "And if we get the goods on this sonofabitch, it'll be worth it to me."

"New York is a big town. Have you ever stopped to think that there might really be a Mr. Gatsby there?" Bill asked. "I'd hate for Coppola's man to make a mistake."

"Yeah, we thought about that," Mike said. "We're going to tell him that we've arranged for Gatsby to be at a certain place at a certain time. There won't be anyone there, of course, so no one will get hurt."

"But what good will that do now?" Bill asked. "If Joe

isn't here to follow the deal through for us, what will we get out of it?"

"I don't know," Mike agreed. "I mean, the fact that he would simply go there intending to commit a murder wouldn't even be admissible evidence in court, under these circumstances," he admitted. "But it would be all the proof we need that Coppola is running a murder-for-hire business. And if we know for certain that it's true, then we won't have to be looking for the answer anymore. All we'll have to do is find the proof."

When Bill returned to the police station he saw that his young friend was back. Boyle wasn't wearing his uniform now, and the expression on his face indicated that he wasn't back by choice.

"What is it, Terry?" Bill asked. "What are you doing back here? I thought you'd be cruising around Steubenville now, with your girl by your side."

"Why didn't you tell me?" Boyle asked. "You could have saved me a lot of trouble."

"Tell you? Tell you what?"

"Captain O'Connell chewed me out pretty good, I can tell you. For 'dereliction of duty,' he said. You know what an entry like dereliction of duty can do to your record? I can sure kiss any promotion good-bye, that's for sure. Why didn't you tell me that Joe Provenzano is an agent for the Bureau of Investigation?"

Bill sat down, slowly. "What makes you think he is?" he asked.

"What makes me think he is? Hell, I don't think he is. I know he is. And you know he is too, don't you?" Terry challenged. "What I don't understand is why you pretended you were going to find out about him, and you didn't say a thing to me about it. You didn't want me to know, did you?"

"No, I didn't want you to know," Bill admitted. "How did you find out he was?" Bill asked.

"I told him," O'Connell said. Bill looked around and saw O'Connell standing in the open door of his office. "You want to come in here, Carmack? I think we have a few things to talk over."

"Yeah," Bill said. "I guess we do at that." He looked at Boyle. "Sorry, kid. I didn't intend to get you in trouble."

"Shut the door," O'Connell said as Bill stepped into the captain's office.

Bill shut the door, then gestured back toward Terry Boyle.

"Don't be too hard on him," he said. "He had no idea Joe was working with me."

"Working with you?" O'Connell said. "Then you don't deny it?"

"No, of course not," Bill replied. He was having to ad-lib all his responses now. It was obvious Joe had been exposed; now Bill had somehow to minimize the consequences. "Why should I deny it?" He continued, "I guess that means I'm going to have to send Joe back to New York now. If you've found out who he is, then Boone probably has as well."

"Who?" O'Connell asked, his face twisted in confusion. "Who the hell is Boone?"

"Charles M. Boone," Bill explained patiently. "He's the reason I'm here, remember? He's the one I told you about, the communist agent Joe and I have been looking for."

"Joe? You mean Joe Provenzano? The man who has been calling himself Joe Faggio?"

"Yes," Bill said.

"And now you are trying to tell me he's looking for communists?"

"Of course he is," Bill said. "I just admitted he was

working with me, didn't I? Hello, hello, are you here?" Bill asked, waving his hand back and forth in front of O'Connell's eyes.

O'Connell stroked his chin for a long moment, glaring at Bill.

"I'm not buying this shit, Carmack," he finally said. "Not for a minute. You and Provenzano are trying to get the goods on Coppola, aren't you?"

"Joe was just using Coppola as a cover. To be honest, we didn't even know Coppola was a communist," Bill said.

"Goddamnit, forget the communists!" O'Connell shouted, banging his hand on the desk. "I want to know what the hell Joe Provenzano is doing sniffing around Ignatzio Coppola! He is an important man, Carmack. A very important man, if you catch my drift. And it's my duty as a police officer to make certain that important men like Ignatzio Coppola don't get harassed by someone from the Bureau of Investigation."

"Like I said, it was just a coincidence that we picked Coppola. But he won't have to worry about Joe anymore," Bill said. "Since everyone knows who he is now, he is no longer of any value to me. If you know and if Coppola knows, probably every communist within a hundred miles also knows." Bill stood up. "If you want me to, I'll drive out and speak to Coppola personally, to apologize for any inconvenience this might have caused. Then I'll pick up Joe and take him to the depot, and send him back to our home office."

"That won't be necessary."

"I don't mind."

"Don't bother," O'Connell said. "Your friend isn't even in town."

"What do you mean he isn't in town? Where is he?"

"I don't know," O'Connell said.

"Does Coppola know?"

"I don't know the answer to that, either," O'Connell said. "But I'll try and find out for you."

"Never mind, I'll find out myself."

"No," O'Connell ordered. "You won't find out yourself. You aren't going to go near Mr. Coppola, have you got that? If I catch you bothering him, I'll put you in jail myself."

"Find out where he is, O'Connell," Bill said, dropping the subterfuge now and omitting the captain's rank on purpose. "Find out where he is and get him back, safely, or I'll throw your ass in jail. And believe me, O'Connell, you don't want to find yourself in my jail."

CHAPTER 11

SOUTHERN PACIFIC DEPOT, LOS ANGELES

Every track that made up the network of iron fanning out under the high tin roof of the train shed was busy. There were several trains at rest, several just arriving and several just getting underway. The ground shook with the power of their rumbling movement, and wisps of steam and tangy plumes of coal smoke drifted across the platform.

When Joe and Carlo left the train, Joe stretched, happy at last to be rid of the motion that had been his constant companion for the last four days. For four days he and Carlo had remained locked into the small compartment, not even leaving it to eat. Carlo had taken care of that problem by paying the porter to bring their meals to them.

It had been a very frustrating trip for Joe, for he had been unable to get any message through to the others. Several times during the trip he suggested that he would like to get off to stretch his legs, have a look around or buy a newspaper, but every time Carlo had said no. His inability to get off the train or even out of the compartment precluded any opportunity of making a telephone call, or sending a telegram or even a letter.

Once Joe even tried to leave a message for the porter, and he wrote, on a table napkin: "Call UN 6-6554 in New York." That was the bureau office number. Joe didn't have time to write anything else. It was his hope and belief that if the porter managed to get the call through, explaining the strange circumstances under which he was calling, the bureau would figure the rest of it out...especially if the bureau contacted Mike.

Joe never had the opportunity to put his theory to the test, however, because the porter discarded the napkin without even looking. Later, Joe had to fish the napkin out of the trash and destroy it before Carlo discovered what he had done.

But now that was all over, and Joe and Carlo were walking down the long concrete ramp that stretched out between the tracks and thus between the trains. To their left was the train on which they had just arrived. It was disgorging its passengers, who were now weary and disheveled from their long journey. To their right one of the trains that were getting ready to leave was receiving new passengers. These were fresh, eager and excited about the adventure that lay before them.

"Make way, make way!" someone shouted, and Joe and Carlo had to step aside as a couple of baggage handlers pushed a large overloaded cart by them, hurrying to the depot and the baggage claim room.

"Busy place, ain't it?" Carlo said.

"Yeah," Joe agreed. "So, what do we do now?"

"Come along with me," Carlo ordered. "I'll just call Mr. Coppola and make sure nothing has changed."

"All right," Joe said. "While you're doing that, I'll go to the rest room."

"Wait for me," Carlo said. "I'll go with you."

"I can't wait."

"You got to," Carlo said. "The rule is, when two people go out on a job, they stay together for the whole time."

"Even when we go take a piss, for chrissake?"

"Even then."

"I'm not sure I like that."

Carlo chuckled. "You're gettin' paid enough, you don't have to like it."

"Why is everything so strict? I mean, Jesus, I didn't even get a chance to look at a newspaper on the way out here."

"Ever'thing is strict 'cause that's just the way Mr. Coppola wants it," Carlo said, as if that were all the explanation needed. "And so far, ever'thing has worked out real good by us doin' just what he tells us to do. Besides which, Mr. Coppola ain't a man you want to piss off, if you know what I mean," he added.

"Yeah," Joe said. "I think I'm beginning to see what you mean."

"Don't worry about it. After a couple of jobs, Mr. Coppola will trust you enough to send you out by yourself. Believe me."

"I can hardly wait," Joe said sarcastically.

Joe followed Carlo on into the depot itself. It was a little quieter inside the depot, though Joe could still feel the floor trembling beneath his feet as, outside, the trains arrived and departed.

"There are the telephones," Carlo said, pointing to a long line of booths near one wall. "I'll give the boss a call an' let him know we're here."

"Okay," Joe said.

The two men walked over to the booths, then Joe

stood just outside while Carlo put through the long-distance call.

When the call went through Carlo shut the door to drown out the noise. That action also prevented Joe from hearing what Carlo had to say. Joe watched the animation in Carlo's face as he spoke, and once Carlo looked up at Joe with an expression on his face that was so curious that Joe looked around to see if Carlo might be looking at someone else. Finally the telephone call was over, and Carlo hung the earpiece back on its hook, then opened the door and stepped outside.

"Is everything okay?" Joe asked.

"Yeah," Carlo said. There seemed to be a change in Carlo, though it was so subtle that Joe couldn't put his finger on it. He wondered what Coppola had told him.

"You're sure?"

"Yeah, I'm sure. Everything is fine," Carlo insisted.

"So, what do we do now?"

"We do what we come out here to do," Carlo said. "Come with me."

Joe followed Carlo out into the street in front of the depot. There were several cars parked along the curb and Carlo seemed to be looking them over very carefully. Finally he stopped beside a maroon-colored Buick.

"This one," he said. "Get in."

Joe got into the right seat, and Carlo got behind the wheel. He leaned over, reached up under the dashboard to cross two wires together, then pushed the starter. The engine caught at once and Carlo pulled out into the street. It wasn't until then that Joe realized Carlo had just stolen this car. Technically that made Joe an accomplice and he looked around with the hackles standing up on the back of his neck. It was a strange and uncomfortable feeling, and he could almost see the owner of the car, screaming for the police and pointing an accusing finger at them. He vowed to himself to see to it that the car was returned to its rightful owner as soon as this incident was over.

Right now, however, being an accomplice in the theft of a car was the least of his worries. There was also a chance that he might wind up an accessory to murder. The likelihood of that was increased by the fact that Joe didn't have the slightest idea where they were going, or who the intended victim was.

"You ever been out here before?" Carlo asked as they drove through the streets of Los Angeles.

"No," Joe admitted.

"We're goin' to Hollywood," Carlo said. He looked over at Joe and smiled. "There's lots of movie stars live in Hollywood," he said.

"So I've heard," Joe replied. He looked at Carlo. "Is that who we're after out here, a movie star?"

"Could be," Carlo said. He turned up an alley. The alley was wide as many streets, but it was flanked on either side by tall wood, brick and concrete walls, so that it gave the illusion of driving down a canyon. The high walls surrounded the formal gardens and backyards of the palatial estates in this neighborhood. Even though they were in the midst of a bustling city, Joe felt a strange sense of isolation in this walled alley.

Carlo stopped the car.

"Why did you stop?" Joe asked. "Is this it?"

"Get out," Carlo said quietly.

Joe got out and closed the door. "What do you want me to do?" he asked.

Carlo raised his pistol, pointing it across the seat and out the window.

"I want you to die," he said. "I just learned from Coppola: you're a goddamned cop!"

Though Joe was always prepared for anything,

Carlo's revelation surprised him. Joe stood there for an instant trying to think of something to say that might defuse the situation. Then he saw the knuckle on Carlo's finger grow white as he started to pull the trigger. There was no time for talk now—Carlo was about to kill him!

Joe had one advantage: Carlo's field of fire was only as large as the door window on the passenger side of the vehicle. Joe threw himself to the ground behind the right rear wheel of the Buick. Carlo fired just as Joe dived; the bullet missed, though it was close enough that Joe could hear the air pop at its passage.

"You sonofabitch!" Carlo shouted angrily.

Joe was on his knees and crawling from the moment he hit the ground. He saw a wooden door leading through a brick wall, and he hurried toward it. It didn't open to his push, so he crashed it open, darted inside, then pushed the door shut. As soon as he was on the inside of the wall he rolled away from the door. It was a good thing he did, because Carlo fired several times into the door. The bullets popped through the wood, leaving behind splinters and ragged holes.

There was a hedgerow growing against the back wall and Joe got behind it, then crawled for several feet until he was well away from the door. When he was halfway across the backyard he dropped to the ground and lay there, gasping for breath, praying that Carlo wouldn't come through the door and start looking around. He could hear Carlo on the other side of the wall, prowling up and down the alley, cursing angrily.

"I know all about you, you bastard," he said. "You're a fed. You were trying to set me up, weren't you? Come on, you bastard. Come on out here and take your medicine like a man."

Joe heard something clang, and he realized that Carlo was kicking the side of the car in anger.

"I gotta go," Carlo shouted. "I got some business to take care of. But you, you sonofabitch. One of these days, I'm goin' to see you again, and when I do, I'm goin' to shoot your eyes out!"

Joe heard the car door open and close, then he heard the car drive away. He lay there for a moment longer, regaining his breath and letting his heartbeat return to its normal rate. He could smell the pungent earth just under his nose and the sweet smell of jasmine from out in the garden. Finally he rose to his hands and knees and crawled out from behind the long line of shrubbery. When he got out into the open, he stood up and began brushing the dirt off his hands and the front of his clothes.

"Who the hell are you?" someone asked.

Joe looked up and saw a very beautiful blond, pointing a pistol at him. He recognized her at once, because he had seen her in dozens of movies. He smiled broadly.

"I know who you are," he said. "You're Kala Sinclair."

"I know who I am, you dumb asshole. The question I'm asking is, who are you?" Kala asked.

Joe started toward her. "I've seen all your movies," he said.

"Stay away from me. What are you doing?" Kala demanded, raising the pistol higher.

"Oh," Joe said. "Well, I'm trying to keep from getting shot."

"You have a funny way of doing that, mister. Because if you come one step closer, I'm going to pull the trigger."

"No, not by you," Joe said. "By the man I got away from. Do you see? He shot at me through your gate." Joe pointed to the bullet holes in the splintered gate at the back of the yard.

"Oh, my gate," Kala wailed. She lowered the pistol

and put her other hand to her mouth. "Look at my beautiful gate."

"Yeah," Joe said. "Well, it's better your gate than me."

"Who are you?" Kala asked, raising her pistol again.

"My name is Joe Provenzano. I'm a federal agent for the Bureau of Investigation," Joe explained.

"A policeman?"

"Yes," Joe said. "A federal policeman. Here, here is my badge." Joe bent down and reached up inside his left trouser leg.

"You carry your badge in your pants leg?" Kala asked in surprise.

"I was assuming a disguise," he said. "I couldn't very well carry it in my wallet." He showed the badge to her and with a sigh of relief, she lowered the pistol.

"Thank God," she said. "After what nearly happened to Katie Starr the other day, one can't be too careful."

"Katie Starr?" Joe said. He knew that she was Katherine Sangremano. "What happened to her?"

"My God, it was in all the papers," Kala said. "Didn't you read the story?"

"I've been on the train for four days," Joe said. "I haven't seen a paper or heard any news."

"Someone tried to kill her," Kala said. "The newspaper accounts said it was a shootout between two jealous suitors, but it was no such thing. One of the dead men was her bodyguard. He and the other man killed each other."

"That's it!" Joe said. "That's who he's after! Where does she live?"

"Oh, I can't tell you that," Kala said.

"Miss Sinclair, you have to tell me. Don't you understand? The man who tried to kill me is here to kill Katherine."

Kala looked shocked. "You called her Katherine," she

said. "How did you know that? Only her closest friends know that's what she prefers to be called."

"I've known her since she was a little girl," Joe said. "Now, please, you must tell me where she lives."

Kala hesitated for just a minute, then she nodded as if she were coming to a decision.

"All right, I'm going to take a chance that you are what you say and that you are here to help her," Kala said. "Come through the front gate," she offered. "You can see her house from here. It's just across the street. I'll show it to you."

"I would think you'd rather have me stay in California than return to New York," Katherine was saying. "I mean, if there really is a war going on, wouldn't it be safer here than back there?"

"You can't stay out here," Johnny said. "The fact that they already tried once should tell you that you aren't safe out here. I want you to come back home where I can protect you."

"Like you protected Clara?" she replied sharply.

"No," Johnny said. Then he pinched the bridge of his nose and sighed. "No, not like I protected Clara," he said. "I didn't do a very good job of protecting her. But I don't plan to make that mistake again."

Katherine saw that her response had hurt her brother and she softened immediately, then went to him and put her arms around him.

"I'm sorry, Johnny," she said. "I didn't mean anything by that remark. I had no right to say such a thing."

"You had every right," Johnny replied quietly. "After all, I'm asking you to come back to New York and put your life in my hands. And so far I don't have a very good record at protecting people. If you are afraid to come home, I'll understand."

"No, it isn't that I'm afraid to come home, It's..." She

stopped. "Look, suppose I did come back to New York? How long would I have to stay there?"

"Not long," Johnny insisted. "Just until this is all over."

"And when will that be?"

"I don't know the answer to that," Johnny admitted. "All I can say is it'll be over when the Vaglichios are taken care of."

"All right," Katherine agreed. "I'll come with you. But Johnny, I'll not destroy my career by staying away too long. If it isn't over in a couple of weeks, I'm coming back."

"It'll be over by then," Johnny promised as he embraced his sister happily.

"Well now, it may even be over sooner than you think," a third voice suddenly said.

"What the hell?" Johnny shouted, pulling away from Katherine and looking in the direction of the sound. He saw a man standing in the arch of the doorway between the living room, where Johnny and Katherine were, and the dining room, which was at the back of the house. "Who are you?" Johnny demanded. "And how did you get in here?"

"The name is Carlo Lambretta. And as to how I got in here, gettin' into places like this is what I do for a living. I'm a death soldier," he added, smiling broadly.

"The Vaglichios can't handle their own war? They have to go out and hire assassins?"

"Well, what can I say?" Carlo replied. "I don't mean nothin' personal by all this. It's business, that's all." He raised his gun.

Suddenly the plate glass window at the front of the house exploded inward with a loud, tinkling crash. The noise distracted Carlo for just a second and he turned his pistol away. That gave Johnny the opportunity to pull

Katherine down to the floor and throw his body on top of hers to protect her. Immediately after that, he heard gunshots, and though he tensed himself for the impact of the bullets, none hit him.

"It's okay now, folks, you can get up. He's dead," someone said.

Johnny looked around and saw a man lying on the floor in the middle of the shattered glass from the large front window. It was he who had crashed through the window and now he was holding a gun in front of him, pointing it toward the death soldier. Carlo Lambretta was belly-down on the floor in the dining room. His gun lay on the floor beside him, about a foot away from his outstretched hand.

Johnny made a sudden and unexpected rolling move, grabbed Carlo's pistol, then rolled over again so that he was now in position to aim it at the man who had just spoken to them.

"Johnny, no, hold it, don't shoot!" the man shouted as he brought his own pistol around to aim at Johnny. "It's me! Joe Provenzano!"

Now it was a Mexican standoff, with both men lying on their stomachs on the floor and both of them holding their pistols stretched out in front of them, each one aiming at the other. Neither fired, though if one decided to do so, he could probably kill the other before the other could respond. It was an eerie and dangerous tableau.

"What do we do now?" Joe asked quietly.

"What are you doing here?" Johnny replied.

"He's the reason I'm here," Joe said, nodding his head toward Carlo. "I came here to keep him from killing your sister. And you too, as it turned out."

"You're a fed, aren't you?" Johnny asked.

"Yes."

"What would keep me from shooting you right now?" Johnny asked.

"Johnny, no, don't!" Katherine shouted. "Can't you see? He saved our lives!"

"Put your gun down," Johnny ordered.

"No," Joe replied. I'm afraid not, at least not until you put yours down."

"I'm not going to do that."

"Then I suppose we're just going to lie here for a while," Joe said.

"Stop it both of you!" Katherine demanded. Then, when neither of them paid any attention to her, she got up and walked over toward her brother.

"Katherine, get out of the way!" Johnny ordered. "Get out of the way! You are in my line of fire!"

"I intend to be."

"Get out of the way!"

"Give me the gun," Katherine said, reaching down for the pistol. When she wrapped her hand around the barrel, Johnny sighed, then gave it up. Katherine turned toward Joe. "Now, Mr. Provenzano, he no longer has a gun," she said. "Will you please put yours away?"

"Yeah," Joe said, smiling sheepishly. "And if you don't mind, I'd like to stand up. Lying in a bed of broken glass isn't exactly my idea of being comfortable."

"You've hurt yourself," Katherine said solicitously. "Let me go into the bathroom. I have some iodine and bandages there. I'll just get them, then I'll take care of your cuts for you."

"Thanks," Joe said. He brushed the little pieces of glass off his body, then sat in a chair and looked over toward Johnny. "Are you all right?"

Yeah, I'm fine," Johnny answered. He pointed toward the body. "He said he was a death soldier. I guess times have really changed. There was a time when everyone fought their own wars. Now the Vaglichios are hiring someone else to do their killing. Who the hell would do such a thing? How could a person kill someone who had done no harm to them?"

"Here," Katherine said, returning with a pan of water, a towel and some bandages. She began cleaning Joe off.

"Am I going to live?" he asked dryly.

"It's amazing," Katherine said as she picked little pieces of glass from his skin, then dabbed at the tiny cuts with a wet corner of the towel. "You don't even have any bad cuts."

"That's because he used his head to break the glass," Johnny suggested.

Before Joe could respond to Johnny's barb, they heard sirens and cars approaching, and Johnny walked over to look out onto the front street through the shattered window.

"Damn," Johnny said. "There are half a dozen cop cars out there. Who the hell called the cops?"

"I guess after the shooting incident the other day, people must think this is turning into the Wild West," Katherine answered. She put down the basin and walked over to look out the window as well. "Someone must have called the police when they heard the shooting."

Several doors slammed shut out on the street, and they could hear the policemen shouting and talking to each other. Joe stood up. "Johnny," he said. "You are my prisoner."

"What? Like hell I am," Johnny replied in a quick flash of anger.

"You have no choice, unless you want to go downtown with these guys," Joe said. "Do you want to go back to New York?"

"I am going back to New York," Johnny insisted.

"Then I'm going to have to tell them you're my prisoner and that I'm taking you back with me. It's your only chance of getting out of here."

"Listen to him, Johnny," Katherine said. "He's right."

"All right, all right, I'll do whatever it takes," Johnny said. "But don't get any ideas that I really am your prisoner," he added, pointing at Joe.

When the police knocked on the door a moment later, they didn't do it gently. Katherine answered the door.

"Miss Starr! Are you all right?" a police lieutenant demanded.

"Yes, I'm fine, thank you," Katherine said. "Thank you for coming so quickly. It makes me feel safe, knowing you are on the job."

"What happened here?" When the officer saw Joe and Johnny standing back in the shadows of the living room, he suddenly shouted and pointed at them. "Cover them, boys!"

Several pistols were leveled at the two men.

"Lieutenant, you are making a mistake," Joe said.

"Who are you?"

"I'm a federal agent for the Bureau of Investigation," he replied. He started to reach for his badge, and the guns were all cocked, clicking menacingly.

"No, wait! Hold it, hold it!" Joe said, putting his hands out in front of him. "Don't get trigger-happy here. I'm just reaching for my badge, that's all."

"All right," the police lieutenant said. "You can get your badge, but bring it out slowly."

Joe did as he was directed. Then, as he was holding his badge out for the police to examine, he pointed at Johnny.

"This man is my prisoner," Joe said.

"Your prisoner? What makes him your prisoner?" the lieutenant asked.

"Because I've been on his trail all the way from New

York," Joe said. "I've chased him this far and I'm not going to let him get away now. He's wanted on a federal charge of violation of the Volstead Act."

"What about the stiff over there?" the police officer asked. "Who the hell is he?"

"His name is Carlo Lambretta," Joe said. "I was after him too."

"And now, the big question. What were the three of you doing in Miss Starr's house?" the policeman concluded.

"Like I said, I was chasing them," Joe said. "They led me here."

"Carlo and me, we was just tryin' to get away," Johnny said, affecting the vernacular of a hood. "This here is where we was when this guy caught up with us. Carlo tried to shoot his way out of it I told him not to, but he don't listen too good, you know what I mean? He don't listen good at all, and now he's dead."

"So what you're admitting is, the shooting of your friend by this federal officer was justified?"

Johnny snorted. "Depends on what you call justified," he said. "If you mean did the federal cop here have to shoot Carlo to save his own life, the answer is, yeah, he had to do that. But you got to look at it from my angle too. From my angle, I don't regard any cop's life all that important. So I don't figure it was justified at all."

Yeah, well, you're comin' down to the station house with me," the policeman said.

"On what charge?" Joe demanded.

"Beg your pardon?" the policeman asked in surprise.

"On what charge are you taking him to the police station?" Joe repeated. "I already told you, he is my prisoner."

"Not yet he isn't," the policeman replied. "When we're through with him, you can have him."

"I ask you again, officer, what are you going to charge him with?"

"What the hell do you keep askin' me that for? There was a man killed here, for chrissake!" the policeman said.

"Yes, I know. I killed him."

"And you killed him in self-defense, right?"

"Yes."

"All right, then, if it was self-defense, that means these men were both tryin' to kill you. So, we'll just hold this jasper for attempted murder."

"This man wasn't shooting at me. If he had been, he would be dead now," Joe said easily. "Carlo Lambretta was the one who was shooting at me and Carlo Lambretta is dead."

"Then we'll hold this man as an accessory to attempted murder," the policeman said.

"Huh-uh," Joe replied. "You can't do that, either. This man surrendered as soon as I challenged them. Carlo acted alone."

"Goddamnit, you sound more like this man's lawyer than his arresting officer. Why are you taking up for him?"

"I'm not taking up for him. I'm telling you, he's my prisoner and you've got nothing to hold him for."

"The hell I don't. If I have to, I'll get him for breaking and entering Miss Starr's home."

"I let them in," Katherine said.

"You let them in? Saints preserve us, Miss Starr, now why would you go and do a damn fool thing like that?"

"I didn't know who they were. I thought they might just be looking for work," Katherine replied. She put her hand on the policeman's arm. "Please," she said. "Don't you see that it would be much better for me if you would just let the federal policeman take this awful person away from here? I had so much bad publicity from that last unpleasant incident that my career wouldn't stand for anything else. It's just my bad luck that these men happened to be here, this time. I don't want to see anything about it in the papers and I won't, if you won't take him downtown."

"What about you?" the police lieutenant asked Joe. "Don't you want at least to come downtown and have a doctor look at your cuts?"

"I've been attended to quite nicely, thank you," Joe said.

He held out his arms. "See, no bleeding. It's almost like it didn't happen at all."

The policeman threw up his hands in disgust. "Let's go home, boys. What are we all doing here, anyway?" he asked sarcastically. "Like the man says, any fool can see that nothin' happened here. Nothin' at all."

"Wait a minute," Katherine said. "What about him?" She pointed to Carlo's body.

"He's not my problem, Miss Starr," the police lieutenant said. "He belongs to the feds, just like the prisoner."

"I would appreciate it if you would take the corpse out of Miss Starr's dining room," Joe said.

The policeman looked at Joe and started to come back with a smart remark. Then, for some reason, he changed his mind. "Yeah, okay," he said. "I guess we can at least take care of the stiff. Pick him up, boys," he said to the other policemen. "Pick him up and let's get out of here."

Later, after the police and Carlo were gone, Joe, Johnny and Katherine, enjoyed a laugh.

"We were pretty good together there, weren't we?" Joe said.

"Yes, as a matter of fact, we were," Johnny said.

"You don't have any more wounds that I don't know about, do you, Joe?" Katherine asked, looking him over.

"I don't think so," Joe answered. He smiled at her. "I'd say you did a pretty good job."

"Then I'll just get this mess out of my living room," she said, picking up the basin and first-aid supplies.

"You know, Joe, there could be a future for you in the family if you were a made man," Johnny said after Katherine left.

"In your family?"

"Yes, of course in my family. Your uncle is my consigliore, my most trusted confidant. But he isn't getting any younger. You could take his job, someday. It's too bad you've chosen the wrong side."

"I haven't chosen the wrong side, Johnny. You have."

"You're a Sicilian, Joe. Don't tell me you've never considered being a made man. You've never thought of joining The Honored Society."

"I have."

"So, why didn't you ever join?"

"Because I already belong to an honored society."

"You're talking about the Bureau of Investigation?"

"No," Joe said. "Something else. Something more honored and more sacred. And more secret even than the Mafia."

Johnny's eyes narrowed. "What are you talking about?"

"I'm afraid I can't tell you any more," Joe said. "For, like you, we have our own code of omerta."

"All right," Johnny said. "All right, I can understand a code of silence. I won't ask you anything else about it. But it's a shame, Joe. It's really a shame that Sicilians like us have to be enemies."

"No more a shame for us than that friends like you and Mike have to be enemies."

Johnny was quiet for a moment. "Yes," he finally said. "Yes, that's a shame too. Ah," he finally said, "If only

Mike could understand that this is just a business, like any other business. I mean, what's the harm? We only give the people what they want; booze, gambling and women."

"And dope?"

"No, not dope," Johnny said. "That's the biggest difference between the Vaglichios and me. They sell dope, I don't."

"And that's what has started this war?"

"Yeah," Johnny answered. "Yeah, I guess it is. I guess that's why they went out and hired a goon like this man, Carlo. Where did he come from, anyway?"

"Have you ever heard of a man named Ignatzio Coppola? Sometimes he is called The Hammer," Joe said.

"Coppola? The Hammer? Yeah," Johnny said. "Yeah, I think I have heard of him. He's got a small family in Cleveland or someplace, I think."

"Steubenville, not Cleveland," Joe corrected. "And while Coppola's family is very small, it is also very powerful. It is even more powerful now than it ever was before, because Coppola is running a murder-for-hire business. Families from all over the country have been using his services. He's done jobs in New Orleans, Chicago and New York. Are you telling me you didn't know that?"

Johnny held up his hand. "I swear to you, Joe. I did not know that," he said.

"I don't know why I believe you, but I do. Anyway, I think he is the one responsible for your wife's murder."

"No, he's not responsible. He may have furnished the muscle for the killings," Johnny said. "But he's not responsible. The Vaglichios are. They murdered my wife, they murdered Vito Patrizzi, they killed Nino LaRosa and Joey Bendetti, and they have tried twice to kill my sister.

It has turned into a full-scale war, just like in the old days."

"Yes, it has," Joe agreed. "Tell me, what started this war, Johnny?"

"That, I don't know," Johnny replied. "Though it may have been because I won't do dope, and I won't let the Vaglichios do it in my territory. What puzzles me most, however, is how it keeps growing."

"Well, that's certainly no puzzle. They hit you, you hit them back, they hit you, and you hit them back again, only each time you hit them harder than you did before."

"Yes, I know that's the way it is supposed to work," Johnny said. "But the funny thing is, Joe, I haven't hit them back. Not once."

"What are you talking about, you haven't hit them back? What about Sollozo?" Joe asked.

"I didn't have anything to do with that. To tell the truth, I sort of suspected that the Vaglichios used that opportunity to take him out themselves. That way they could kill two birds with one stone, so to speak. They could get rid of Sollozo, if that's what they wanted, and they could blame it on me. But when Maria Vaglichio was also killed, it really threw me for a loop. I mean, I know Mario wouldn't kill his own daughter."

"What!" Joe gasped, his face turning ashen. "What... what did you say?" He sat down, hard, in the chair. Katherine, who was just returning to the living room now, saw Joe's strange behavior.

"Joe, what's the matter? Are you all right?" she asked, solicitously.

"Did you...did you say Maria was killed?" Joe asked Johnny in a choked voice.

"Yes, a couple of days ago. You mean you hadn't heard?"

"No," Joe said, so quietly he could barely be heard.

Katherine was studying him intently through narrowed eyes. "That was really a shame. She was a good kid."

"Oh, God, no," Joe said. He pressed his fist against his forehead and tears welled in his eyes.

"Hey, what's wrong with you?" Johnny asked, surprised by Joe's reaction.

"Hush, Johnny," Katherine said quietly. "Can't you see he was in love with her?"

"In love with her?" Johnny replied. "Jesus, I'm sorry, Joe. I didn't know."

"How...how did it happen?" Joe asked.

"I'm not really sure," Johnny replied. "I was on the train on the way out here when I heard about it. They said she was in the mission when it happened. Officially, she was killed by one of the bums, who went crazy. And who knows, maybe that is what happened. I just know that the Vaglichios will blame it on me, even though I had nothing to do with it."

"All this time I've been thinking of her as if she were alive, but she wasn't. She was dead. And I didn't even know."

"Oh, Johnny, and you were so insensitive as to just blurt it out like that." Katherine accused.

Joe began to pull himself together. "There is no way you could have known," he explained. "Nobody knew. We couldn't let anyone find out about us. I'm a cop and her father...well, you can understand, he would never have approved of me."

"No, I guess not," Johnny said.

I'm going to find out who did it," Joe said determinedly.

"I hope you do," Johnny replied. "Like I said, I didn't have anything to do with it."

"I'm sorry for you, Joe," Katherine said, putting her arms around him to comfort him. "I am so very sorry."

"Joe, you said something about going back to New York," Johnny said. "When can we go?"

"Come on," Joe said. "We'll go now. The quicker we get started, the quicker we get back. There's a train leaving at eleven, tonight."

Johnny smiled. "Who needs a train?" he asked. "When we can fly."

"Fly?"

"I have a plane at the airport," Johnny explained. "If we leave now, we'll be in New York before morning."

"You mean to say you are going to fly from here, all the way to New York?" Joe asked in surprise.

"Why not? It's been done before. Now, do you want to ride with me, or what?"

"Yes, all right, I'll ride with you," Joe agreed.

Johnny smiled. "Good. You come along too, Katherine. You're going with us. You promised me you would spend a couple of weeks in New York, and I'm holding you to it."

CHAPTER 12

"Wake up, Joe," Johnny said. "We're coming into New York." Joe opened his eyes and rubbed them to get the sleep out, then he looked through the silver disc of the spinning propeller, toward the towering buildings ahead. When he had gone to sleep a couple of hours ago, lulled by the incessant drone of the engine, it had been dark. Now it was light, and the towering skyscrapers of New York were before him, glowing in the golden blush of dawn.

"Damn, it's morning already," Joe said. "It sure seemed like a short night."

"Not if you'd been sitting here holding on to the wheel all night," Johnny replied.

"No, I guess not."

"I wonder if your friends will be there to meet us?" Johnny asked.

"They said they would be there, so they'll be there," Joe replied.

"You have a lot of faith in them."

"Yes, I do," Joe said, simply.

"Wake my sister, will you? We're about to land."

Joe twisted around in his seat, then reached back to gently shake Katherine awake. She opened her eyes, then smiled at Joe.

"Good morning," she said. "Where are we?"

"See for yourself," Joe invited.

Katherine, who had almost managed to lie down in the back seat, now sat up to look out the windows.

"Oh, it's beautiful, isn't it?" she said.

The sound of the engine changed pitch as Johnny came back on the throttle, then the nose pointed down as they started their long descent into Roosevelt Field.

"You know, you fly this thing pretty well," Joe said. Johnny looked over at him and smiled. "Yeah," he agreed. "I do. I wish things were..." he let the sentence die and shrugged.

"You wish things were what? Different? They could be, you know? You don't have to..."

"There they are, over there," Joe said, pointing to a group of men standing in front of a couple of cars.

"I see them," Johnny said, taxiing the plane in the direction indicated by Joe. When he reached his destination he touched the brakes, then pulled the fuel mixture control to idle shutoff. When the engine stopped he turned off the magneto switch. After so many hours of the engine's roar, the quiet seemed almost deafening. "'Lafayette,'" Johnny quoted, "'we are here.'"

Mike, Bill and Jason came over to the plane as Joe, Johnny and Katherine climbed down. Johnny turned to help Katherine out of the plane.

"Are we happy to see you!" Mike said, shaking Joe's hand happily. "For a while there we were afraid we might have lost you."

"Here I am, in one piece, you see," Joe said, smiling broadly. You know Johnny, of course. And his sister, Katherine."

"Hello, Mike," Johnny said.

"Hello, Johnny. Miss Sangremano," Mike said, greeting Katherine as well.

"I owe you guys my thanks," Johnny said. "For my life, and my sister's life. If you hadn't been on the ball, if Joe hadn't arrived when he did, the Vaglichios would have gotten us both."

"I'm glad he got there in time. But it wasn't the Vaglichios," Mike said.

"The hell it wasn't. Who else could it have been?"

"Why don't you ask Luca Vaglichio?" Mike asked. He held his hand up toward one of the cars and waved. The car door opened and Luca got out.

"What the hell is this?" Johnny demanded angrily. "What's going on here? My God, Mike! Have you set me up?"

"Johnny, you know better than that!" Mike shouted. "Will you, damnit, just listen to me for a minute?"

"Give me one reason why I should."

"Because one time I pulled your naked ass out an Illinois cornfield when a farmer wanted to blow you apart with his shotgun for dallying with his wife," Mike said. "Is that reason enough?" he demanded.

Johnny and Mike exchanged long looks and, for just a moment, time and events rolled away to let the two men be as close as they once were. First Johnny laughed, then Mike joined him. The others, especially Luca Vaglichio, looked on in confusion.

"Yeah," Johnny finally said. "Yeah, I guess that's reason enough. But you're going to have some explaining to do as to why this man is here." He looked over at Vaglichio.

"He is here because I want him to hear your answers," Mike said.

"My answers to what?"

"To a few questions that I want cleared up," Mike replied. "Johnny," he went on, "I would bet my life that you didn't kill Maria Vaglichio."

"I didn't," Johnny replied.

"And you didn't have her killed."

"No, I didn't do that either."

"And I'd be willing to make the same bet that you didn't kill Amerigo Sollozo."

"You'd win that bet too," Johnny said. "No matter what Luca Vaglichio might tell you." Johnny looked directly at Luca. "I didn't have anything to do with killing either one of them."

"I know you didn't, Johnny," Luca replied. "And I have already told him that."

"What did you say?"

"I said, I don't believe you killed Amerigo or Maria."

Johnny's eyes narrowed as he studied Luca's face. "What's going on here? Why the sudden turnaround? You used to think I did it. What caused you to change your mind?"

"Because I know that the person who is responsible for the deaths of poor Amerigo and Maria is the same person who is responsible for killing Weasel and your darling wife."

"Coppola?" Johnny replied. "Yes, I already know that."

"No, not Coppola," Luca said, waving his hand. "Oh, yes, he was the instrument. But he wasn't the cause. He wasn't the man who set it all in motion."

"Then who did?"

"Who is the one man who would benefit most if both our families were destroyed?" Luca asked.

"I can't think of anyone," Johnny replied. "I mean, Don Pietro Nicolo's territory is contiguous to ours, but

Don Pietro is a peacemaker. I can't believe he would be behind all this."

"He isn't."

"Then I don't know who else it could possibly be," Johnny stated. "I mean..." He paused in midsentence. "Son of a bitch—it's Enrico, isn't it? That wormy little bastard always has been a sorry specimen. Enrico has been behind this all along and not even Don Pietro knows about it."

"That is true," Luca said. "I know it for a fact because Ben Costaconti's niece is married to a man who works for Enrico. When he found out what Enrico was doing, he came to Ben and asked if we would take him in."

"And you went to the cops with this?" Johnny asked. There was an accusing edge to his voice.

Luca began speaking in Italian. "Who are you to find fault with me?" he asked. "Do you think I have violated the code of omerta because I have spoken with these men? They came to arrest me. If it is a question of my neck or the neck of someone like Enrico, then I say it is his neck."

"Why did you tell them anything?" Johnny replied, also speaking in Italian. "Would it not have been better to take care of this thing ourselves?"

"One does what one must do," Luca replied.

"Speak English in front of me," Mike demanded.

"All right, I'll speak English," Johnny replied. "So tell me. Do you go along with Don Vaglichio? Do you believe it is Enrico?"

"Yes, that's the way we have it figured," Mike said.

"That means he is the one responsible for having Clara killed," Johnny said bitterly.

"And Maria," Luca added.

"Then what are we standing around here for? Why don't we go out to his place and get him?"

"We need proof," Mike said.

"Proof? Maybe the law needs proof. I don't. I'm going to—"

"You're going to do nothing," Mike said sharply. "Except sit back and let us finish this case."

"Do you have something in mind, Mike?" Joe asked.

"Yes. We paid Coppola to kill a Mr. Gatsby. All we have to do now is wait for one of his hired killers to show up."

"One of Coppola's hired killers?" Joe said. "As far as I know, right now he has only one left."

"Yes, we know that too," Mike replied. "His name is Clyde Tunstul. Do you know him? He has very pale skin, pink eyes, white hair."

"Yes. I know him. Only I know him as The Albino. He's a creepy sort of person."

"Tunstul, or The Albino as you know him, matches the description of the man who killed Maria," Bill said. "At first, no one believed the witness inside the mission house. He's an alcoholic and he thought he was seeing a ghost. But someone out on the street saw him also, and when we put the two descriptions together, we knew we were dealing with an albino."

"And I found records on all of Coppola's men in the classified files of the Steubenville police force," Bill added. "We just fit all the pieces of the puzzle together and we came up with Clyde Tunstul."

"A.k.a. The Albino," Jason added.

"The Albino killed Maria. I knew it," Joe muttered. "I knew it."

"What are you talking about? You didn't even know Maria was dead until I told you," Johnny said.

"No, but there was something about The Albino when I was near him," Joe said. "Something dark and foreboding, like a sense of death."

"They were all killers," Bill reminded him. "There would be a sense of death about all of them. I don't know how one could be any more so than the others."

"I used the wrong word," Joe said. "I should have said the stench of death." He looked up. "I'm sorry, I interrupted you. Now, tell me how this is going to work."

"We have sent word that Mr. Gatsby will be waiting for The Albino in the parts room in the rear of hangar number three," Mike went on.

"And who is this Mr. Gatsby who is brave enough to be the bait?"

Mike and Jason both laughed. "Don't tell me you don't read the popular novels," Jason said.

"What's so funny?" Joe asked.

"The Great Gatsby, by F. Scott Fitzgerald," Johnny put in. "Is that the Gatsby you're talking about?"

"Yes," Mike replied. "I hope The Albino isn't as well read as you are. Coppola didn't seem to be."

"So, when The Albino gets here, there won't actually be anyone for him to meet, is that it?" Joe asked.

"Oh, but there will be. He's going to meet Enrico Nicolo," Mike said.

"Yeah!" Johnny said. "Yeah, you're setting the son of a bitch up to be killed by one of his own hired killers! I like that!"

"No, that's not what we're doing," Mike said patiently.

"It isn't? Then what the hell are you doing?"

"We're setting him up, all right, but not to be killed. All we want is to be able to get the goods on him. On both of them, in fact. So Bill, Jason, Joe and I will be hiding out in the parts room," Mike explained. "If we're lucky one, or both, of them will say something during that first few moments that will be incriminating enough to use in court."

"If you're lucky? That's a pretty iffy proposition, isn't it?" Johnny demanded. "What if you aren't lucky? Do they both go free?"

"Not entirely," Mike explained.

"What does that mean, 'not entirely'?"

"Even if we don't get enough incriminating evidence to put them in jail, we will know that they are guilty... and they will know that we know. That should slow them down quite a bit, and eventually, we will get them. You can rest assured on that, Johnny, we will get them."

"I'll believe that when it happens," Johnny growled. "When is the meeting supposed to be?"

"At eight o'clock this morning," Mike answered. "Now, I would appreciate it if you would take your sister and clear the area."

"You're not getting me out of here," Johnny said.

"Johnny, please," Mike said, changing his tone from demanding to pleading and using the tact that he knew would get a response. "It could be very dangerous and your sister has already been exposed to enough danger." Johnny looked over at Katherine, who had been standing by quietly, taking in everything.

"Yeah," Johnny said. "Yeah, I guess you're right. Okay, I'm goin' to take her home. But you don't let these creeps get away from you, you hear me, Michael? You don't let these creeps get away!"

"We'll do our best, Johnny," Mike answered. "Mr. Vaglichio, I'm going to have to ask you to leave too," he said.

"Yeah, yeah, I'm going," Vaglichio said.

"Don Luca," Johnny said, speaking again in Italian. "If Coppola has only one hired killer left, how is it that he filled the cars with gunmen when Vito Patrizzi was killed?"

"This, I do not know."

"I know—that wasn't Coppola, was it? It was you?"

"It was the vendetta. I did not know about Enrico Nicolo then. I ask that you forgive and that there be peace between our families once again."

"I will do what I can with Vito's men," Johnny said. "But I cannot promise anything."

Suddenly Johnny looked over toward Joe and realized that he had been listening to everything. "You heard, didn't you?" he said.

Joe smiled. "I have always loved the sound of spoken Italian," he replied, speaking in that language. "I could listen for hours."

"What are you going to do about what you just heard?" Vaglichio asked.

"Nothing, for now," Joe said. "The others would not understand but this is something that is best for you to work out between you."

"You are a good man, Joe Provenzano," Vaglichio said. "A good friend."

"I am a good man," Joe said. "I am not your good friend."

"Come on, Katherine, I'll take you home," Johnny said, returning to English. Then he stopped and looked back toward Mike. "How am I supposed to do this without a car?"

Mike reached into his pocket and tossed a car key to Johnny. "Use the blue Essex," he said. "I'll pick it up later. It would be better not to have any cars around anyway."

Johnny chuckled. "How about that?" he said. "Me, borrowing a car from a fed."

Mike, Bill, Joe and Jason watched as the two cars drove away, Vaglichio in his own car, and Johnny and Katherine in Mike's official car. When the sound of the retreating engines was gone, it grew very quiet at the field.

"What was all the Italian about?" he asked.

"We were practicing our Latin," Joe replied.

Mike smiled. "I'm not Italian, Joe, but I am Catholic. I know Latin when I hear it and I know Italian."

"It was nothing, Mike."

Mike looked at him for a long moment, then he smiled. "Okay," he finally said. "Then what do you say we back into the parts room and find us someplace to hide."

They went to all four corners of the parts room, the better to have the area completely covered. Each of them found a place of concealment, then they just settled back and waited.

The smell of motor oil and gasoline, castor oil and fabric dope brought back hauntingly familiar memories to Mike. As he waited for The Albino and Nicolo to show up, he whiled away the time by recalling the hours and days he had spent rebuilding the DH-4 he and Johnny had used during their barnstorming trip across the country.

Finally Mike heard a car pull up out front and stop, then a car door open and close. A moment later someone stepped inside the building. It was Enrico Nicolo. Mike had lured him here by sending a message, purportedly from Ignatzio Coppola, saying that he had a matter of great importance to discuss.

"Don Coppola? Don Coppola, are you in here?" Enrico called. He walked across the concrete floor until he reached the middle of the room.

"It's Enrico, Don Coppola. Enrico Nicolo. I came, like you asked."

At that moment another car drove up outside. Enrico paused in the middle of the concrete door and turned his head toward the door, like a rabbit caught in a beam of light.

Joe, too, looked toward the front door. When he saw The Albino come in, he drew a short, ragged breath, then held it, biting his lips to keep from shouting out in his rage. This was the man who had killed Maria!

"Who are you?" Enrico asked as The Albino walked across the floor toward him. "Are you from Coppola?"

"Yes, Coppola," The Albino said. He continued to walk slowly toward Enrico.

"What are you doing here?" Enrico asked. "I deal with Coppola, do you understand? All of my dealing is with Coppola, not with one of his hirelings. You tell Coppola if he wants to meet with me, he must come in person."

"Mr. Gatsby?" The Albino asked.

"What?"

"Are you Mr. Gatsby?"

"No," Enrico replied.

"It won't do you any good to lie," The Albino said. He pulled a knife from his jacket pocket "It won't save you."

"What are you doing?"

"Nothing personal, Mr. Gatsby," The Albino said. "It's just business."

"I told you, I'm not Gatsby. My name is Nicolo, Enrico Nicolo. Don't you know who I am? I've been doing business with your boss for over a month now."

"Business? What business?" The Albino asked.

"You know what business," Enrico replied. "The film distributors, the policy man in the back of the laundry, the woman on Long Island, the one in the mission house, those were all my contracts. Don't you know about any of them?"

The Albino stopped. "The women," he said. "Yes, I know about the women."

"Then what are you doing here? What's going on?"

"Mr. Gatsby," The Albino said, coming toward him again. "I came here for Mr. Gatsby."

"Well, there's no Gatsby here. Wait a minute," Enrico said. "That's not even a real name. It's from a book. What is all this about?"

The Albino stopped. "A book?"

"There is no Gatsby, don't you understand, you dumb son of a bitch! You've been set up. We've been set up."

"That's right, Enrico," Mike called, stepping out from behind a large crate. "You have been set up. You two are the settees, and we are the settors." Joe, Jason and Bill also stepped out into the opening.

When The Albino started to move his hand toward his pocket, Joe raised his pistol and pulled the hammer back. The metallic click sounded extraordinarily loud in the confines of the parts room.

"I want you to try it, maggot," Joe growled. "Please try it." The Albino's hand moved away.

"Disarm them, Bill," Mike said.

Bill walked over to the two men and took a pistol from Enrico, and a knife and a pistol from The Albino.

Johnny stood just outside the hangar. He had taken Katherine only as far as the nearest cab stand, where he put her on a taxi for home, then he returned. At first he didn't have a clear idea of what he was going to do. Then he saw something in Mike's car that helped him formulate his plan.

What he saw were two tear-gas canisters and a gas mask. At first Johnny was surprised to see them, then he realized that this was, after all, a police car, and tear gas was a standard weapon for forcing a criminal out if he was entrenched in a building somewhere. Johnny was going to make just a little different use of it.

As soon as Johnny saw that both Enrico and The Albino were disarmed, he tossed in the two canisters. The effect was dramatic and instantaneous. The hangar was filled with a huge, irritating cloud of gas, so strong that everyone inside immediately covered up his face, then started running for the front of the hangar. Johnny, using the mask to his advantage, came into the hangar through the back door. Covered by the cloud and the confusion, Johnny slipped up behind Enrico, knocked him out with a blow to the head, then tossed him over his shoulder like a sack of flour and carried him out the back way.

Once he was outside and sure he wasn't being followed, Johnny carried Enrico's limp form over to a two-seated, open-cockpit biplane. Enrico was still groggy from the blow and from the gas, so he offered no resistance as Johnny stuffed him down in the front cockpit and strapped him in. Quickly Johnny propped the engine, then, once it was started, jumped into the back cockpit and opened the throttle.

By the time Mike, Bill, Jason and Joe got their eyes cleared of the tear gas, Enrico and The Albino were both gone.

"Mike, who threw those canisters?" Bill asked.

"I don't know. I didn't get a look at him."

"Hey, look over there," Jason shouted, pointing to an airplane that was just beginning to move. "Isn't that Nicolo in the front?"

"Yes, it is!" Bill said. "Mike! The son of a bitch is getting away!"

The biplane, with Nicolo in the front seat, started its takeoff run heading west, on the east-west runway. In addition to the biplane, there was one other airplane in sight. It was a large tri-motor Ford transport plane, and it was making a landing. There wasn't much wind, but what wind there was, was blowing out of the east. Therefore the Ford, which was on final approach, was landing to the east, on the same runway as, but in the opposite direction of, the departing biplane. The pilot of the tri-motor was not only landing into the wind, he was also landing into the sun, so he didn't even notice the biplane. It was now tail-high on the runway below and just in front of him, at about the speed necessary to get airborne.

The first thing Enrico saw after he regained conscious-ness was a large, three-engined airplane coming right toward him. It took him a second to gather his senses, then he screamed in terror, just as the airplane he was in lifted off the ground and banked sharply to the right. The tri-motor slipped beneath them, coming so close that Enrico could see each individual ripple on the corrugated skin.

Where the hell was he? How did he get here in this airplane? Enrico wondered. He twisted around in the front cockpit and looked back to see who was flying the plane, but the pilot was wearing a gas mask, and Enrico had no idea who it was.

"Who are you?" Enrico shouted. "Who are you?"

The pilot just stared at him through the goggles of the gas mask, looking for all the world like some gigantic insect flying the plane. Enrico knew there was no way he could be heard over the roar of the engine, so he turned back around to enjoy the flight. Whoever the pilot was, it had to be a friend, because he had just rescued him. They were almost killed during the takeoff, but one had to take chances at such times. Nicolo would see to it that the pilot was properly rewarded.

Back on the ground, almost every breath The Albino took burned his throat and chest as if he were breathing fire. He could still smell and taste the tear gas. Whoever the son of a bitch was who threw that, nearly killed him. But then, he thought, the tear gas was also what enabled him to get away.

The Albino was hiding just around the corner of the

hangar, but he knew he couldn't stay there very long. He had to get over to where the cars were parked. All four of the feds were watching the airplane take off. If he was going to go, he had to go now. He took a deep breath and started running.

"Hey!" he heard someone call. "Hey, there's The Albino!"

"He's trying to get to the cars! Head him off!" another shouted.

The Albino realized then that his pursuers could get to the cars before he could. His only chance was to turn and run the other way.

"Look out for that plane!" someone screamed at him. The landing airplane was coming too fast and the warning came too late. The Albino had been looking back, trying to gauge how much of a lead he had on the others, and he ran wildly, right across the runway. The pilot, who had just missed the departing biplane, was unable to avoid the runner. He heard a sickening thump, then his left cabin window and the windshield in front of his face went red with blood as the propeller on his left engine took off The Albino's head, left arm and shoulder.

"Oh, my God!" Jason said. "Did you see that?"

Jason's observation wasn't necessary. All four had seen the impact, the spray of blood and the flying pieces of The Albino's body. The plane was traveling much too fast to stop, and it continued to roll down the runway, the left side of its fuselage dotted with splashes of red, while behind the airplane, lying in two obscene lumps on the grass, was what was left of The Albino.

Enrico knew nothing of what had just happened on the ground. The biplane continued to climb in wide, lazy circles until it was very high. It was, in fact, the first time Enrico had ever been up in an airplane, and though it was a little frightening to him, he found it thrilling too.

Finally, when they were so high that Enrico could see all the way to the other side of the city, and into New Jersey, where his uncle had a small truck farm, the noise of the engine stopped. Enrico looked around in alarm. He didn't know anything about airplanes, but he knew they couldn't stay in the air if the engine wasn't functioning.

"Hey!" he shouted. "Hey, what happened? The motor quit!"

"It didn't quit. I shut it off."

Enrico looked around again and saw that his pilot was no longer wearing a gas mask. Now he recognized him.

"Sangremano!" he said. He forced a smile. "Sangremano, so, you're the one rescued me from those guys. Listen, I want to thank you."

"No thanks needed," Johnny said. He climbed up to the rim of the rear cockpit and sat there for a moment while he began tightening several straps that crisscrossed his body.

"What's that? What's that you're wearing?"

"A parachute," Johnny replied.

"What are you doing sitting up there like that?" Enrico asked. "What's goin' on here? Who's flying this airplane?"

"You are," Johnny replied.

"Me? I don't know anything about flying an airplane!"

"I guess you're going to have to learn," Johnny said. "It's easy, you just pull back on the stick when you want to go up and push it forward when you want to go down."

Enrico looked back around into the well of his cockpit. "Stick?" he shouted. "What stick? There's no stick up here!"

"Oh, isn't there? Yes, I guess I forgot to tell you. In this model, there is only one stick, and it's back here. When I leave, I guess you're going to have to crawl back here to get to the controls."

"Crawl back there?" Enrico forced a laugh. "I get it. You are joking with me, aren't you?"

"I guess I am," Johnny said. "But it's going to be a lot funnier to me than it is to you." He stepped out onto the wing.

"What? What are you doing?"

"I'm trying to get you to listen to reason," Johnny said coldly.

"Listen to reason?" Enrico screamed. "What do you mean? What do you want? I'll do anything! Anything! You just name it!"

"I want my wife back," Johnny said. "You bring my wife back and I'll get in this airplane and fly it."

"You're crazy! I can't do that," Enrico said. "Your wife is dead! There's nothing I can do to bring her back."

"Too bad," Johnny said. He pitched back off the wing, then disappeared, leaving Enrico in the airplane alone. Even above the sound of the wind in his ears, Johnny could hear the ear-piercing, blood-curdling scream as Enrico went mad.

Steubenville, Ohio, three days later

Stewart Dempster was just approaching the twelfth hole when he looked up and saw the four men coming toward him. "Mr. Jarvis, Mr. Wodehouse," he said. "What can I do for you?"

"It isn't Jarvis," Mike said, showing Dempster his badge. "I'm Mike Kelly, federal agent for the Bureau of Investigation."

Dempster's face turned ashen and his hands started to shake as each man, in turn, identified himself.

"What...what do you want with me?" he asked.

"We want Coppola," Mike said.

"I, I don't know anything about his business," Stewart said.

"That's bullshit, counselor. You represent him," Mike said.

"Yes, in certain matters," Stewart said. "Matters that, under the client-attorney relationship, should be kept secret."

Bill looked over at Mike. "I told you, Mike," he said. "Guys like Coppola always manage to find young fools like Dempster to take their fall."

"I guess you're right," Mike said. He sighed. "All right, cuff him. All we have to do is make a case, it doesn't matter whether it's Coppola or Dempster. One of them is going to jail for thirty-five years."

Bill put his handcuffs on Dempster.

"Wait!" Dempster said. "Wait. Suppose I become a friendly witness. Could we work something out?"

"It depends on what you have," Mike said.

By now another group of players was approaching the green.

"Could we, could we get out of here?" Dempster asked. Joe chuckled. "You worried about your reputation, counselor? After this, you aren't even going to have a reputation."

"No," Dempster said, quietly. "I'm not worried about my reputation. I'm worried about my life."

"Well," Mike said. "That sounds pretty serious."

"It is," Dempster said. "Can we deal?"

"What can you offer me?"

"Coppola's head on a plate," Dempster said.

"And Charlie Matranga?" Mike asked.

"You mean the gentleman in New Orleans?"

"I'd scarcely call him a gentleman."

Dempster shook his head. "I'm afraid not. Mr. Matranga, like Mr. Capone, is an exceptionally clever fellow who leaves no trail," the young lawyer said. "I can't help you with him. But I can give you Captain Jock O'Connell."

"Yeah," Bill said enthusiastically. "Mike, I want that son of a bitch."

"All right," Mike agreed. "If you can deliver what you say you can, counselor, I think we can deal."

"What kind of deal? What will I get out of it?"

"A reduced sentence."

"A reduced sentence?" Dempster said, weakly. "That's the best I can hope for?"

"That's it."

"But you don't understand. If I have a felony conviction on my records, I'll never be able to practice law again."

"Mr. Dempster, I believe that would be the law profession's gain," Mike said.

"But what will I do? How will I make a living?"

"How are you at frying hamburgers?" Bill asked.

GRAND CENTRAL STATION, NEW YORK

The floor echoed with the footsteps of throngs of passengers who were hurrying to and away from the trains while the track-caller's amplified voice added to the din. Katherine, as Katie Starr, posed, smiling prettily, while a throng of press photographers took her picture. She was just about to board the 20th Century Limited for the long trip back to the West Coast.

"Just one more, Miss Starr, please," someone called and, dutifully, Kathryn struck one more pose.

"Just one more."

"Oh, please, let me spend a few minutes alone with my family," Katherine protested.

"It won't be long."

"No," Johnny said, stepping in between Katherine and the press. "You've got enough pictures now. Give her a break."

"Yes, Mr. Sangremano," one of the photographers said and he started gathering his equipment.

"Hey, who are you to talk for the lady?" a brasher, younger photographer asked. "Why don't you just stay over there out of the way and let us do our job?"

The photographer who was gathering his equipment grabbed the brash young man by the arm. "Don't pay any attention to him, Mr. Sangremano," he said. "He's new."

"What are you buttin' in for?" The photographer started to protest, but the older man leaned over and whispered something. The younger man blanched, then looked back toward Johnny. I'm...I'm sorry," he said. "I didn't mean anything by it."

"It's okay," Johnny said easily. "Just go away now. Go away and let my sister have a few moments of peace."

"Yes sir," the young man said. "Yes sir, we're going." Within a moment all the photographers had withdrawn, leaving Katherine, Johnny, their mother and Nicky Tortora, a soldier who had recently "made his bones" and been promoted to take Weasel's place. Nicky stood a respectful distance away from his godfather and the family. His back was to them while he kept an attentive eye on everyone in the crowd, alert to anyone who might mean harm to his boss.

Katherine smiled. "You would have a hard time getting on as a press agent," she said. "Sending them away like that."

Johnny chuckled. "Well, it depends on what you need a press agent for. If you are looking for newspaper coverage, that's one thing. But now you're so popular that you need to push them away so you can have a little privacy now and then."

"That's the way it is now," Katherine said. She sighed. "It probably won't be that way much longer."

"What do you mean? Why not?"

"Talkies."

"Talkies?"

"Movies with sound," Katherine said. "That's the coming thing, Johnny. Two or three years from now, there won't be a silent film made. And when that happens, I may be on the outside looking in."

"Why?"

"Why? Do you have to ask? You've heard me talk."

"You talk fine."

"I talk like a wop from Brooklyn."

"Katherine!" Mrs. Sangremano gasped. "Why do you say such a thing?"

"Because it's true, Mama."

"There's nothing wrong with the way you talk," Johnny said. "Lots of people talk just like you. I'd think that would be an advantage."

"Yes, well, that's what I tried to tell Sid Friedman," Katherine said. "He's going to be casting for Molly Pitcher next month. Johnny, I'm perfect for the part, and the funny thing is, I'm sure the real Molly Pitcher talked just like me. But Friedman has this idea that everyone who ever utters one word on screen must have the diction of a graduate of Oxford or something."

"Who is Sid Friedman?"

"He is the director."

"And he's the one who can make the decision as to whether or not you get the part?"

Yes," Katherine said.

Johnny reached out and took Katherine's hand in his own, then looked his sister right in the eyes. "Katherine, are you asking me for help?"

"Well," Katherine hedged. "If you think there is anything you can do that may be of help, I'd be a fool to turn it down. The only thing is, I don't exactly know what you could do. I mean, Mr. Friedman is such an unreasonable man."

"Don't you worry about it," he said. "Nicky and I will take a little trip out there this week, and I'll talk to Mr. Friedman." He smiled. "I think we can make him listen to reason."

"All aboard for the 20th Century Limited!" the track caller called, and the amplified metallic voice echoed throughout the chamber.

"You write to your mama," Katherine's mother said, giving her daughter a hug.

"I'll give you a call when I get out there," Johnny said. "Everything will be fine, you'll see."

"Thank you, Johnny, you're a dear," Katherine said as she started toward the gate.

Katherine walked away quickly, hearing Johnny soothe her mother's cries behind her. Her mother always cried when Katherine left and sometimes Katherine felt a sense of guilt for not inviting her mother out to California to live with her. The sense of guilt wasn't enough, however, to overcome the crimp her mother's presence would put in her lifestyle. A lifestyle that was guaranteed to continue, now that she was sure she would be able to make the transition into talkies. Johnny had promised her that he would talk to Sid Friedman, and if there was one thing Katherine had learned, it was that when Johnny talked to someone, he could always make them listen to reason.

A LOOK AT: THE BROKEN COVENANT

WHEN HONOR DIES BOOK THREE

In the glamorous world of Hollywood, loyalty is as fragile as fame.

As the roaring twenties usher in a new era of glitz and greed, the Mafia sets its sights on taking control of Tinseltown. At the center of this deadly power struggle are two men bound by a lifetime of twisted loyalties: Johnny Sangremano, the son of a notorious Mafia boss, and Mike Kelly, the federal agent sworn to bring the mob down.

Hollywood's allure draws both men into a web of betrayal and ambition, where the lines between law and crime blur. As rivals close in, Johnny and Mike face an impossible choice: remain enemies or unite against a common threat. But in a world where trust can get you killed, even alliances come at a price.

With the Mafia tightening its grip on Hollywood, how far will Johnny go to protect his empire? Can Mike uphold the law without losing his soul?

AVAILABLE DECEMBER 2024

ABOUT THE AUTHOR

Robert Vaughan sold his first book when he was nineteen. That was several years and nearly three-hundred books ago. Since then, he wrote the novelization for the mini-series Andersonville, as well as written, produced, and appeared in the History Channel documentary Vietnam Homecoming.

Vaughan's books have hit the *New York Times* bestseller list seven times. He won the Spur Award, the Porgie Award in Best Paperback Original, the Western Fictioneers Lifetime Achievement Award, the Will Rogers Medallion Award, the Readwest President's Award for Excellence in Western Fiction, and is a member of the American Writers Hall of Fame and a Pulitzer Prize nominee.

Vaughan was also a retired army officer, helicopter pilot with three tours in Vietnam, who has received the Distinguished Flying Cross, the Purple Heart, the Bronze Star with three oak leaf clusters, the Air Medal for valor with 35 oak leaf clusters, the Army Commendation Medal, the Meritorious Service Medal, and the Vietnamese Cross of Gallantry.